EAT THE MOON

A CLIMATIC LOVE STORY TO SAVE THE WORLD

BY PORTIA D. SYKES

Published by:
Carrots and Stick Publishing
P.O. Box 767
Aztec, NM 87410

www.portiadsykes.com
portiadsykes@outlook.com

Printed in the United States.

ISBN: 978-1-7362920-0-6

Cover Design by Lori Patton O'Hara at Design5sixty4
Interior Design by Portia D. Sykes
Backcover Photo by Jamie Boone

I DEDICATE THIS BOOK TO THE BEST IN ALL OF US

Ad astra per aspera

Chapters

"My children, war, fear and disunity have brought you from your villages to this sacred council fire. Facing a common danger, and fearing for the lives of your families, you have drifted apart, each tribe thinking and acting only for itself. Remember how I took you from one band and nursed you into many nations. You must reunite now and act as one. No tribe alone can withstand our savage enemies, who care nothing about the eternal law, who sweep upon us like the storms of winter, spreading death and destruction everywhere. My children, listen well. Remember that you are brothers, that the downfall of one means the downfall of all."
- Hiawatha, Onondaga message from the Creator

❖

Foreword

This book began in the summer of 2017 when I realized I was sharing memes about climate change without knowing exactly what was being forecasted for the future, and not nearly enough about what to do about it.

It was an epiphany that packed a punch.

I knew then, in my bones, the world isn't in danger simply because of the Deniers among us, but instead, because the majority of us are Avoiders. It was a hard truth, because I was guilty. I'd avoided in-depth books, articles and documentaries on the subject because it's difficult to look at, even painful.

After my little 'Awakening', I faced the mirror and asked myself as a mother, "What harm is coming towards my family, what danger am I not adequately preparing for, just because I'm choosing to be willfully uninformed?"

Well, okay, those probably weren't my exact words, but it conveys the feeling. The answer to this question was that my ignorance could prove catastrophic. I decided to learn everything I could about climate change and how to survive it, vowing to use this information to protect my children.

There is no nice way to say this, so I'll be brutally honest, most of what I learned made me want to curl up into the fetal position and hide under the covers. One out of four days that summer I succumbed, rolling into a ball with despair in my stomach.

In a nutshell, I learned that the scientific community is screaming in their matter-of-fact, Vulcan-like, data-driven way, that it's going to take ALL of us to fix the problem, and there's little time to act.

The 'window of opportunity' is rapidly closing.

Fighting my instincts to move onto more pleasant topics, I dug deeper, reading projections of how things could shake out in the coming decades. Let me tell you, there are many, many shitty ways this can all go in the crapper, but only a few positive, ethical, logical and challenging ways to get it right.

I'll be honest, I worked the knowledge I found has hard as I could, like a dog with a bone, looking for loopholes, searching for ways I could get around the predictions. My urge to run and hide that year was a ten alarm fire inside me, but I could not find a place on the planet which would survive without damage.

Here's something to know about me: I don't do victimhood. During this time, a fierce desire to fight played alongside my fears. (Let's pray the world never nears true anarchy because the things I'm capable of and the rage I sometimes feel could unleash a monster. My soul, however, doesn't want to go that route.)

So, running was out and turning mercenary/angry-goddess/warrior-queen, fighting in do-or-die situations in a dystopian future, was a Big Nope on my life's wishlist for me and my kids.

Epiphany numero dos was realizing my family's safety was integrally tied up with how well others, my fellow earthbound neighbors, did in the world. (If you struggle, it increases the chances my family will struggle, and vice versa.) It therefore stood to reason that to solve the problem effectively for myself and my own children, I also had to figure out how to help the world. *Gulp!*

Luckily, my inner Mama Bear told me to "toughen the hell up", "to put on my Big Girl Panties" and to "look this Beast dead on in the eyes." I actually said that last one out loud to myself, and I was kind of mean about it, but sort of impressive like my best mom voice and some gladiator had combined; picture Clint Eastwood and Zena the Warrior Princess. I believe I even answered myself, "Yes, ma'am."

I imagine many of you will feel some degree of insanity and despair as you learn more about our environmental crisis. Please be strong. Remarkably, I uncovered a deeper truth which is that humans are remarkable and resilient creatures. There's irrefutable evidence we've overcome insurmountable odds, over and over again, by reinventing ourselves and adapting our culture. We fixed what was broken. Learning this truth of history's tendency to repeat gave me hope.

What we've done before, we can do again.

I wrote the intention for this book before I ever wrote a sentence. It stated that I wanted to write a popular love story that would wake up the masses to the coming changes and help us engage in the discussions we needed to be having. This novel is meant as a conversation starter, as an inspiration for others to look closely at what scares them and to rise up to the circumstances.

This love story contains a certain degree of sexual content; consider it a morality tale with fellatio and cunnilingus. You can think of it as a Scooby Snack reward for doing the hard work of thinking about tomorrow. I also just love sex, and since I wanted to write a life-affirming book, I decided it should have some good and healthy, but kind-of-naughty, intimate moments.

(NOTE- wearing condoms is an important protection against disease and unwanted pregnancies; they are invaluable in real life, but I dispensed with them in fiction. This book has enough tough subjects, so I decided to run with a virginal, multi-orgasmic male character and an experienced, Vixen-esque, infertile female, who engage in latex-free lovemaking. Please be smart with your own body and with others, always practice compassionate safe sex, and have fun allowing your mind and imagination to run wild!)

I also love music; it's unifying and helps us transcend our differences. Embedded in this story are many songs and musical artists whom inspired my writing. My deep gratitude to the artists who agreed for their lyrics to be included. I had oodles more initially, but ran out of time to get permission. (Next time, Jack Johnson and Neil Young...next time.)

I have purposefully avoided talk of politics and government, which was not an easy feat. In our current culture, the topic is beyond divisive. Instead, I wanted to focus on what unites us since I believe all humans are worthy of dignity and respect, regardless of whether they are moderate, conservative, progressive or balanced somewhere between. We cannot save the planet without all of our talents, insights, perspectives and wisdom.

Lastly, there's a fair degree of religious and spiritual messages in 'Eat the Moon'. In my musings, I simply could not see a solution which didn't include improving our conversations about God and the Universe. There are literally thousands of belief systems and religious denominations today, and many, many more in the past eons. I encourage people to be more accepting of differences and to embrace faith of one kind or another, even if it's a humanist belief in the goodness of our fellow men and women.

Currently, we are in the middle of a pandemic. COVID-19 has rocked our world. This book was almost finished before I ever heard the word, coronavirus. I've spent the past few months thinking long and hard about weaving it into the story, but ultimately decided to let this timeline exist as I had foreseen, a different version of the world before we ever got stuck in lockdown and witnessed so much death.

Like many of you, I'm grappling with the repercussions this disease will have on society, but I'm hopeful it may speed along the shift we need to create. As the character, Zia LeMay, states, "The world's going to shift and change no matter what happens, and some of those changes are going to be positive, even in a shitstorm. Focus on that. Always on the good."

This is my first novel, a three and a half year adventure from start to finish, from 'epiphany' to publication. During which time, not only did I radically change, but concurrently, the world did too.

In some ways, I am horrified by how crazy life has become these days, however, I'm more heartened now than when I started this project; people are growing gardens, playing music and being creative; the media is talking more about climate change, and elected officials are finally speaking up; where I live in San Juan County, New Mexico there are now more positive signs of making the transition from an oil and gas economy to a renewable energy one; even some 1%ers appear to be waking up.

It's a new day, but global warming is still a threat; not an existential one, but an honest-to-God, as-I-live-and-breathe crisis.

There's lots of work yet to be done, ladies and gentlemen. The changes in our systems and in our thinking which need to occur will be hampered by the natural law of inertia. None of us can accomplish this on our own. Personally, I believe we can move mountains…if we work together. Let's create a future we want to live in.

Ready, steady, go….

"I'm not afraid of storms,
for I'm learning how to sail my ship."
- Louisa May Alcott

Chapter 1: Eye of the Storm

Colton took his hands off the wheel and killed the boat's engine. He didn't have to look behind him to know the storm would hit any moment; he could feel it coming, like a remnant from a bad dream. His ears rang with its heart-stopping roar, the hair on his arms raised, skin tingling, a metallic taste in his molars. Reluctantly, he turned to watch the wall of advancing rain battering Navajo Lake, slapping and pounding the surface as if it were miraculously solid enough to walk upon.

With little time to act, he raced to the edge of the boat, searching the starboard side for the stranded woman in the water. Peering down, he found her, wide-eyed and pale-faced, fighting wildly to right an overturned kayak which was still buoyed by trapped air. Seeing him, her grim look of raw desperation was replaced by a bright light, as if the sun shone inside of her.

For a brief moment, Colton thought he'd seen the face of an angel.

In the east, lightning exploded, crackling with foreboding energy.

The mist thickened into a fog, obscuring his vision, before changing into a merciless pelting like a faucet turned on high. Reflexively, he gasped as he was instantly chilled and soaked to the bone by the unexpected and unwelcome baptism.

Struggling to see, he reached down into the dark and difficult waves, his fingers momentarily brushing against hers. The yellow kayak lost its battle and transformed into a yellow submarine, plummeting into the depths of the lake. Suddenly, her strong hand grasped his own, and under the torrential downpour, he helped her climb onto the deck.

Above, thunder cracked like a god with an urgent message.

The storm surged ahead, its clouds swirling in an arc, high in the sky, up and over them in a downdraft, its forceful tailwind driving the rain parallel to the lake.

To Colton, it felt like a perverse tidal wave descending from above as a high-pressured firehose assaulted him simultaneously.

With no other option for escape, they hid under the small roof of the center console, huddling together for shelter, but the wind and rain came at them from all directions, seeming to defy the law of gravity. Heads down and bodies entwined, they curled on the floor as the boat lurched and swayed with a stomach-churning recklessness.

Colton felt the young woman shaking in his arms, then realized the sensation was coming from himself. His breathing was hitched, ragged with adrenaline as unwanted memories of a past hurricane hijacked his mind; the raging wind and turbulent water were overwhelmingly familiar.

Please God, he thought and prayed, *I don't want to die!*

Fighting his escalating panic, he looked up with half-closed eyes through the gloom to gauge their position.

His boat had been driven like a child's toy towards the steep walled portion of the Pine River Pass. Sandstone cliffs enveloped them on both sides as they swiftly drifted towards the rain-slicked rocks.

"I have to stop the boat!" he yelled over the tumultuous noise.

The young woman released her arms which had been clutching him tightly around his waist.

The two untangled clumsily and stood up together to face the next challenge.

"Oh, shit," she said, cursing as the cliff face sped towards them.

Clambering to the front of the craft, she searched the bench seats for padding and quickly attached them to the sides of the boat as a cushion against the shock of impact.

Colton turned towards the steering console. He tried starting the engine, but it remained stalled. Irrevocably, the rocks drew closer. Bending down, he grabbed a rope, making sure the knot was secure, then wrestled the anchor overboard, the line unfurling rapidly at his feet.

The boat snapped to a halt, jarring both passengers, a mere four feet away from the canyon wall.

Time stretched and held its breath, the way Time sometimes does. Three minutes passed in slow motion before the apocalyptic rain dialed down to a typical summer thunderstorm, still intense but no longer of biblical proportions.

"That was close," the young woman said, looking up at the sky.

Her voice was direct, like she was making a calculated observation, but there was a slightly haunted look in her blue eyes as she contemplated the receding storm.

Her lips were a cherry red and her hair was an amber glow of wet tendrils down her shoulders. She was petite and curvy, what cleavage dared to show from the top of her dark green t-shirt was wet with rain and sun-kissed with light freckles.

On her shirt was a picture of the planet Earth with the words, 'Save Me'.

How ironic, he thought.

He watched her take a deep breath and stretch her body, raising her arms above her head, her feet up on tiptoe. Holding the pose, she balanced upon the waves and gazed appreciatively around her as if it was the most beautiful view she'd ever seen.

When her eyes finally settled on his, her smile broadened.

Colton's heart clichéd and skipped a beat.

"Hi," she said, reaching for his hand. "I'm Saffron."

"Every dream begins with a dreamer. Always remember, you have within you the strength, the patience, and the passion to reach for the stars to change the world."
- Harriet Tubman

Chapter 2: Dawn of a New Day

Saffron LeMay awoke to the soft glow of a Himalayan salt lamp, its rosy light growing steadily brighter upon the curved dome of her bedroom. As always, her first conscious thought was, *'This moment is a gift'.* The practice was a trick she'd learned from her mother, choosing to start each day with gratitude instead of dread and irritation. The habit helped clear the unease from her last dream, a reoccurring one she hadn't had in awhile.

She'd never considered it a bad dream, but it had never felt particularly good either.

Her thinking was interrupted by her cat, Bucky, rising from his perch at the end of the bed and draping himself across her in true Ragdoll fashion.

Like a limp lion, she thought sleepily, crushed by his weight.

Named after R. Buckminster Fuller, the visionary futurist who'd inspired her geodesic room, Buckminster the Cat was, at least in Saffron's opinion, worthy of a Nobel Prize for Best Pet in the World. She stroked his soft fur, feeling his purrs vibrating into her chest. Cat-like, she too languidly stretched; her lithe, nude body lengthening to touch the coolness outside the body-warmed sheets beneath her.

Her cornflower eyes opened onto a triangular skylight. In the light of day, she could view the sage-strewn bluffs wrapped around the tiny town of Navajo Dam. At 5:00 am, however, only the starlight from the nearest neighbors in the Milky Way could be seen in the still-darkened sky.

"Well, boy," she said quietly as her fingers worked into Bucky's fur, his fat plume of a tail swishing in feline delight, "I guess it's time to get moving."

She gave him one last tussle on the head and got out of bed.

Descending a spiral staircase, she plunged into the darkened room below her bedroom, knowing the timer for the salt lamp would soon shut off in a conservation of energy.

At the bottom of the stairs, she flipped a switch, revealing her living space by the haunting light of Moroccan lamps which cast tiny diamonds across the stacked books and extinguished candles on the coffee table. Near the stereo and turntable were a microphone and guitar for when the urge to make music called, which was often. The adobe walls were adorned with bookshelves, scarves and tapestries, her favorite depicting a large, bejeweled elephant; her own private Ganesha.

She passed her plush sofa with its cushions in varying hues and styles to make a Sultan swoon: gold and teal, mustard and fuchsia, mandalas and paisleys. In the center was one with a peacock boastfully displaying its plumage. Next to it was a heart-shaped pillow that read in hand-stitched cursive, *Fuck The Rich*.

Saffron liked to think of her home, with its Bedouin feel and hippie-punk flare, as a true Bohemian Rhapsody. Constructed with earthbags then buried under dirt berms, her Hobbit-like house felt like a warm, insulating blanket.

At the end of the living room, pale moonlight shone through a large picture window and an open door leading to a greenhouse. A half-crescent moon hung low on the horizon, silhouetting the bountiful indoor plants in a dim, silver light.

Inside the atrium, windows and vegetation traversed the full length of the Earthship, providing a riotous glory of food, flowers and oxygen. Somewhere in the greenery, a cricket chirped.

Saffron padded down the long hallway to the first door on the right, a layer of turquoise patina over its aged wood. Inside the restroom, she kept the dimmer switch low. Her reflection swam mysteriously in the mirror as her liquid eyes held the last remnants of sleep in their depths. Her strawberry blonde hair looked darker in the light from the stamped tin sconces, the play of shadows making her appear underwater.

Water itself had a full life and history in her house. Rain, falling onto the high desert, was captured by a collection system before being routed to a cistern buried deep in the coolness of the earth. The rainwater was then filtered before its use in the sinks and showers.

Saffron thought it was the best tasting water in the world.

Drains led to the greenhouse plants in the front atrium, the gravelly soil cleansing out the biodegradable soaps the LeMay household used. The grey water was then collected in tanks for use in the toilet; the resultant black water, finally pumped to the front yard, to the plant life her father affectionately called 'The Shit Eaters'.

With the morning's urgency completed, she turned off the light and continued down the hallway to the main living quarters; her mother's domain.

The air was lightly scented with Tibetan incense. Numerous rugs invited her bare feet to explore the natural fibers woven by practiced hands. Artwork from Santa Fe and various Indigenous people littered the space like a gallery. Tables and countertops were graced by bright, hand-painted tiles; the walls and ceiling, sculpted with nooks, crannies and swirls her mother alone had envisioned and coaxed out of the clay, then brought to life with jewel-toned pigments.

Overall, the home had a reverential, sacred air to it.

Saffron considered it a sanctuary from the outside world, a haven from all that was broken and wrong. The warm feeling extended towards her neighbors who shared the intentional community with her.

Most of the planning, the real estate acquisition, and the construction of 'The Colony' had been her mother's idea, discussed in rooms redolent with marijuana smoke and the laughter of friends whom Zia had loved and admired. If the Sweetwater commune had been a child, Zia LeMay was surely the Mommy.

No one could accuse Zia of lacking in dreams; she practically crackled with the fire of creation, like an archaic goddess.

Saffron's father, Jack, the smitten yet practical one, had always been at her mother's side to help her dreams come true; at least, the ones within reason. The last project on her honey-do list had been an outdoor oven for use during the summer, but he'd not yet staged the weeklong music festival she'd requested.

Wood-fired pizza, however, was a testament to their enduring partnership.

In the kitchen, Saffron took a green mug from a cabinet teeming with handmade pottery and put a tea kettle onto a hot plate. By the bluish glow of a solar lamp, she took hard-boiled eggs with golden yolks, added homemade mayo, mixed in relish from a Ball glass jar, then wrapped the egg salad in fresh lettuce from the greenhouse. Delicately, she took a crunchy, satisfying bite.

As the tea kettle began its shrill cry, her dad emerged groggily down a wrought iron staircase from another dome above. He wore a Johnny Cash t-shirt and cargo pants, but would have looked equally at home in simple cotton trousers, suspenders and a coonskin cap, like his great-great-great-grandfather, Jacques Francois LeMay, a French-Canadian trader and trapper, may have worn.

Jack's dirty-blond hair, with the inevitable greying of a fifty year old man on the sides of his still youthful face, was sticking up in a faux-hawk, either by the whim of his pillows or by his own hands. The stubble on his jaw seemed undecided as to whether it was there for the long haul or if it would be clean-shaven by afternoon. With Jack LeMay, it was a toss of the dice.

"Mornin', Saffy." Only her parents called her Saffy. "Did you sleep well?"

Saffron swallowed and said hesitantly, "Sort of. I had that crazy dream again about finding dozens of fish tanks hidden in closets and piled high in secret rooms I didn't know existed. As usual, they were filthy, and some of the fish were weird and mutated-looking, but they're all still alive. I always wonder what they've been eating and how they've survived without me."

Saffron had been having this same dream throughout her teenage years. Self-diagnosing, she typically associated it with an uptick in anxiety, her long-standing worries that life and its delicate ecosystems were out of balance.

Fear for the future was never far from her mind.

"Sounds to me like it's time to clean the tilapia tank," Jack said.

"I did that last week," she said grumpily. "I think it means I'm overwhelmed. Too much is beyond my control."

She let her statement drop like an anvil, but Jack didn't let her words carry them down; worrying about the state of the world was common for the LeMays, but beginning the day talking about it was against family rules.

"I think it means you're avoiding something," he said. "All this heat, hotter than last year, that algae could get out of control. But sure, we can put it off for another week or two."

Saffron rose and turned her back, her mouth stubbornly working the soundless words, *Dreams aren't literal, Dad.* Lifting the kettle, she poured the hot water over a tea ball full of fragrant oolong leaves, herbs and spices.

As they sat quietly, sipping masala chai and gazing out the picture window at the sunrise's golden ascension, animation returned to her father's good-looking and good-natured face.

He sighed contentedly, a man at peace, and gave her a loving smile, his blue eyes so similar in hue to her own.

She smiled back and let her negative thoughts drift away.

Zia glided down the spiral staircase in a swirl of red, orange and white from the koi fish adorning her Japanese silk kimono. Her auburn hair was tossed into a messy bun, errant waves cascading down her slim shoulders. Exuding health and vitality, she looked fresh and ready to devour the day, even at dawn and fifty-five years of age.

"Good morning, Beautifuls!" her mother's lilting voice sang out.

The cricket began chittering its own song.

"Oh!" she exclaimed, her green eyes sparkling with delight. "We have a visitor!"

Saffron sighed. "Crickets are annoying, Mom."

"Crickets are good luck," she retorted. "Today is a good day."

Zia used the phrase, 'Today is a good day', with the precision of a Swiss-made watch. One could count on her uttering the phrase daily, regardless of whether 'good' or 'bad' things were occurring.

Saffron smiled and shook her head.

All in all, she loved her parents, and their quirks.

Jack rose from the table to sweep his wife of twenty-five years into a deep kiss and embrace. Unapologetically enamored, the heat between them was sometimes palpable from afar.

Saffron carried her dirty cup to the kitchen and left them to their affections.

If asked, she would've said she admired their continued passion for each other. Sex had never been a taboo subject growing up and the frank discussions from a young age had developed her confidence, helping her avoid the misery and frustration of many of her peers.

At the age of eighteen, she'd demanded to have her tubes tied. The doctor had vehemently argued with her until her parents were called in to say she was perfectly capable of making the decision for herself and, 'would they please refrain from calling in matters of their adult daughter who was of age and no longer a minor'.

Saffron had relished in the blustering look of frustration on the physician's face.

Her parents had just smiled, kissed her on the top of her head and left. She'd never told anyone outside the commune this story, knowing most people wouldn't understand.

She hoped one day they would.

Bringing more children into this world was not something Saffron intended to do. If she ever found true love, she thought maybe she would be open to adoption or fostering, to care for an unwanted child who hadn't asked to be alone in this world. She considered it a strong possibility for some future time, but for now, sex was a hedonistic distraction from the seriousness of life and a wonderful way to connect and elevate on a higher, more intimate plane.

Unfortunately, she briefly thought, *I haven't gotten lucky in awhile.*

She returned to the table with a cup of tea for her mother. With Zia's inexhaustible energy, she certainly didn't need the caffeine, but frequently choose it for the sheer pleasure of drinking hot tea with milk and honey.

"Thanks Roni," Zia said, using Saffron's other nickname. She took a sip and smiled, eyes closed, savoring the exquisite scent and taste. Cupping the warm mug with both hands, steam rising near her face, she opened her eyes and asked, "So, what's on your agenda today?"

Saffron's pulse quickened as she remembered what she had planned.

"*Eeeeeee*!!!" she squealed, an impromptu dance erupting from her body. "I'm taking the kayak out on the lake for her maiden voyage!"

"Nice," said Jack enthusiastically. "I wish I could join you, but I've got to muck out the chicken coop before it gets too hot. The compost heap is going to love that manure. And, I think your mom is picking zucchinis for the farmers market. There's a ton this year."

"Oh, I'll be back in a couple of hours to help," Saffron said. "I was planning on working in the greenhouse this evening after it cools down."

She spent most of her time working in Sweetwater, along with teaching yoga in nearby Aztec. With no private classes planned for the day, she was looking forward to the inaugural use of the new kayak she'd bought in Durango; many downward dogs and sun salutations had gone into its procurement.

Her mom smiled and absentmindedly reached for Jack's hand. Today was a good day.

"The secret of getting ahead is getting started."
- Mark Twain

Chapter 3: Rise and Shine

Colton James Miller was an early riser, but thanks to yet another nightmare, he was rudely awoken hours before dawn.

He rarely remembered his bad dreams, only the panicky and disoriented feelings they left behind, like he was racing in the wrong direction down a fast-moving and turbulent train; lurching unsteadily while something sinister followed him, step by step, gaining speed.

Alone in the dark, Colton shuddered, feeling off-kilter and ill-equipped to handle whatever was coming.

Realizing he wasn't going to fall back to sleep, he turned on a light and bounded out of bed, dropping to the carpet for his daily push-ups. Eager for his anxiety to go away, he refused to recall any details of the nightmare. Instead, he let the memories turn fuzzy as he focused on his form and breathing.

The exercise worked, and with a clearer head, he went outside in the pre-dawn twilight. A sliver of moon sliced the starry sky. Crossing the gravel yard towards a white metal barn, he appreciated the cool, summer air on his face; the day ahead was expected to be a scorcher.

It was smart to muck the horse stalls and lug straw bales before it got too hot.

Inside, the barn smelled of sweet hay. He took a deep breath and let the last of his lingering unease disappear. Tending to his horses, Dusty and HoneyLemon, always made him feel better.

In truth, just being outside usually did the trick.

"Good mornin', ladies," he said in a gentle voice to a painted quarterhorse and a palomino mare. Both stretched their necks and nuzzled his hands. "Be glad you're not human, girls. It's not an easy job."

HoneyLemon bobbed her golden head as if in agreement.

When his chores were completed and his bad dream long forgotten, he relaxed and soaped himself clean in a long, hot shower. Steam clouded the stone-tiled bathroom. Over the steady pulse of the water, he sang with a passion he rarely displayed in public. The one exception being the previous winter during a pub crawl in Durango for his twenty-first birthday; that night, he'd gotten drunk for the first time in his life, and had fearlessly sung his heart out in a country and western karaoke bar.

The memory of that night was foggier than the vapor-filled room.

Still humming 'Hands on the Wheel' by Willie Nelson, Colton pulled the curtain aside and grabbed a worn towel to wrap around his firm waist. He rubbed a forearm across the mirror, revealing his day old scruff.

His hazel green eyes shone brightly in the mirror with a pleasant inner thought.

Many of his thoughts lately centered on Kaelynne, his girlfriend, who herself was nearing her twenty-first birthday. Fantasizing of how they might celebrate the special day together made him hard under the cotton towel.

Whoa, whoa, whoa, CJ, he said, willing his erection to disappear. *Remember...no ring-a, no vagin-a.*

The words 'resist tempation' and 'sin no more' from a church pamphlet came to his mind. Obediently, Colton cut off his sexual train of thought and focused his attention on shaving. Halfway through however, with white cream on the left side of his face and some in his hand, temptation won out.

Somehow, imagining Kaelynne's wedding gown tossed haphazardly on top of a chair made him feel less guilty and shameful as he emptied himself into the sink.

During high school, every student had been asked to sign a chastity agreement, promising to refrain from sex until marriage. Abstinence-only curriculum had been taught in the area for decades, even after many schools in the country had abolished it. Many of the churches preached it as well, including his.

Colton even knew couples who were waiting for their wedding vows before they ever kissed, which seemed totally extreme to him.

He was fine with waiting for marriage, however. All of his three older siblings had married their first loves and he was intent on doing the same. With time however, it was getting harder to remain chaste. Thankfully, Kaelynne wasn't opposed to other forms of touching as long as it wasn't 'all the way'.

Lately, she'd been dropping hints she'd waited long enough.

Lord knows I have, he thought, and immediately regretted it.

The pressure to marry her had been mounting. Several of their friends were either engaged or married already, but Colton couldn't seem to wrestle the courage to pop the question. The timing never felt right, especially while working in his family's struggling business.

His grandfather, Alton Justice Miller, had started their company during Farmington, New Mexico's heyday years. Miller Gas Supplies operated as a service and repair company for the natural gas and oilfield industries; however, the good old days of making a killing in the Four Corners area had been over for awhile.

It was the unfortunate curse of living in a boom and bust town; it was easy to slip from glory to ruin.

Colton didn't exactly feel like he was setting the world on fire.

In truth, he often felt like the sky was falling; it was getting harder to ignore the uncertainty in the world, as well as the increasing pushback against fossil fuels.

Usually he chose not to dwell on it, avoiding the tension in his house and the office by busying himself with other things, but admittedly, there was an emptiness in him that he couldn't adequately describe, a feeling that things wouldn't quite right themselves in the unknowable future ahead.

Proposing to Kaelynne, while he felt so lost and unsure, had never felt like a good idea.

Without a wedding ring however, he had to control his desires.

Dressing quickly in a white t-shirt and dark blue jeans, he donned his favorite cowboy hat, not the going-out one, but the comfortable, perfectly-fitting-his-head one, and headed downstairs.

He was hoping today would be a good day. He had his sights set on boating at Navajo Lake with a cold six-pack, his pole in the water, and the lull of the waves rocking his boat while he enjoyed a fresh breeze; a simple day without complex worries.

Humming under his breath, he strode down the wide staircase, past intricate crosses and numerous family photos, many in frames that Colton and his brother and sisters had crafted when they were younger. School pictures, baby pictures and a few wedding photos vied for space along with ones of the Miller children roping and riding, hiking and camping, smiling and posing. Near the bottom of the staircase, he gazed at one of himself, an ear-splitting grin across his youthful face, as he held up a large bass with one hand and a rainbow trout with the other.

He hoped to catch similar ones later in the day.

Hurrying through the great room with its cathedral ceilings and large dark windows, he moved towards the kitchen, the smell of rich coffee making his mouth water. Scrolled above the kitchen sink window were the words *God Bless Our Home and Family* in beautiful calligraphy.

Currently, he shared the home with both his parents and his sister Meaghan, whose marriage had recently ended in divorce. She practically oozed disappointment and negativity. Colton's attempts to comfort her had failed miserably. She preferred to hide in her room watching television, possibly adding rum to all of the Cokes she was downing. For certain, large amounts of junk food were disappearing into the sanctum of her grief-filled room.

Colton's mother, Cricket, was mourning the 'loss of her unborn grandkids' by throwing herself into baking, and had even started bugging Colton about having kids of his own. Closer to the oven, he could detect the faint smell of blueberry muffins beginning to brown.

He was aching to move out next summer. Asa, his dad, was going to give him a large bonus when he turned twenty-two, like he'd done with his other three children. Some days, Colton worried the family business wouldn't be worth much by then. Unfortunately, he had no other choice except waiting until, as his father had once said, 'the wild oats of being young' were worked out of his system.

Whatever the heck that means, Colton thought bitterly.

Typically, he spent five long days every week doing his dad's bidding, with his weekends spent either with Kaelynne or Gage Stockton, her brother and his best friend. Last Saturday, the two young men had spent hours four-wheeling at Chokecherry Canyon. Afterwards, he'd taken Kaelynne out for dinner and a movie, followed the next day by Sunday worship and a potluck meal with church friends.

From his perspective, he wasn't living recklessly, and he resented the wait to be acknowledged and treated like an adult. In his mind, the sooner he had a bigger paycheck, the sooner he would move out and propose... and the sooner he could cease being a virgin.

Maybe then the nightmares will stop, he reasoned.

With a steaming cup of coffee in hand, he popped a bagel into the toaster on the granite countertop, stopping at the fridge for cream cheese and a six pack of Coors for the boat.

His mother walked in from the laundry room adjacent to the kitchen, her arms wide with a basket of folded clothes. Her silver-blonde hair was perfectly curled in waves down to her shoulders, her L.L. Bean outfit tailored to downplay her middle-aged paunch. Even at this early hour, her make-up had been expertly applied.

"Good mornin', Colt," her southern accent sang. "I was just headin' up to your room. Luckily, I was able to get that oil stain offa your shirt."

Colton had changed the oil in his Ford F-150 a couple days earlier. He hadn't cared much that it had gotten stained, since technically it was a work shirt, but he knew it was in his mother's nature to try.

"Thanks, Mom," he said graciously.

His father sauntered in from the great room and looked surprised to see him.

"What're you still doing here?" he said gruffly, his blue eyes glinting like ice chips while lines of disapproval knitted his brow. "It's after 5:30. I thought you'd left by now."

Asa still maintained a full head of brown and greying hair. His beard was clipped cleanly on his sun-weathered face. He too carried a little more around the middle, but he refused to go on the multitude of diets his wife was always trying.

People frequently said he had a stubborn streak, but his mother often remarked that his bark was worse than his bite. Colton took it to mean his father was intimidating without necessarily meaning to be.

Sometimes, it was hard to remember.

"What're you talking about, Dad?" he responded sheepishly. "It's Saturday. It's my day off." He instantly regretted how whiny his voice sounded as he watched his father's face darken.

"Colton! I sent you a memo yesterday that the Turkey Hill pump had gone offline. If we don't get that son of a bitch up and running, it's going to be a sad an' sorry day for you." Asa paused, then let each syllable of his next sentence come out with the impact of unquestionable authority. "Now-git-out-there-and-git-her-runnin'."

Colton had completely forgotten about the broken pump. He pictured the long haul to where the remote patch resided on federal land.

"That's more than thirty minutes each way," he said. Again, the whine was minimal, but still there. "I was planning on taking the boat out on the lake."

"Tough shit, tough guy. No excuses," Asa said, passing him on the way to the coffeemaker, ostensibly dismissing him with that parting remark. "It won't get fixed on its own."

"Yes, sir," Colton said, grabbing the keys by the back door and letting himself into the three car garage. His gleaming white truck stood on the pristine gloss of the carport next to his father's King Ranch model and his mother's red Explorer.

The Millers were Ford people.

He loaded his cooler and placed his fishing gear in the back. The garage door eased up quietly, revealing the break of sunrise on the horizon. Strapping on his seat belt and sighing deeply, Colton realized he didn't mind hard work, but he definitely hoped it wouldn't be long before he got a chance to play too.

"Stop acting so small.
You are the universe in ecstatic motion."
- Rumi

Chapter 4: Kundalini Kayak

Saffron strolled outside in the early morning air on her way to the orchard. Her home in Sweetwater was located on a small rise below Navajo Dam where the San Juan river spilled down, creating an oasis in the desert.

She didn't talk about it often, but she'd always felt like there was a pulse, a force, beating just under the surface; a primal feeling that behind an invisible veil, there was power.

For the ancestral people, the Puebloans or Anasazi, this land and its abundant river waters had been a Holy Land; for the Spanish conquistadors, a potential goldmine; and for the early pioneers, a Manifest Destiny. Over the last one hundred years, the region had drawn even more settlers. Nearby Farmington had grown and prospered, originally full of apple orchards and ranches, and then as the age of modern living had taken over, farming had been replaced by coal, oil and gas.

Zia had purchased the sixty-acre parcel with several of her friends when Saffron was eight years old. The planning and construction of the many different dwellings had taken time and a lot of sweat equity. In total, there were twelve homes; two 'tiny' houses, a half dozen dome homes, a few traditional, round hogans which were native to the area, and two other Earthships. These were similar to her own house with the exception of the two white domes on the second level, a rebellious architecture which her mother's feminist friends adored.

A drone from above would be ogling two tits with triangular areoles.

The site built homes were either painted white to reflect back the sun's merciless rays, or else they were a natural adobe stucco, blending with the sandy dirt around them. The tiny homes were both tall with rustic log siding and clerestory windows at the top near their loft areas to ventilate out the heat. Every home was outfitted with solar panels.

Throughout Sweetwater were colorful, sailcloth awnings to cut down the sun's glare, minimizing the heat load on the homes and structures, as well as creating shady spots for the residents to enjoy. Benches and mismatched chairs clustered chummily together out of the summer's fierce brilliance.

The communal spaces included a large yurt for gathering, two commercial-sized greenhouses, a wood-fired hot tub, and a stage which had been constructed from strawbales, plaster and tree limbs; wavy blue lines mimicking the river were painted on the back wall.

Pathways of stones and pebbles crisscrossed the commune, edged by borders of drought-loving plants. As Saffron passed by, the rain barrels dotting the landscaping stood empty and ready to collect any precious drops that the Sky might have to offer.

Everywhere, honeybees had their attention drawn to the siren song of fragrant blooms before they returned to their hives under a large cottonwood. In the shade below, they worked their magic, transforming pollen and nectar into beeswax and fresh honey. When the wind was just right, the golden scent would drift across the field, creating a mouthwatering temptation.

As with the bees, today's opened flowers beckoned to Saffron. She deeply inhaled the perfume of a pink blossomed rose before leaving the orchard with a ripe peach in hand.

Food abounded on the property. Permaculture and smart water techniques were practiced for both the ornamental plants along the pathways and in the greenhouses and fields. Herbs and medicinal plants grew root to root and leaf to leaf within a multitude of garden beds.

For years, the people in Sweetwater had been collecting, hunting down ancient, heirloom seeds from nearby locales as well as varieties from intensely arid locations such as Australia, Egypt and Iraq. They'd gone looking for the Heat Lovers, the Sun Worshippers, and the Water Deniers.

They hoped they had found The Survivors.

Sustainability may have been the backbone of Sweetwater, but music was its heart. All of the residents participated in its creation and enjoyment in some form or another. Saffron had been singing long before she had learned to strum a guitar. As was typical on a Saturday night in the summer, she planned to join the others to jam under the stars.

Licking peach juice from her fingers, she glanced down below the rise of Sweetwater's compound. Russian olives and majestic cottonwoods towered along the riverbed line. On the opposite bank, a stunning craggy bluff rose up, boldly displaying the geological layers of millennia past.

The entire area had once been under an ancient ocean.

Saffron sometimes mused if this land would once again succumb to the sea as the planet continued to change.

Her new kayak was set up on a small trailer hitch near a shed on the side of her house. It was bright yellow and fairly lightweight. Pulling it with her bike gave her some hesitation, yet she was determined to try it before giving in and using a car.

Most of the Colonists had electric ones they recharged with solar panels. Saffron, instead, had a hand-me-down Hyundai that got great gas mileage, but it still irked her to use it. Plus, she feared that the sun-scorched, peeling paint job did not say, 'Reduce! Reuse! Recycle!' like she wanted it to, but rather screamed, 'Poor Ass Hippy!'

Ready to enjoy the day, she hitched the trailer to her bike and pedaled out of the gate for the trek to the marina. The sun rose over the rolling desert much to the excitement of a bevy of quail; the line of seven birds burst from under a cholla bush, leaning slightly forward like mimes in a windstorm, the tiny curls on their heads bouncing with each step, until they disappeared under the cover of a large sage bush.

The cool breeze felt good on her face and shoulders as the day was already beginning to warm as if the sun had stored its heat all night and was ready to unleash it, like pouring water out of a bucket, drenching everything in sight until it boiled. She planned to be home in the coolness of her buried house during the height of the day for a summertime siesta, a family tradition during months when the afternoon heat made so many outside tasks unbearable.

The steep climb to the dam was indeed challenging, but she was pleased that she could do it, albeit with concentration and exertion. At the marina, she dropped her kayak at the water's edge and tied the bike and trailer to the fence near the dock. Holding the paddle against the side of the Hobie, she pushed off the rocky shore, climbed in, and aimed herself for the deep blue waters in front of her.

The lake was far from placid, but it wasn't terribly choppy either, only mild swells.

After a minute, she stopped and took a large sip of water before heading deeper out. Her small backpack included a pouch and straw so she could drink without the risk of dropping a bottle into the lake. Littering made her crazy. She always kept a bag with her to gather whatever garbage came her way. Most days, it would be full of styrofoam and plastic by the time she was done.

Some people didn't seem to share her hatred for throwing stuff away without a care.

She resumed paddling, and soon the rhythm of her body's movements, coupled with the *slap swoosh slap swoosh* timing of the paddle, allowed her to slip into a blissful meditation. Taking in big belly breaths and exhaling slowly through her nose, her eyes softened and slipped out of focus to enjoy the play of colors reflecting back at her.

The dawning light kaleidoscoped along the surface of the water like a mirage, appearing to reveal dimensions beyond this one.

Saffron had heard stories about a sacred site, Tohe-ha-glee, that was hidden somewhere beneath the lake. No one she'd asked was exactly sure where it'd been located. When the dam had been built back in the 1960's, the valley had been purposely flooded and the magical area which had been called 'Shining-Sands-located-at-the-Meeting-Place-of-Waters' had been drowned under its depths along with several pioneer homesteads.

Her mother had told her that before the water burial, the site had been where purified medicine men, bearing songs, prayers and offerings, had come to be provided with insights about upcoming changes; disastrous changes in particular. They'd come to hear the warning call and be granted visions for what needed to be done in order for them to be spared. Zia herself claimed to have been given a prophecy on the lake many years ago.

Saffron could not fully explain how deeply pulled she felt to this place. She often came to meditate and pray, beseeching God and the angels, the spirits and deities, to show her 'the way'. She liked to imagine this powerful location was below her whenever she was out on the lake. She dreamt it still emanated a force, like a holy beacon, calling to those who could hear its cautionary song.

Realizing she was humming again, the vibrations lightly tickling her lips, Saffron began her morning mantras.

"Onnnggg," she chanted and inhaled.

"Naaaammmo." The syllables were held long as she slowly exhaled.

"Guru…Dev…Namo," she sang.

This Kundalini mantra meant 'I call upon Divine Wisdom', and the chanting worked to expand her consciousness. She felt her solid form melting, dissolving into the lake beneath her, the arid land surrounding her, and the blue sky above her. After a few minutes of quiet meditation, she switched to the Guru Gaitri mantra which was supposed to unite the two hemispheres of her brain for better logic and creativity, as well as to expand her heart chakra.

It was designed to increase compassion, tolerance and patience, three traits she wanted to work on strengthening.

"Gobinday, Mukunday, Uderay, Apaaray," she sang, hearing the lyrical Sanskrit words carrying out over the waves. "Hariang, Kariang, Nirnamay, Akaamay."

The Guru Gaitri mantra had several translations. Most were about truth-seeking. The definition Saffron liked best was 'sustainer, liberator; enlightener, infinite; destroyer, creator; nameless, desireless.' It was one she frequently used to increase her resilience and quell her fears.

She used it to prepare her soul for the sufferings and sacrifices of tomorrow.

At a young age, too young probably, Saffron had learned that the planet was nearing a cataclysmic end. The orgiastic usage of fossil fuels, along with the contributions of tipping points across the world, was driving temperatures higher. Her parents and their friends had been activists, trying to manifest changes and raise awareness before the climate destabilized to an unstoppable status, called runaway global warming, or, as they often called it, The Hot Mess.

As carbon dioxide levels kept creeping up, unresponsive to any changes or lack of changes that the world's governments were making, the emphasis in her family and group had shifted more towards survival, to a more concrete plan of action, and to finding peace within, peace in the moment, peace in the Now.

It took practice to find this peace because underneath the surface, Saffron brewed an intensely hot, bitter-tasting anger and resentment. Meditation was one of her antidotes to the rage. Sex was also a useful tool, as well as music and dancing, and laughter.

Last night, the group had projected the cult classic, 'Hitchhiker's Guide to the Galaxy', on a big, white sheet spread across the back of the stage. The film made light of planets being destroyed with an absurdity that rang a bit too close to home.

Saffron felt her center slipping as the negative thoughts pulled her away from the peaceful place within. Her 'connection-to-all' feeling dissipated as she found herself slipping back into the 3D world, back into her blood, bone, and body with its accompanying thoughts circling like buzzards.

Desperately, she wanted to return to her relaxed state. Taking in the quiet of the lake, she let it suffuse her being. Her perception again extended out beyond the sensory nervous system contained by her skin. Her spine straightened and she felt a pulling sensation up through the top of her head through the crown chakra. Saffron allowed herself to let go, giving herself permission to dissolve into nothing and everything at the same time. Her nagging thoughts and fears drained effortlessly away as the kayak glided blindly ahead.

With closed eyes, she listened to the paddles slipping in and out of the granite-colored water.

Slap swoosh.

Slap swoosh.

Slap swoosh.

The rhythmic sounds of her paddle interspersed with her deep breathing. Her spine and torso twisted gently side to side in a rotational dance, like an undulating cobra under the spell of a flute. Her skin tingled as if an invisible, electric current passed millimeters above it; an energy field she could suddenly feel expanding well beyond her, touching all other beings on the planet.

Her spirit soared away, high out of her body.

Saffron felt like the embodiment of Love as the shoreline receded farther and farther behind her, never once glancing back. The new yellow kayak cut a trail of sliced water in its wake while the sky darkened ominously above her.

Slap swoosh.

"A person often meets his destiny
on the road he took to avoid it."
- Jean de La Fontaine

Chapter 5: Bumpy Road

The Turkey Hill well site was in the middle of nowhere, even by local standards; an isolated patch of stamped-down dirt in an otherwise empty landscape. Everything in the yard was painted green and tan in an attempt to blend with the scenery, but no amount of camouflage could disguise the machinery's man-made, metallic nature, nor hide its insistent and unnatural drone.

With a non-functioning pump jack, however, the quiet was almost palpable.

To an untrained eye, the view would've been described as barren, but life did its best to exist. Outside the perimeter of the fence, where routine weed spraying couldn't reach, were strongly determined flora and fauna spread amongst the sandstone and rocks, intent on surviving under the sweltering sky.

Above, a red-tailed hawk resolutely searched for its unlucky prey.

"Bumblefuck with a capitol B," Colton mumbled irritably as he drank the last slug of black coffee. With his poor night's sleep, he was already craving more and was yearning to be done with the work so he could get to the lake. The heat on his bent-over back felt like it was increasing exponentially by the minute.

After half an hour of kneeling in the hot sun and dust, Colton made what he hoped would be his last repair. He'd finally located the broken part only after checking several technological, electrical and mechanical possibilities to blame for the pump's immobility; every second of its inactivity, evaluated, recorded and transmitted by a computer which was powered by a solar panel.

The sun never breaks down and quits working, he thought grumpily.

The job had taken much longer than he'd hoped.

Like everything else in my life, he lamented.

And every minute this pump stays down, his father's gravelly voice reminded him, *is a dollar lost!*

With frustration and perspiration mounting, Colton dropped his wrench and picked up a handful of rocks. Hurling each stone as hard, as fast, and as far as he could, he broke the silence by yelling into the desert, "I...want...a...better...life!!!"

The urgency in his voice, as well as the words themselves, took him by surprise.

This time he heard his mother's voice, "*My, oh my, aren't we in an ill temper?*"

Sighing heavily, he resumed working.

With the replacement of the broken equipment, a gear he felt fortunate to have found in his supply box instead of left behind at the warehouse, the pump sprung to life. *Up, down, up, down, up, down, up, down.* Colton felt extraordinary relief when the computer confirmed the flow of natural gas was being extricated and sent down the line to the processing center. He was free.

Back in the truck, he resisted the urge to gun the engine. Arduously, he began the jarring and sinuous route back to civilization along the forsaken dirt road. After twelve minutes of bumping and banging, the ruts finally evened out and his tires hit smooth asphalt. Colton pressed the truck hard to make up for lost time, racing blindly ahead, determined to be on the water by 7:30.

Quickly, he sped past drab, olive-colored chamisas, twisted junipers and sandy arroyos, evidence that floods sometimes swept through the dry river beds. The solitary road thread its way like a black snake along the open expanse of high desert country.

The way ahead was clear, like he was the only person left in the world.

The emptiness of the land began to mirror how he felt inside. His irritation went deep into his bones, his bitterness like a toothache. Wanting to be out of his head, he blared the radio, locked his gaze ahead, and let the speedometer climb higher.

Topping the ridge of the dam, he looked down upon the southern portion of Navajo Lake, its blueness piercing the earth around it like a sapphire eye.

The Miller family boat was docked at the marina along with the expensive play toys of nearby wealthy residents. As he walked briskly towards the slip, he noticed a darkening in the sky behind the steep bluff surrounding the lake. The change in light only spurred him to move faster, driven by his eagerness to be on the open water.

Once clear of the marina, he raced to get far away from the shore, away from his family, away from his obligations, and from his discomfort about the future. Towards what end, he didn't know. He simply let the wind, roaring in his ears and face, carry him away from his thoughts, as the engine pulled him farther out.

Unfortunately, the feeling of freedom and escape did not last long.

Colton noticed the light around him palling into a greyish-green as the waves multiplied, rippling and buffeting against the hull of his boat with increasing violence. Casting a look behind his shoulder, he witnessed an immense tower of dark clouds amassed high above the marina. They swirled with a comic book fierceness, rolling and boiling, almost too perfect to be real, as if they'd been created for a disaster movie by a CGI department.

Realizing the vulnerability of his position, he slowed down considerably, a flutter of fear in his gut; Colton had hated storms ever since his teens. With his heart pounding, he watched the oncoming tempest swallow the marina; it disappeared into an advancing wall of rain.

A wall.

One moment, the boats were shimmying in the dock, rocked by the intensity of the wind, their moorings put to the test. The next moment, everything was obliterated by a deluge of smoky mist and rain, the full force of it speeding towards him with no safe place to run. The only thing ahead of him were white-capped waves crashing onto the rocky cliffs in the distance, and a bright yellow kayak struggling in the swells.

The passenger had long blonde hair glinting with a golden red sheen against the dull grey of the water. The waves pulsed sickeningly below the little boat. Colton watched as it listed precariously sideways before flipping over in the gale. The person was lost from view, and the storm continued to advance.

Without thinking, he rushed forward, his own boat lurching in the lashing from the wind. Silently, he prayed he'd be able to help in time.

"Time has been transformed, and we have changed;
it has advanced and set us in motion;
it has unveiled its face, inspiring us with
bewilderment and exhilaration."
- Kahlil Gibran

Chapter 6: Aftermath

Saffron steadied herself, stretching towards the heavens in gratitude. The storm had passed, and she had survived.

"Hi," she said, extending her hand towards the young man who'd helped her. Facing him directly, her already racing heart accelerated a fraction more with an extra *ba-bum ba-bum*.

He was about her age, taller by several inches, and soaking wet. Droplets glistened on his tanned arms; his muscles, glossy with rain and the sheen of a young, athletic build. Though his body appeared hard and capable, there was no trace of hardness in his kind, worried eyes which were a lush and complex hazel. Water dripped from his dark blond hair onto his nose and shoulders; his legs, stiff with drenched denim; his shirt, semi-transparent and clinging to his body like a second skin.

Glancing down at her own saturated t-shirt, she briefly thought, *Thank God I'm not wearing white!*

"I'm Saffron," she said, smiling and suppressing a giggle.

Her rescuer's look of concern vanished as an infectious grin erupted across his clean-shaven, chiseled face. Like a model from an 'All-American Boy' calendar, his friendly expression and fit physique conjured images in her mind of quarterbacks, cowboys and prom kings; the type of guy with gold medals on a shelf in his room.

Noticing his large belt buckle, she thought, *Yep, definitely the cowboy-type.*

"Saffron," he repeated in a husky voice with a hint of country song sweetness.

He rubbed his hand on his thigh as if to dry it before touching hers, then seemed to realize the ridiculousness of the attempt. With a sheepish grin, he shook her hand, his touch instantly warming Saffron's cold fingers.

"Th-that's a beautiful name," he said shakily. "I-I'm Colton. Colton James Miller."

Clearing his throat, he gently squeezed her hand, holding it a moment before letting go.

"Sometimes my buddies call me CJ," he said nervously, backing away and tripping over his feet before resting against the side of the boat. "Wow, that was something else! I've never seen a storm like that before in my life." He swallowed noticeably before adding, "I mean, well, once I have...a-a hurricane actually, but who ever heard of one in the desert?

"Are-are you okay?' he asked, his face reddening. "I'd offer you a towel, but I don't think anything I own is dry at the moment."

"I'm fine," Saffron answered politely, thinking his embarrassment and self-consciousness were kind of cute. "Thank you."

There was no denying the proximity and intimacy of their circumstances since the moment they'd first met. Pitching erratically on the waves, she'd felt so helpless. All she'd been able to do was hold tightly to this stranger's strong body, her face and eyes down, willing the storm to stop.

She suddenly recalled the sensation of his arms wrapped protectively around her. From the way he was looking at her, or trying not to, she wondered if he was thinking the same thing.

The noise and chaos were completely gone, replaced by a peaceful quiet and a hint of blue sky. Suddenly fatigued, she sat down, cross-legged, resting in an inch or two of cold water.

"I'm pretty sure that was a derecho or a supercell," she said, watching the dark clouds speed away. "I'm not sure which...I've only read about them. I'm leaning towards a supercell because of the backdrafts we experienced.

"Sadly," she paused and sighed heavily, "it's not the last megastorm you'n'I'll see in our lifetimes." *And, they're gonna be a hell of a lot worse, too,* she thought, choosing to keep her morbid thoughts to herself. She bit her lip, as if to seal it against further words, and changed the subject. "You haven't seen my kayak, have you?"

She scanned around and Colton did the same. They were alone in the Pine River Pass. Towering bluffs came steeply down on either side of them, as if they'd been transported into a canal.

"I'm sorry," he said. "I saw it go under." He moved to the center console and put his hands on the steering wheel. "We can go back and look for it, if you'd like."

"No," she said sorrowfully, "you're right. I know it's a lost cause."

It hurt her heart to think of it residing at the bottom of the lake for hundreds of years.

With minimal deterioration, her inner voice snarled.

In her opinion, nothing came as close to immortality as plastic; it lasted well beyond our time to make use of it.

Damn it, she thought angrily. *I frigging know better. Next time I'll get a wood canoe!*

To quiet her mind, Saffron took a deep, cleansing breath.

When she was little, her parents had taught her the Buddhist principle of 'lack of attachment' which didn't mean one shouldn't own things, they'd said, but rather, people shouldn't place too much value on objects, outcomes, opinions or particular ways of living, they'd told her.

Life was constantly changing, forever evolving. Being too rigid, unadaptable, often increased suffering. It stopped one from being free.

Although she knew not to get too upset, her emotions were still shaky. She'd felt so well, so alive, during her meditation in the kayak; completely at peace, unified, connected to Everything on a deep, cosmic level. It was one of her favorite feelings in the world, the boundary line of enlightenment.

Then, the world and its fury had crashed in on her reverie.

When the wind had begun whipping her, she'd opened her eyes onto the force of the storm bearing down on her. The shoreline had appeared miles away as she'd struggled, fighting for her life to stay upright and afloat while the waves had abused her. Capsizing into the cold, dark lake, her worldview had drastically narrowed from the expansiveness of the Universe into the depth of her bones.

This is not how it ends, she remembered screaming inside her skull. *I have so much more to do!!!*

Suddenly, when panic had started taking control, Colton had appeared, arriving at the exact moment she'd needed saving.

Saffron let out another long sigh, wanting to shake the negative feelings of fear and loss out of her body. Turning away from her memories, she focused on her breath, in and out, in and out.

The air smelled like fish and algae, and something hard to describe like positively charged ions.

Consciously, she relaxed her muscles which were beginning to ache from tension and exertion. Stretching her arms towards the sky, she stretched again, rotating her torso and spine, releasing the stress from her tissues. The returned sunshine melted into her exposed skin and wet clothes. Listening to the sound of the soothing waves, her pulse rate steadied.

Yes, she reminded herself, *my kayak is gone, but I'm still here and today is truly a good day.*

"I hate to tell you this," Colton said, as he fruitlessly twisted the key in its ignition, "but the boat's dead. We're not going anywhere for awhile." Picking up his cell phone, he began pushing buttons, over and over, his expression growing more frustrated as he fought the blank, unresponsive screen.

Saffron thought he looked like a chain smoker staring morosely into an empty pack of cigarettes. She felt herself guarding for what she knew was coming.

"Hey, is your phone waterproofed?" he asked. "Mine's fried."

"Oh," Saffron hesitated. "Umm, I don't have a phone," she said hesitantly. "Sorry."

"Wait," he said, looking up with incredulity, "you don't have a phone...or, you don't have it with you?"

"No, actually," she nervously admitted. "I don't have a cellphone. Of course, I have a regular phone at home, you know, a landline." She didn't like the sound of defensiveness in her voice. In her experience, the world was full of judgmental people who had a hard time understanding her.

It wasn't always easy to be different from the masses.

Colton's hazel eyes went wide and his mouth hung open a little.

She braced herself for his teasing, and possibly, his insults.

"Wow," he said, sounding pleasantly surprised. He gave her another one of his heart-warming smiles. "You're a rebel!"

Saffron laughed unexpectedly, the sound amplifying and bouncing off the canyon walls.

"A rebel!?!" she repeated, immediately at ease when he hadn't criticized her. "Well, that may be true, but right now, with the world the way it is, there're worse things to be."

Suddenly, she realized she was sitting in a puddle and rose up to sit in one of the chairs, falling back into the leather seat with a splooshy, flatulent sound.

She giggled and felt herself blushing.

Colton's grin stretched from ear to ear.

"Well," he replied, again trying to start the stalled engine, "it seems like we have time for you to tell me about yourself, while I figure out how to get us movin' again."

In the back of the boat, he lifted a seat cushion and hefted out a worn red toolbox.

Saffron let her gaze linger on his back, taking in his easy yet efficient manner and his strong, sculpted body. It had been awhile since she'd met a new guy, let alone a local one. The last time she'd hooked up with someone had been in Albuquerque at a protest rally. Her 'type' tended to be on the radicalized side, not usually found in San Juan County, which was populated mostly by rugged, rural, conservative types. She didn't have any problem with them as a rule, but she'd never met any who were like the intensely analytical and revolutionary guys she leaned towards.

Still, there was an ease in his nature that appealed to her; nothing derisive nor condescending about his personality that she could tell. As he shuffled through his tools, she found herself open to the idea of getting to know him as well; a man who knew how to fix things had always been appealing to her. It was a happy bonus he was attractive and seemed genuinely interested in her.

Unconsciously, her tongue skimmed along the back of her teeth, creating a tantalizing tickle. She particularly liked the way his rain-soaked jeans hugged his long legs and cute butt.

Hmm, her inner voice thought, *he is pretty tasty.* Her mind began slipping into images of seducing and ravishing him on the deck.

Down girl, her more rational mind interrupted. *Now's not the time for a Fifty Shades of Grey fantasy.*

"Oh, my goodness," she replied, "you want to know about me? Where do I start?"

Saffron considered what to share. She knew she could be a little intense at times as she despised small talk. It was in her nature to get to the meat and bones of a discussion and say all the things that needed saying, qualities which were a bit much for most people.

Experience had taught her to keep her opinions to herself, but the urge to be authentic frequently had her spilling her guts anyway.

Most people however didn't know what to say when she brought up global warming.

Even with information on climate change coming out more regularly, the mainstream media didn't discuss it to the depths it needed discussing; plus, there was still a lot of pushback and false information circulating from groups that denied it was even an issue. Most people lived without worrying about it for long. They moved on to the next catastrophe in life, then the next, not seeing the overall whole and pattern.

They won't be able to ignore it for much longer, her inner cynic chimed in.

Saffron promised herself to avoid controversial subjects at first, especially if it turned out he vehemently disagreed with her views. She didn't want to end up stuck on a boat with him for hours if he was going to argue with her.

That'd be a shitty way to spend a beautiful day with a good-looking guy, she thought.

With the sun on her skin, Saffron came to the conclusion to enjoy the day and the company as much as she could, and do a little bit of flirting... just in case.

"Well, Colton James Miller," she said with a coy smile and a lusty, southern-belle drawl, "my full name is Saffron Jolie LeMay." She winked and added coquettishly, "And my friends sometimes call me Roni."

Colton reacted to her sexy, come-hither answer like the air had been punched out of his lungs, nervously swallowing, clearing his throat, and chewing on his lip.

Saffron laughed, her seduction immediately dissolving.

"Sorry," she said apologetically, "I'm just messing with you." Then, realizing she had not properly expressed her gratitude, she leaned towards him. "Thank you for rescuing me," she said sincerely. "I've never really considered myself the 'Damsel In Distress' type before," she said, making air quotes. "Most of the time I'm pretty capable and self-reliant."

"Somehow," Colton said, looking steadily at her, "that doesn't surprise me."

"If I'm being totally honest," she said, "I usually think of myself more as the superhero type." She flexed her biceps, looking up towards the sky and adding theatrically, "Destined to save the world!!!"

Her declaration carried across the water and echoed up the canyon walls.

She was being silly, but in truth, it wasn't far from what she really believed.

In her opinion, perceptions were the backbone of reality; people saw the world the way they wanted to see it, through their own lens. Since no one could control everything that happened to them in life, one only had the power of how to react to their experiences. Saffron felt better imagining herself as a fierce warrior, one whose purpose was to make the world a better place. It felt better than picturing herself as a victim, one who gave in to the numbing realities of a collapsing world.

"I-I'm glad I was there to help," Colton replied.

"Me, too," she agreed, taking her eyes off his distracting smile to better look around. "By the way, I like your boat."

Typically, she used an old, battered fishing boat her dad had gotten in trade for some cabinet work. To be fair, it was still functional, adequately serving its sole purpose as a fishing boat, but that's where the compliments ended.

Colton's boat however glistened with chrome and luxury.

She didn't consider herself a materialistic person, but she'd always appreciated beautiful things. She could recognize the aesthetic qualities in the design, the richness of it, without feeling the need to possess one herself. Envy was not an emotion she frequently indulged in. Her main flaw, in her opinion, was the occasional derision she felt for the greed and ignorance of others, especially those she blamed for creating the situation the world was currently in.

This hatred was an ugly feeling she fought hard to overcome.

Briefly, she wondered if Colton was just another rich Farmington guy.

Saffy, her inner voice kicked in, the one that sounded like Zia, *maybe you could just relax and enjoy the Now? He saved you. Give him a chance.*

"It's my dad's boat," Colton answered, shrugging his shoulders. "I'm sorry about yours," he added with a look of genuine concern, like he meant what he was saying.

See? He seems nice, she thought. *Someone who deserves to know the truth.*

Saffron made a split second decision to open up a figurative can of worms.

"You can't get too attached to things in life," she said matter-of-factly.

"So much more is going to be taken from us, a hell of a lot actually, but no one seems to really believe it. Most people just push it out of their minds."

What happened to taking it slow, she reprimanded herself as she considered changing the subject again, to avoid the difficult discussion and keep her fears buried. Then, the part of her that wanted to run screaming through the streets, alerting everyone she possibly could like a modern-day Paul Revere, said, *If we don't start talking about it, then nothing's going to change.*

"How much do you know about climate destabilization?" she asked. Without giving him a chance to respond, she added, "It's okay. I realize few people are studying the science of it like I do. Everything I've learned over the years says it's gonna be a real shitshow, but I try not to get too down about it.

"I have the belief," she continued, nervously but resolutely, "that to truly survive and thrive in life, you need to be informed with what's going on, but you can't let it own you. And every day, it's important to appreciate, to fully *enjoy,* all that has been given to us in this life while consciously letting go of what's lost or in the past. Then, the basic job of being human is to work towards making yourself and the future a better place.

"It's like the old prayer," she said. "God, grant me the serenity to accept the things I cannot change, the courage to change the things I can, and the wisdom to know the difference."

She suddenly felt dulled by sadness, older than her years.

"Otherwise," she said tiredly, "the darkness will open up and eat us."

Colton stared quietly into the distance, not looking at her. His face had fallen, an ashen tone obscuring his healthy tan. His far-off look and total silence made Saffron anxious.

He doesn't think you're a rebel, she thought derisively. *He probably thinks you're mentally deranged.*

She shifted uneasily in the wet seat.

Damn it, she berated herself. *Why do I feel the need to talk about this so much?! Get it under control and stop being a buzzkill!*

"What lies behind us and what lies ahead of us
are tiny matters to what lives within us."
- Henry David Thoreau

Chapter 7: Lost and Found

The voice of Colton's dad sounded in his head, *Ahh, she's one of them Alarmist folks.*

The term was frequently used on the television programs Asa liked to watch, a derisive word for people pushing for changes in the government and industries like the ones Colton worked in, in an effort to stop global warming. Most of the people Colton knew thought it was hogwash.

It was true Colton had never looked deeply into the science of climate change. He'd never heard the term 'climate destabilization' before. Mostly, he'd glanced at a few articles his dad had left lying around, all of which had debunked the possibility that mankind was responsible.

However, Saffron's words conjured images from the news he'd been watching all week long from Billings, Montana; the entire Western town, consumed by wildfire; the sky, menacingly dark; the people, ashen and tear-stained, having lost homes, possessions, and loved ones in a losing battle with Mother Nature. On the television, the burnt landscape had appeared apocalyptic.

His mom, in conjunction with their church, had been collecting donations to send to a local Baptist church for their recovery efforts and emergency aid. She was talking about sending more money to Florida too, which was nervously watching a tropical storm building up steam over the Atlantic. The Sunshine State had barely survived the previous year's hurricane season, the one that had left Orlando's Disney World in ruins for months; the iconic theme park had been stripped bare of its lush palm trees and glamour; its favorite attractions, splintered and collapsed; the magic of the place, reduced to rubble.

Colton considered the intensity of the storm they'd just survived and his memories of a different storm and boat resurfaced. In 2017, he'd been visiting his older brother, Dylan, in Houston, when the hurricane hit. Dirty water had raged into the home, flooding it quickly. In a panic, they'd had to evacuate onto the roof. In mere hours, his world had turned upside down as the house had submerged, his sense of security washed away.

The wind and rain had been relentless, much like it had today.

Colton had had nightmares for months afterwards. His parents had almost taken him to therapy. He remembered they'd prayed a lot that year. His grandfather had started coming by on the weekends, taking him on adventures in the wide, open beauty of the countryside, telling him tales of the rich history of the area. They went horseback riding, hiking and fishing until life had finally become normal again. Sadly, in the past two years, Colton had lost both of his grandparents to cancer.

He was at a loss of words to describe what he was thinking, but he felt like he knew plenty about the darkness.

"I was homeschooled," Saffron said, breaking the silence and blushing minutely. "It meant I could basically study anything I wanted to. Fair warning, I read a fuck-ton of books, anything I can get my hands on. History, physics, nature, philosophy. I've always felt pulled to know and understand as much as I can. I tend to work with a lot of different, complex ideas at once, you know, trying to solve all of the world's problems. Most people usually think in a vacuum, but the things that happen to us are more like a spiderweb. So many things interconnect. I probably come off as flighty or scatter-brained, I don't know. I think people can sometimes get a little overwhelmed by me."

Her blush turned from pale pink to crimson.

"Sorry for rambling," she added.

"Don't be sorry," Colton answered quickly. "I was homeschooled too, when I was younger. I don't read as much as I probably should, especially about the climate, but I love history and old-fashioned things. I'm sorry, I should be the one to apologize to you for being so quiet. I-I got triggered by a memory." He paused, swallowing a lump in his throat, then continued, "I was in one of the houses that got flooded during Hurricane Harvey. This storm reminded me a lot of that day."

He looked away from her, peering at the reflective water, feeling vulnerable but wanting to face his fears. He disliked feeling weak.

"We had to be rescued from the roof," he said quietly. "My nieces and nephews were little and they were crying so hard...I-I don't know if you know this, but there's no sound in the world to compare to the screams of a terrified child." He shuddered, the old anxiety creeping into his skin. "We tried consoling them, but deep down, we didn't know if we were going to make it."

Usually, Colton was more guarded around people, but in the moment, he didn't feel like he had anything to hide.

"I-I thought I was going to drown," he added, his eyes turning from the lake to rest upon hers. "I'm very glad I was there to help you today," he said. "It feels like I finally got a chance to pay it forward. You're right. I don't really know anything about climate change. What word did you say? Destabilizing?"

Saffron nodded and kept quiet.

"But," he slowly admitted, "even I can see something isn't right."

"Well," she said, a loud sigh escaping her, "it's too pretty of a day to bum ourselves out, especially since we survived this round." She paused, watching him intently like she was sizing him up. "Do you like Johnny Cash? Storms like that always make me think of this song."

To Colton's amazement, she began singing 'Five Feet High and Rising' in a strong and sure voice. It'd been one of Grandpa Miller's favorites. They'd often sung it together while riding in the boonies as part of Colton's healing from the trauma of the flood. Colton knew all the words. On the next verse, he began singing baritone and Saffron stopped to listen. She smiled with approval, then joined him in the final verse for a duet.

He thoroughly enjoyed the sound of their harmonizing voices; it was a wonderful release from his stress. When they finished, they each sat quietly, listening to the gentle waves lapping in a slow, rocking motion against the boat.

"Man, I wish I had my guitar," she said with a wide grin and a laugh, "but then again, I wasn't exactly planning on meeting you today."

"You're an amazing singer," he said, feeling a little bit star struck.

"So are you," she said enthusiastically. "I love music. I play almost everyday. Mostly guitar and singing, but I know some piano and mandolin."

"I'm more of a singing-in-the-shower kind of guy," he shyly admitted.

"Well, you should do it more often," Saffron said. "You have a great voice. Do you realize every culture on this planet enjoys music? No matter what else divides us, most people have songs and rhythms inside them. It's a universal law. Plato even called music a moral law. He said it gave 'soul to the universe and wings to the mind'. No matter what language we speak, we typically have this love of music in common.

"And what's even more cool," she said, her eyes widening with excitement and a passion that made Colton a bit dizzy, "is that on a subatomic level, smaller than atoms and electrons, physicists speculate all matter in the universe is created by varying frequencies of vibrations. Superstring theory." Saffron was animated, her arms opened wide, gesticulating as she talked. "So, in essence, everything in the cosmos may be one big, happy symphony!"

Becoming self-conscious, she dropped her hands into her lap and shrugged her shoulders.

"Sorry," she said, "I warned you. Homeschool."

"Don't apologize," he said. "You're right, maybe I will sing more often. How do you keep yourself from being nervous?"

Or making a fool of yourself?

"It only takes a little courage," she said, moving forward in her chair, closer to him. "Singing and playing in front of others is good practice for being brave in other ways. My mom and dad used to talk about courage a lot when I was growing up. Along with resilience, fortitude and duty. They always wanted me to be optimistic, too." Her gaze returned to the water. "Why is that the hardest one to maintain?"

A-men to that, Colton thought.

Life in the Miller household had been similar.

On Sundays, when he was very little, the family had gone to his great-grandparent's ranch, a sprawling two hundred seventy acres of scrub, rock and cowpatties. Great-Grandma Miller, his GG, would always read from the King James Bible, an old family heirloom. He could still hear her lively reading from its well-worn pages, *'Have I not commanded thee? Be strong and of good courage; be not afraid, neither be thou dismayed; for the Lord thy God is with thee whithersoever thou goest. Joshua 1:9.'*

Colton became conscious of the sun spilling onto his body, warming him.

From the corner of his eye, undetected, unapologetic, unable to look away, he observed her as she sat, quietly thinking to herself. Her gaze had a dreamy, far-off quality, like she was peering into a crystal ball. He noticed the bare foot of her crossed leg making tiny, circular motions; her delicate toenails were painted an iridescent blue.

"May I get you something?" he asked, his good manners kicking in as he stood and moved towards his cooler.

"Sure," she said, "I could totally go for a cold beer."

"Well, you're in luck twice today, because I came out here to fish," he said, pawing through his ice chest, "and drink beer. I've even got some barbecue potato chips."

Saffron took off her backpack and reached inside.

"And I've got homemade trail mix, venison jerky and an apple," she replied. "Voila! Breakfast of champions!"

Walking towards him, she took a loud, crunchy bite out of the pinkish-red fruit, then offered it his way. He took it without hesitation, bit into it, then passed it back.

"I sthee no eason why we shouldn't ish right naw," she said with her mouth full. "Izz ah bootiflull day." Swallowing dramatically, she said with a smirky grin and a raised eyebrow, "Now that we've survived death and all." Bouncing on the balls of her feet with girlish glee, she added, "Can we do it right now? I love to fish."

Colton couldn't help grinning as he licked the sweet juice from his lips.

"Good thinking, Rebel," he agreed wholeheartedly, offering her a cold can of Coors. "It's beer:30 somewhere," he said, taking a long, satisfying drink before grabbing the fishing poles. "So, tell me more about you. How'd you get turned into a damsel in distress?"

"Oh," Saffron said with a chuckle, "I was out contemplating the secrets of the universe. You know, the questions of life itself."

"Oh, really?" Colton said, wondering what was going to come out of her brain and mouth this time. "And the answers?"

"Have you read or seen 'The Hitchhiker's Guide to the Galaxy?'" she asked.

"Um," Colton said hesitantly, "I've heard of it."

"Well, there you go," she said cryptically as she shrugged her shoulders.

"Huh?" he responded in confusion.

He must have looked funny because she threw back her head and let out a mirthful, full-throated laugh. The sound twinkled and burst over him like champagne bubbles of light.

"I'm sorry," she giggled. "I'll have to show it to you sometime. The basic premise is our whole planet gets destroyed by overtly bureaucratic aliens and by the whim of a narcissistic, self-absorbed supreme leader. Only one man and woman survive and are given a back-up Earth by The Planetmakers, sort of like a Garden of Eden story." Her eyes still radiated the light of her laughter, as her face took on a wistful look. "I was out on the lake dreaming of a much different world."

"I can drink to that," he responded.

I'd love to see a much different world.

"Here," she said, reaching for his fishing poles. "I can work on these while you work on the motor." She took them from him and squatted to have a look inside his tackle box. With her attention on his hooks and bait, she asked, "Have you heard of Sweetwater?"

"Sure," he replied, resuming his examination of the engine with stolen glances at her bent over form. "It's that commune near here."

He'd heard of Sweetwater, mostly from his father who complained about the environmentalists who were making it difficult for them to make a living.

Damn tree-huggers, Asa would say, *they're constantly bitching about fracking, that everyone knows is as safe as kittens, just to further their liberal agenda,* and other things to the same effect.

Colton tended to stay out of these conversations, mostly because he didn't like argumentative discussions and politics. He tried to avoid watching the pundits on television as much as possible. There was too much division in the world, in his opinion. He was more of the live-and-let-live type.

"Most people around here call it a commune," she said, holding up a neon orange rubber worm, "but it's best described as an intentional community. My mom started it several years ago."

"So," Colton asked, "you live with a whole bunch of other people?"

He looked up to see the water reflecting sparkles of sunlight onto her glowing skin as the sun turned her hair into gold. He worried he was staring, or worse, drooling. To distract himself, he focused on the repair job.

"Well, technically," she said, casting her line out into the lake, "the others have their own homes, so we only have to share the communal spaces. I live in a house with my parents but I've got my own separate area that's all mine. I go to Aztec a lot to teach yoga and work at the farmers market on Wednesdays. My dad's a carpenter, among other things, and my mom is a bodyworker slash energy healer. We each have our own things, so we don't crowd each other too much."

"Well, that's better than I'm doing," Colton admitted. "I'm with my family all the time, it seems. I work with my dad in the family business and I'm still stuck in my parents' house, plus one of my sisters just moved back in. I'm dying to get out. Sometimes I feel like I'm suffocating."

Normally, he wouldn't have revealed something so personal, but with her, he didn't feel like there were there any walls around him. He felt free.

"I guess that's one of the cool things about communal living," she said, "there's a comfort to them. You're accepted, given space, but also involved with your friends. What needs to get done, gets done together. Most of the people living there are killer smart, really funny too. And it gives a sense of peace, you know? Knowing you aren't alone in the world. I don't think I'll ever leave, except for maybe during Phase 4, if I make it that long."

"Phase 4?" he asked, unsure of what she meant.

"Oh, never mind," Saffron said, shaking her head briskly. "Ignore me. Tell me more about you."

Colton took another gulp of beer. His brow knitted in concentration, thinking about what to reveal about himself.

"I-I'm just ordinary," was all he could think to say. Shrugging, he wiped his dirty hands on a rag and stood up to stretch his legs. "Let's see if this thing works, so we can head back."

The engine started up without a hitch, purring deeply in a macho way that only an expensive powerboat is capable of.

"Oh, no you don't," she scolded, an exaggerated pout on her face. "We've got beer to drink, fish to catch, and secrets to tell. Spill it, CJ," she commanded. Just then her line gave a sharp tug. "Oh! I've got one!" she squealed, bouncing excitedly as she began reeling in a green and glistening small-mouthed bass.

There was no more mention of heading home for another couple of hours. Conversation came easily and naturally, with many silent moments as they listened instead to the quiet lapping of the lake; its soothing rhythm, a perfect accompaniment to their casual talk.

As they got too hot, they playfully dove in the calm waters to cool off. The six-pack became a memory, all the snacks consumed. Collectively, they pulled five beautiful fish from the lake; two smallmouth bass and three rainbow trout which flashed and whirled in a bucket.

"Would you like to come to my place," Saffron asked, "and let me cook you fish?" She bit her lower lip and looked at him expectantly.

"Umm, yeah," Colton said, hesitating only for a second, his mind having already decided to continue spending time with her sometime between learning she played music and watching her exuberance as she caught her first fish.

Her hair was a mess, her armpits stained with sweat, her freckles darkened in sun-exposed places, but her blue eyes were warm and her smile was an invitation to happiness.

Colton was hooked. "That would be great."

"We must, indeed, all hang together or, most assuredly,
we shall all hang separately."
- Benjamin Franklin

Chapter 8: Sweetwater

Colton strapped Saffron's mountain bike and trailer safely in the back of his truck. It'd been quite a day and it wasn't even close to over. The drive back along the river was beauty incarnate with nature showing off with lush green trees, slick brown rocks, and striated red bluffs.

Due to the storm, the San Juan river was higher than usual. Runoff water sluiced up the embankments, a muddy force straining downstream carrying flotsam and jetsam along the way. Standing still on a cottonwood branch, a spindly white heron peered dejectedly into the murkiness below; the fish, hidden by the darkened water, temporarily free from the threat from above.

Once in town, the effects of the storm were less appealing. Plastic bags swung from branches like dispossessed jellyfish gone missing from the deep sea. Garbage cans spilled their week's accumulation of household waste along the curbsides. A stop sign by the Sportsman's restaurant was missing and the restaurant itself, with its attached fishing shop/convenience store, was dark inside, even though a handful of cars stood in its parking lot.

As they passed the fly fishing and raft rental shop, they saw an electrical pole lying aslant on a pale yellow mobile home; a sizable dent in the single-wide's middle making it resemble a big fat banana. Colton could only imagine the sound the impact had made and hoped to God no one had been inside at the time.

Deep grooves striped the dirt roads where fast rivulets of storm water had cascaded. Along the side of the road was a Toyota truck, its front end teetering into a ditch and its ass end hanging a foot above the asphalt; black skid marks in the street were evidence of its fishtailing journey.

Trees had blown over, shingles had flown. Mud covered crosswalks and had buried downhill gardens. Detritus and branches abounded, but at least the homes were still intact, minus The Big Banana.

A few people stood outside their homes with their necks craned at their rooflines, assessing damages. With worried faces, most of them clutched their cell phones to their ears or peered into them like a talisman;

modern day mystics divining the wisdom of the ages in a palm-sized device.

The greatest damage appeared to be lost power. Colton predicted by evening the air would be suffused with the smell of barbecue as people grilled their refrigerated meat before it could go bad.

One, big, post-apocalyptic afterparty, he thought as his stomach grumbled.

He drove up to Sweetwater's gates which were an interlocking sun and moon made of wrought iron. Yuccas and other desert greenery, radiating new lifeforce from the rain, grew around a thick adobe wall which enclosed the front of the property. Sporadically embedded within the natural bricks were openings barred with branches. Colton could almost picture rifle barrels sticking through them to ward off attacks, although this particular fence had not existed during the area's Wild West era, when fighting off bandits or raiders may have been a necessity of life. Instead, it was a nostalgic reminder of that forgone and more violent era.

He stopped next to a solar-powered control pad. Saffron undid her seat belt and murmuring a soft "excuse me", she crawled over his lap, leaning out the window to tap in the number. Colton's throat constricted, his breath suspended as her petite body crushed him into his seat. As she withdrew, she turned to face him, biting her bottom lip for an instant before smiling and averting her eyes to the opening gate.

Colton shifted in his seat and had to remind himself once again about temptation and unclean thoughts.

Saffron pointed out her house to the right of the entrance. The greenhouse windows glinted with the afternoon light, refracting tiny rainbows and the blueness of the expansive sky. Two white domes rose above it on the second level and were connected by a deck. Red and teal lawn furniture had tipped over while a large patio umbrella teetered over the edge, its colorful mandala pattern fully displayed.

He parked to the side under a turquoise blue sail shade and took a look around at the beautiful, park-like setting. Meandering paths connected the homes and common areas, weaving through natural landscaping and colorful gardens. Many of the houses were hogans, circular buildings with straight walls and a round roof, while others were fully domed in a sphere.

The ancient past, mingling with the futuristic.

He saw two other Earthship houses nestled on a terraced ridge near the bluffs that towered on the back half of the immense property.

No fence is needed to keep intruders out from that side, he thought.

On a lower level, next to a vintage Ford pick-up in sunshine yellow, were two large commercial greenhouses, their hoops covered with semi-translucent plastic. Black and white goats frolicked in a pen nearby, ambling up the sandstone boulders and leaping off in games of you-can't-catch-me. A rustic lean-to provided shade and shelter for the less energetic and older ones.

Off to the left, near the entrance and abutting the adobe fence was a pavilion, a bandstand with a cobbled area encircled around it. Christmas lights dripped from its curved half shell overhang. Most of the chairs were tipped over in disarray.

Colton admired a copper-coated Kokopelli sculpture playing a savage blue guitar instead of a flute. Near it was a large fire pit surrounded by simple wooden benches and Adirondack chairs.

Here and there, some sail shades hung down, flapping lightly in the breeze. A couple people were working to reattach them. He saw a bearded, lanky man and a lean, long-haired brunette wrestling to get a blown-down fence back up as a dozen or more tittering chickens scampered around.

The heat hit as they exited the coolness of the vehicle, the sun's rays bearing down on them, unopposed by clouds. The rich, humid scent of happy dirt, long parched and now infused with the wellspring of life, rose up to greet them.

Saffron led Colton down the front path; brightly painted stones lined the pea-gravelled pathway to the entrance; the yard was a mecca of butterfly bushes aflame with purple flowers, irises of orange, red and purple, and yuccas with cream-colored stalks flowering and stretching towards the sun; under the eaves, oak rain barrels caught the last drops of rain from the copper chain links hanging above them.

The front door, a vibrant indigo blue, was unlocked.

He followed behind her into the lushness of the front foyer and was greeted by the light passing through the home's many plants which greened the long hallway. Sixties' surfing music blared as they entered a door to the left, this one a deep burgundy red. Inside the shadowed room, a sexy woman wearing yoga pants and a form-fitting shirt was gyrating to the go-go music in the kitchen, a mountain of vegetables on the counter before her. Her back was turned and her long, auburn hair shook in concert with her swiveling hips as she swirled, eyes closed and mind lost in the music and her movements.

A man with dishwater blond hair sat on a stool with his back turned to the front door. The back of his shirt said 'Make Music Great Again'. He was busy chopping cucumbers and tossing them into a large wooden bowl brimming with varied greens.

The red-haired woman burst from the kitchen and shimmied across the thick rugs, twisting and turning her body in concert with the driving rhythms. Each hand was shaking stalks of celery like little green pompoms.

Uma Thurman would have been proud.

Voyeuristically, the man watched her dancing until he noticed the young couple at the entrance. A look of relief passed over his face, his eyes crinkling into a wide smile.

"Saffy!" he happily exclaimed as he came to embrace her.

The woman's movements immediately ceased, her green eyes opened like pie plates, as her hands, full of celery, came up to her mouth to catch a sob.

"Saffy!" she choked.

"Thank goodness you're home," her father added, his arms around his daughter. "Your mom and I've been worried. I think she's stress-cleaned every inch of the place and channeled every ounce of power she has. I'm surprised you aren't glowing in white light." He kissed her forehead. "I was finally able to distract her with music."

"Hi, Dad. Hi, Mom," Saffron said, her words muffled by her father's shoulder. After the hug, she turned to look behind her. "This is Colton. Colton, this is my mom, Zia, and my dad, Jack."

"Welcome Colton," Jack said, his blue eyes as warm as the hand he extended in greeting. "Nice to meet you." He turned again to look down into his daughter's face, peering at her as if he had x-ray vision which could spot any flaw. "Are you all right," he asked. "We've got the lake patrol out looking for you."

"Sorry for making you worry," she responded guiltily. "I'm alright," she continued, 'but the kayak's gone. Colton helped me during the storm but his phone died and the boat wouldn't start right away." She turned towards her mother. "Are you okay?"

Zia's held breath released in a rush as her body seemed to shrink in some minute way, a cloud passing briefly in front of the sun; the next moment, the light was back. Shoulders straightened and head high, she came and wrapped her arms around Saffron and Jack, a beatific look of relief etched into her high-cheek-boned face.

"Yes. I'm okay," she said, "especially now since you're home. Tell us what happened."

Saffron relayed the details of the storm with a methodical precision, mentioning the wind speed, the wall of rain that had battered them, all with a journalistic style and very little melodrama.

Colton briefly thought of how shook up and disturbed Kaelynne would have been, how helpless and frightened if she'd been out on the boat with him. Saffron made it sound exciting, almost as if she'd been involved with a scientific experiment and had witnessed the results to support her hypothesis. She was animated and comfortable talking to her family who had resumed lunch-making, seemingly for an army.

Grapes piled high in a stainless steel colander. Pickles, olives and roasted red peppers sat in a colorful dish next to various cheeses and crackers. Zia took a pot that had been cooling on the counter and dumped the contents into a ginormous wooden salad bowl, mixing quinoa with the rainbow of veggies.

At the beginning of her account, Saffron had reached back for Colton, guiding him to her side so she could look up at him for confirmation and occasionally squeeze him in a sideways hug around his waist. It reminded Colton of their embracing during the storm.

It felt as if they'd known each other for years; comfortable, natural, organic.

Even the retelling of the demise of her new kayak and her harrowing rescue didn't cloud her countenance. She took it in stride with the calm acceptance of a monk. Finally, she finished talking and the room returned to the sounds of ceramic dishes being placed on the glazed concrete counter.

"Plus, we have fish," Colton interjected into the brief silence. "So the day wasn't completely ruined."

"Oh!" Zia exclaimed. "We would love to invite you to dinner, fish or no fish." Her piercing green eyes blazed into his own, leaving little room for dissent. "Let's start with lunch. Roni, go ring the bell and let the others know we're ready. Jack, please get the feta from the fridge." Turning to Colton, she said, "We make it fresh from our goats. You should try it, unless of course, you're vegan?"

"No, ma'am," he answered politely. "It sounds delicious. I'd love to try some."

"Oh, good," she said, placing a large stack of fabric napkins next to the plates, "because it's amazing."

Saffron went to the front stoop and rang a large cowbell.

Jack handed Colton a bottle opener and gestured him towards some wine bottles on the counter.

The Sweetwater inhabitants began filing in, their boots and sandaled feet muddy, yet their spirits high, smiles on every face. All stopped to hug Saffron, expressing their relief she wasn't harmed. Saffron went deeper into the belly of the house to an old landline phone to call off the rescue squad.

Colton was warmly welcomed by the eight or so people who streamed in, loaded up with food, then retired into the living room to eat. The tall, dark-haired woman he'd seen outside introduced herself as Kristen. Her eyes were glacier blue brimming with a sunny disposition. She urged him to eat up and put a plate in his hands; handmade pottery in a bright jade color, slight imperfections in the glazing and form, but ultimately quite beautiful. He filled his plate and went to sit on a curved banco.

Everyone was discussing the storm.

Somberly, the group shared a report from the solar radio that two hikers had perished in a flash flood in an arroyo not too far from Farmington. There was no word yet on whether they were from out of town or not. They also said that Navajo Dam had been lucky and had only experienced the outer edge of the twenty mile wide squall. The brunt of the storm had barreled farther south with hail, torrential rain and a windspeed of almost seventy miles per hour. Most of the county had been hit hard. There was a lot of reported damage and a vast portion of the surrounding community was without electricity; the biggest blackout in the county's history.

Colton learned that Sweetwater hadn't been affected much since it was off-grid. They'd suffered only minor damages and the loss of some lightweight items, like Tao flags and a patio table umbrella.

A statuesque, dark-skinned woman, Marlowe Worship, wearing long necklaces, corn rows and a voluminous skirt told the group about a leak in her roof. They all agreed to address it in the early evening.

Dick Dale's hip-thrusting surfing music ended and gave way to the laughter of good friends and the clink of forks.

Jack walked to a wall of shelves loaded with books, albums, CDs, as well as a collection of southwestern pottery displayed randomly throughout. He picked an old vinyl record and placed it on the tabletop turn-station. A tiny, scratching, hissing sound, followed by Neil Young's fervent voice and message, soon joined the mirthful noise of the room.

Zia cruised past Jack at the bookcase, squeezing his butt before moving a Magic 8 ball and a Guy Fawkes mask, aka the Anonymous 'mascot', out of the way to reveal an ornate glass bong hiding behind it. The sweet and skunky smell of cannabis mixed in with the smell of burned incense and fresh food.

When the bong came around to Saffron, she simply passed it along, her eyes meeting Colton's with a devilish smile curling her lips. He also passed it without smoking, and her smile widened as she tried not to laugh in her good-natured way.

His nerves had been on red alert since the moment he'd realized what was going on. Pot was not a part of his typical crowd.

With her easy manner, Saffron turned back to the group.

A skinny, bespectacled man wearing a Bernie Sanders 2020 shirt who'd introduced himself as John Perry, was making an argument that if they ever had to build an ark, there would be certain creatures he would leave behind.

"Fuck peacocks," he said.

Everyone in the room laughed in a knowing way.

"Seriously," John Perry continued dryly, "they can't come on."

Clay, the lanky man who had been working on the fence with Kristen, rested his arm around her shoulders and asked, "What about mosquitos?"

"Fuck mosquitoes," John Perry replied with deadpan seriousness. "Peacocks and mosquitos can't come. I've got no interest in either of them."

Laughing with a mouthful of salad greens, Saffron told Colton that the winery down the road kept peacocks. If the wind was right in the summer time, and the windows open at night, Sweetwater could hear them squawking up a storm.

Lighthearted and witty conversations continued as the meal was graciously consumed. Listening to them, Colton felt himself relaxing, enjoying himself, even enjoying the food. The feta was indeed delicious mixed in with the veggies and quinoa. At the end of the meal, Saffron plucked an olive pit from her mouth, licked the last remnants of lunch from her lips and reached for his empty plate.

"Come on," she said, her blue eyes flashing enticingly. "I'll show you around." She stood up from her cushion and asked, "Wanna see The Bunker?"

Her eyebrows lifted and fell in a Groucho-Marxian way; her blue eyes rolling in her head like someone in need of an exorcism while her Kewpie doll lips and nimble fingers pantomimed sucking on a large cigar.

Colton couldn't hold back a laugh.

"Why, c-c-certainly," he responded in a falsetto voice, hoping she would get the Three Stooges reference. His family had watched a lot of black and white movies when he was younger. From Saffron's look of recognition and giggle, he knew she must have too.

They deposited the dishes in the kitchen where Lydia and Nick, both schoolteachers in the elementary and high school respectively, were doing their part and washing up.

In the back of the house, Saffron grabbed the thick handle of an old barn door, heaving it along a track to the side.

Colton saw shelf upon shelf of homemade canned goods and dehydrated foods in glass jars. Like a work of art, golden peaches nestled against raspberry preserves. Green beans rubbed elbows with yellow corn kernels. Pickles neighbored with deep orange carrots while tomatoes showed off their myriad forms- diced, puréed, sauced with fresh herbs, and salsafied with onions and jalapeños. Multiple bags of flour, boxes of pasta, and canisters of olive oil kept company with honey, rice and beans.

Saffron flicked a light switch, revealing more shelves deeper in, loaded with household supplies, stored water jugs, camping gear, as well as the battery panel and mechanicals for the Earthship. There was even a small desk and a computer at the far back. The whole space was well organized and wonderfully cool.

"It's not really full right now," Saffron said. "We still have a lot of harvesting to do for this year's crop. I usually can on Thursdays and Fridays after the farmers market in Aztec. We gotta put up whatever we don't sell." Her face lit up as a new thought seemed to cross her mind. "Hey, let's put your phone in some rice to dry it out!"

Colton passed her his phone and looked around as she scrounged for an empty Mason jar.

"Are we in a semi-trailer?" he asked, noticing the walls behind the stored goods were a maroon corrugated metal.

"Yep," she replied. "Buried in the back of the house, it spans over 20 feet."

"Wow," he said appreciatively, "my mom would kill for a pantry like this."

Probably my dad, too, he thought. *Who doesn't want a bunker?*

"She cans in the summer, too," he said. "Her applesauce is my favorite. I should bring you some." His eyes swept and fell onto a gun safe. "Does your dad hunt?"

"Sure," she said with a shrug, "not a lot, but sometimes. Maybe once every three or four years. It's more my thing. I got my first elk when I was fourteen."

"Um, you don't look like the hunting type," he said, looking down at the petite pixie, feeling equally skeptical and impressed.

Her face lost some of its softness, replaced by a determination bordering on fierceness.

"I'm a southwestern girl," she said bristling, "born at the beginning of an apocalypse! You're damn right I know how to hunt and shoot." Her small frame expanded as if daring him to attack so she could prove how strong and capable she was.

In the relative dimness of the room, her eyes were a deeper blue than he'd seen before, like the hidden depths of the oceans where fantastical creatures of evolution were at home. In them, Colton saw strength and composure swimming in the cobalt blue.

He pictured her with a gun in her hand, focusing, steadying her breathing like she'd done on the boat, before taking aim and firing.

He suspected she'd be a good shot.

"Nice," Colton said approvingly. "I like to do some target practice at a spot not too far from here. Hey! Maybe we can go together sometime? You know...before the apocalypse?" he added jokingly before realizing how his statement could be interpreted.

Wait, he thought with surprise. *Did I just ask her out!?*

"Ha, ha, funny boy," Saffron said, narrowing her eyes. "We'll see who's laughing later." Teasingly, she stuck out her tongue and turned away, delicately lengthening onto her tiptoes like a ballet dancer, reaching for a bottle of wine. Bottle in hand, she spun gracefully to another shelf for applesauce.

"Come on," she said, leading him towards the door. "I've got more to show you."

Colton gulped reflexively.

Get a grip, CJ, his inner voice commanded. *You have a girlfriend!*

The living room had emptied out. Jack was alone with his feet on an ottoman, a Howard Zinn book in one hand and a glass of wine in the other. On his lap lay a large, orange-striped cat. It jumped down and went to Saffron for some loving.

"Hi, Chomsky," she said, her fingers caressing the cat's fur as he sinewed underneath her outstretched hand.

Colton heard a low, guttural purr emanating from his eighteen pound girth like a lusty lion.

"Wow, Mr. LeMay," he said, "that's an amazing space you have back there, sir. Did you design this house?"

"Call me Jack," he said. "Well, Zia was pretty much the creative force. I'm simply the carpenter, and the plumber, and the electrician." Smiling broadly, he added. "Oh, and the painter, too!"

His pleasure and pride in his wife and home were clearly outlined on his face.

From the turntable, 'Harvest Moon' floated like an ethereal cloud. Zia's lyrical voice melted out of the kitchen as she sang confidently along. She'd resumed her dancing, only with less fervor, as Neil Young grooved to a more mellow beat than the legendary Dick Dale.

"I'm taking Colton on the tour, Mom," Saffron said, interrupting her performance as they headed back to the atrium.

"Nice," Zia said, her hips resumed their swiveling to the beat as she emptied the leftovers into a bowl. "I'm going down for a nap as soon as I give these scraps to the chickens. I hate working in this heat," she grumbled. And with that, she waltzed out the front door, her arms wrapped around the large wooden bowl and the remnants of the feast.

Saffron sashayed down the tiled hallway, humming along with the music. At the last door, she turned to Colton.

"I want to tell you again how grateful I am, truly, that I met you today," she said. "Things could be a hell of a lot suckier right now. I underplayed how dire my circumstances were this morning. That was for my parents' benefit. I, however, know how quickly things could have turned tragic for me."

She stood in the green shadows under a tree with clusters of bananas; her skin had burned a light red; freckles dotted her nose and cheekbones; sincerity shone with an inner light through her warm, penetrating eyes.

"Thank you for saving me," she said quietly.

Colton shuffled his feet and looked down, a wellspring of emotion releasing in him. His memory flashed on the stark white look of desperation he'd seen on her face before he'd been able to get her safely on board. He hoped never to see that look of fear from her ever again.

I barely know her, he thought with incredulity. *Why do I feel so connected?*

When he raised his eyes to hers, the sexy smile was back on her face, the one that made him a bit weak in the knees.

"It, it was nothing," he was able to stutter, with his own fair share of sincerity. "I'm glad I could help."

"Well, come on, cowboy," she said as she opened an emerald door with the Tree of Life carved into it. "Welcome to my Secret Lair."

"You only live once, but if you do it right, once is enough."
- Mae West

Chapter 9: Secret Lair

Saffron stumbled as she closed the door behind her. Heavily buzzed from the wine at lunch on top of the two and a half beers she'd had on the boat, she felt invincible and blessed to be alive, confident and comfortable in her skin...with a strong urge to touch Colton's.

Occasionally when she was drunk like this, her vivid imagination would picture herself as a belly dancer, a geisha, or a harem consort; sauntering with a dainty swish in her hips as if draped in rare silks and jewels; an exotic goddess in her mind's eye. Other times, her alcohol-infused brain skipped demure female archetypes and brought out a more Bombshell/Betty-Page-like inner persona; an erotic minx.

Behave, she warned herself sternly. *No full-throttle vixen action!*

She could almost feel her inebriated libido pouting and giving her the middle finger.

Well, okay, she rationalized, *keep options open, but take it slow.*

"Make yourself at home," she said, pulling aside the blackout blinds in the compact kitchen, allowing sunshine to spill into the whole room. She placed the applesauce on the counter before grabbing two hefty goblets created by her next door neighbor, Alice Cardeñas, whom had made the handmade pottery used at lunch; Alice's beautiful dishes were a hallmark in most of Sweetwater's kitchens.

"Here," she said, turning towards Colton as she poured him a cup of white wine, this time a local vintage with the clever name of 'Girls Are Meaner', a play on the sweet German wine, Gewürztraminer. "I get all my rescuers drunk."

"I thought you said you didn't get rescued a lot?" Colton said teasingly, a smile playing on his lips, his hazel eyes bright.

"Nope," she said after a sip of the honey colored wine, "you're my first, but I plan on setting a precedent."

I'd like to give you even more, she thought silkily.

"Oh! That reminds me," she suddenly exclaimed, turning to search her bookcases.

Her fingers and eyes began roving the many titles; fiction and nutrition, poetry and philosophy shared the shelves with bleak predictions of the future; utopia flirting with dystopia.

Saffron considered books to be a wonderful tool; they transported the soul, fired the imagination and threw light into the dark; they were portable, never needing batteries; wisdom and whimsy both could be passed from one person to another, one generation in the past to some generation in the future; a smorgasbord of thoughts, visions, and messages to be shared. She loved it when they conspired in serendipity, one book's message on the edge of another; one thought, one theory, strengthened by the next. It happened more often than to be true coincidence.

Books were one way Saffron communed with the Divine, very often receiving the guidance she needed in that very moment.

Finally, she found what she was looking for, a rag-eared copy of Douglas Adams' 'The Hitchhiker's Guide to the Galaxy'. She brought it to the kitchen for a pen. On the inside cover, she wrote, *'To My Hero- May Good Fortune Be Yours In The Universe.'* She signed it, *'Your Damsel'.*

As she closed the book, the words on the first page caught her eye. Reading them, a mischievous idea came to her besotted mind. Pulling the blinds again to dim the light, she turned on the Moroccan lamps and returned to the living room with the gift.

Colton was at her bookshelves, head tilted, looking intently at the titles.

She guarded, feeling slightly exposed, naked, as he was potentially learning quite a bit about her interests, desires and quirks by searching her collection. However, she realized it was also an opportunity; a pragmatic way for him to get to know her mind quickly; a method possibly more efficient than speed-dating.

Hey, if he likes me, Saffron reasoned, *he should at least like the real me. I'm not going to pretend to be someone I'm not!*

The irony of what she was about to do next was not lost upon her and she giggled. Sweeping a billowy blue scarf from the wall, she wrapped it around her body like a toga and stepped up to the microphone.

"Ah-ah-hem," she said, clearing her throat, "may I please have your attention?"

Colton turned, a finger casually tucked into a loop of his jeans, cupping his goblet with the other. He looked relaxed, and very much at home in her space. Seeing her, he broke into a big grin; the same soul-touching smile he'd given when they'd first met.

Damn, she thought, her stomach filling with butterflies, *he's so cute.*

"Please, sir," she said, gesturing theatrically towards the couch. "Have a seat."

"Yes, ma'am," Colton replied, bowing playfully. He beamed at her and sat wide-legged on the many-pillowed sofa.

Saffron gulped and curtseyed in return as she tried to stop thinking about jumping him.

"I, Saffron Jolie LeMay," she said regally, holding the book up to the meager light, "would like to give you my rendition of an amazing cult classic."

"By all means," Colton responded with a courteous nod.

"And then," she began melodramatically in an upper-crust British accent, as if delivering a Shakespearean soliloquy, "one Thursday, nearly two thousand years after one man had been nailed to a tree for saying how great it would be to be nice to people for a change." Breaking character, she smiled and added in her own voice, "Boy, wouldn't that be amazing?"

"Ha! You got that right," Colton offered, looking pleasantly amused by her over-the-top performance.

"Where was I? Oh, yes," Saffron resumed, "a girl, sitting on her own suddenly realized what it was that had been going wrong all the time, and she finally knew how the world could be made a good and happy place. This time it was right, it would work, and no one would have to be nailed to anything! Sadly, however, before she could get to a phone to tell anyone about it, a terrible, stupid catastrophe occurred, and the idea was lost forever.

"This," she said, pausing for effect as she stared into Colton's rapt eyes, "is…not…her…story,"

Bowing low, and feeling a bit self-conscious, she added, "End. Scene."

"Encore! Encore," Colton said, clapping and whistling loudly. "Bravo! Bravissima!"

"Here," she said as she reverentially offered the book, "I hereby bequeath this cultural treasure from our cousins across the sea to you, noble sir, for your compassionate act of bravery committed this day of our Lord. Please accept this as a token of my deepest appreciation."

Colton's eyes sparkled with humor, however, as he read the inscription, his face softened, becoming more serious.

"Thank you," he said, looking and sounding genuinely touched as he raised his glass and clinked it against hers. "Cheers."

Saffron met his eyes, looking deeply at the paradox before her. Here was a man she hardly knew, yet she felt closer to him than to many of the people she encountered on a regular basis; more natural with, more at ease.

It felt *authentic,* she decided.

"Cheers," she said, breaking eye contact first, and turned towards a bookcase loaded with CDs.

They too ran the gamut; dance music rubbed shoulders with punk; classical with blues and country. She reached for one of FY5, a bluegrass folk band from Colorado. At the stereo console, she pushed play and the sounds of Americana filled the room. Fiddles and banjos, crooning male and female voices, conjoined in an uplifting beat which was somehow new and old at the same time. She began swaying to the music, her eyes closed, her lips resting in a comfortable smile.

This was her space, and it was a good day.

Colton surprised her by wrapping an arm around her waist and clasping her hand with his. He dipped her other hand to the bookcase so she could put her wine goblet down. With confidence and a bit of a swagger, he began two-stepping with her around the living room.

Saffron was less than confident. She loved to dance, but considered herself more of a free-spirit, one-woman-show type of dancer. Trying to follow his steps left her with the feeling of two left feet.

"Relax," he said, smiling widely, his eyes glimmering. "Let me guide you."

Focusing more on his body next to hers instead of her feet, Saffron found herself swinging and spinning with less effort and concentration. She actually felt like she was getting it, until she inadvertently tangled her leg up with his, and almost fell over.

"Oops!" she gasped.

Colton's strong arm held her steady until she righted herself.

"Well, well, well," she said, her voice laden with flirtation. "Look at that…you saved me again."

Standing on tiptoe, she pressed herself against his chest. Her mouth suddenly ached to taste him. As she moved in to kiss him, she was momentarily distracted by his intoxicating scent, although there was nothing in particular about it she could put her finger on.

Probably a pheromone thing, she thought briefly in a remote part of her brain which was still sober and steady.

Inexplicably, Colton dropped his arms from her waist and turned away.

Saffron's pending kiss morphed into a frog in her throat.

"I'm sorry," he said hastily, sitting on the edge of her sofa and looking up at her sheepishly. "I-I should have mentioned I have a girlfriend."

Saffron took a step back, her shoulders sagging.

Colton wouldn't look at her face.

"And this is why drinking to excess in the middle of the afternoon is not a good idea," she said with a self-deprecating laugh. "I'm sorry, I can get a bit randy when I drink too much. You may have a different adjective to use, but I'll stick with 'randy', thank you very much. My apologies for being too forward. It's one of the main reasons I don't smoke weed too often. Well, first I don't do it regularly because if you're under twenty-five, it can diminish brain capacity. And I require a full-capacity brain. Can't get muddled and damaged if I want to survive and thrive. That's sort of my motto. So, I avoid it unless I want to feel super-connected to the cosmos. It can be amazing during a full moon. And, as you've seen, I already lack a certain level of inhibition, so sobriety is something I have to hold onto. Otherwise, I might be coming on to random strangers. Which, technically speaking, you qualify for. So, yeah, forget about me trying to come on to you, okay?"

She'd been walking around the room as she delivered her tirade; straightening up, fluffing pillows, folding blankets, and taking her wine glass to the kitchen sink; all with her gaze diverted from him until her last sentence when she raised her eyes to his.

His verdant eyes hid pain in them, embarrassment too.

Saffron could relate. Her skin felt hot.

"Today's been a day of revelations," Colton said sighing. "Why stop now?" He stood up from the arm rest and sat at one end of the sofa, gesturing for her to sit at the other. "Come, sit down. Please."

She returned with a glass of water.

"I'm the one to apologize to you," he said, looking down into his wine. "In all the talking we've done today, not once did I mention Kaelynne. That's her name," he said uncomfortably. His hands gripped the goblet as his eyes shifted to the coffee table where his newly inscribed book was resting next to a stack of Mother Earth News magazines.

"Why?" he asked, seemingly to himself was well as her. "I'm not entirely sure, but it wasn't being honest with you. I-I guess I don't know what I'm feeling."

"Well, that my friend, makes two of us," she said. "I only know that I don't know you, but I'd like to know more. This 'revelation'," she said with air quotes, 'just solidifies that we're meant to be friends, not lovers."

Colton's face fell at the word 'lovers', like his throat and groin were simultaneously contracting. Looking mildly ill, he nervously took a gulp of wine.

Time to change the subject, she thought morosely. *Again.*

"So," she asked, digging herself deep into the soft cushions, expanding the space between them, "do you like to travel?" Resolutely, she threw her thoughts of seduction aside and resolved to put him in the friend box.

"Um, well, sure," he stammered. "We go back to Texas pretty regularly, mostly for business and to see my brother. Once in awhile, we go up north to Montana and North Dakota. Also, mostly for business, but sometimes just to camp and fish. When I was younger, we did some traveling for barrel racing and rodeo around the Four Corners."

Taking a sip of water, Saffron swallowed and said, "I don't remember much of Montana and North Dakota except they're big states with lots of open land. Basically, a lot like here."

"Oh," he asked, "you've been up there?"

"Oh yeah," she said, feeling herself lighten up. "I love to travel. I've been to all fifty states plus across Canada from Vancouver to Halifax, Nova Scotia."

"Whoa," Colton interrupted, looking somewhat bewildered.

"Well, yeah, I know. It's crazy," she said. "At sixteen, I was traveling with a punk band called Last Generation. We flew through most places, like a torpedo, just stopping to play before heading on. It's not like I truly got to explore and enjoy it fully."

"You? You were in a punk band?" he asked with incredulity.

"Umm, yeah," she said self-consciously. "Just some back-up harmonies and second guitar stuff. I grew up with Ayden, the lead singer, here in Sweetwater. It was his band really."

"What happened?" he asked.

She thought a moment before speaking.

How can I explain Ayden when I barely understand him myself?

"I guess I grew tired of the anger. Oh," she added, "believe me, I'm still armpit deep in anger some days, but I came to the conclusion, if I only have this one life to live, it'd be better off spent on creating connections with people, rather than focusing on all the things which disconnect and divide us. Soooo, long story short, I dropped out, studied yoga in Santa Fe, came home, and here we are."

"Well, I got nothing on that, I don't think," he said. "My life's pretty boring."

"What's wrong with boring?" she said, edging out of the cushions and leaning towards him without realizing it. "There's beauty and perfection in the little things in life, too. Growing food, caring for animals, catching fish, that's about all I do these days, and I wouldn't change it. I made the decision to come home, care for the land around me, do my duty and contribute to my community. There's immeasurable value in just being there for others, keeping a low carbon footprint, and living lightly on the land. It's a type of grace, and it's how I keep my anger and resentment at bay these days."

Question after question seemed to swirl through Colton's head. Finally, he asked, "So, where's the band now?"

"Oh, somewhere on the East Coast," she said. "Last I heard, Ayden was in an Occupy-type movement called TimeBomb near Washington DC. He's still trying to save the planet, in his own way."

Shifting lower on the couch, her head rested on a pillow and her feet glided towards his thigh; her blue toenails flashed in the light like little minnows.

"You know what? I'm exhausted," she said. "Would you like to stay and take a nap? No more funny stuff," she added, trying not to blush. "After dark, we usually cook and eat together while we jam and play music. You're welcome to join us."

"Honestly," he said, "that sounds wonderful, but I should probably be heading home."

Saffron found herself swallowing a lump which had magically appeared in her throat. She looked in his kind eyes, remembering how he'd pulled her from the water, how his strong arms had held her tightly as the waves and the wind had tormented them. In those dark and frightening moments, it had been just the two of them, two souls in jeopardy. Separating now felt like a part of her was being ripped away.

That's totally ridiculous, she told herself. *We're nothing alike. Plus, he's taken.*

"Well, Colton James Miller," she said, sitting up and squaring her shoulders. "It's been a revelation." Tilting her head to the side, she added slyly, "Thank you for the fish."

"The Lord is my Shepherd; I shall not want;
God makes me lie down in green pastures.
The Lord leads me beside the still waters."
- Psalm 23:1,2

Chapter 10: Crossroads

Colton had no clue how late it was. He only knew that his dark bedroom was stifling hot and that his multiple prayers for a cool breeze had not yet been granted. Wide awake and spread-eagled in bed, he wore wet washcloths on his chest and neck while mentally kicking himself for turning down Saffron's offer to play music under the stars.

No matter how hard he tried, he could not get Saffron out of his mind. Over and over, he had replayed the day, remembering her laugh, her energy, and her sexy self-assurance. His heart raced repeatedly with these memories before dropping into his stomach; his mind, guiltily ricocheting back to Kaelynne with dizzying speed, back and forth between the two women like a spectator in a tennis match.

It was exhausting.

Damn it, Colt, he thought shamefully. *You have a girlfriend for heaven's sake!*

Dancing with Saffron had been totally spur-of-the-moment, born of the playful, light-hearted mood, the music and alcohol. When she'd fallen against him, angling for a kiss, his knees had almost collapsed. It had taken every ounce of his strength to turn away from her cherry lips and milk-white skin. Even sitting, he'd felt winded, his heart hammering in his chest.

Recalling that moment in his hot room, he noticed an uncomfortable pulling sensation in his gut, a wrenching pang of regret. Surprisingly, he realized it wasn't because he'd almost cheated on Kaelynne, but for the simple reason that he was dating her in the first place. Suddenly, their relationship seemed so trivial, so paper thin, a gossamer facade of love.

What he had with Kaelynne had never been passionate. It had never felt this alive.

This...connected, he thought with amazement.

Gazing out the open window at the still night and waxing moon, he imagined Saffron's pale skin glowing under its light only a few miles away. He pictured her sitting in the pavilion, a sultry smile turned his direction as if she knew intuitively that he was thinking of her.

His groin began to ache. Quickly, he moved the washcloths over to his pelvis and eyes.

He'd deliberately left his cellphone in the jar with the rice, reluctant to call Kaelynne until he'd sorted out his jumbled feelings. With no electricity or phone, he had little else to do but toss, turn, and think.

The night's humid air wrapped cloyingly around him.

Colton felt squeezed and constricted, as if he had ill-fitting skin.

Never had he felt so restless, but the feeling seemed to shake something loose in him. He could finally admit things hadn't felt right for awhile. For one thing, his nightmares had been occurring more frequently, even if he was choosing to ignore them. On most days, he admitted he felt stressed, like he was never going to measure up somehow.

This isn't working, he thought with frustration, kicking away his sweaty sheets. *Something has to change!*

Like a bolt of lightning, Colton realized his life no longer felt like the right path; he wasn't living the life he wanted to live.

This truth unearthed an avalanche of clarity.

For one, his feelings for Kaelynne were best described as lukewarm. Compared to the richness of his transient experience with Saffron, the relationship with his girlfriend was a dull and comfortable beige.

For as long as Colton could remember, his eventual marriage to Kaelynne had been hinted at. The Miller and Stockton families had been close friends for decades. Her brother, Gage, had been his best friend since preschool. They worked together and even attended the same church. When he and Kaelynne had finally made it official, many members of the congregation had remarked with "it's about time."

Breaking up with her was going to have multiple repercussions. Not only would he be hurting her, but his decision would disappoint his own family, her family, and some members of their congregation.

Lots of people were not going to understand his change of heart.

So, he asked himself contemptuously, *I stay with her out of fear, even if I'm unhappy?*

It was another truth bomb. He wasn't happy in their relationship.

Even though Kaelynne was pretty, and smart, and got along with his family, oftentimes she could be demanding and occasionally, downright mean-spirited.

One of the things which had always annoyed him was that he could only call her Kaelynne, no other name was tolerated. He knew it was only a minor irritation, however, once he was being honest with himself, he could see that intolerance was practically her middle name. When things didn't go the way she thought they should, Kaelynne could be overtly critical and acerbic, like when he missed a day to call her.

He predicted he was going to get scolded in the morning for avoiding her.

For months, he'd been practicing forgiveness and acceptance, trying hard as a Christ-loving man to elevate his love for her simply because it'd felt like the right and responsible thing to do. Lying in the dark, in the quiet solitude, he realized it'd also been killing him inside.

His life was at a crossroads; he could continue down his current path which led to marriage with Kaelynne, something everyone expected him to do, or he could free himself to explore new and uncharted territory; to walk a new path that was poorly defined, yet wide open in its possibilities.

Colton wished for a crystal ball to help him see into the future.

He looked out the window into the night. With no streetlights or houselights, copious stars shone unrestricted. For some reason, their twinkling made him think of Sweetwater.

The event-filled day had been a catalyst for revelations. Colton realized it wasn't only the attraction he felt towards Saffron that excited him. Astoundingly, he'd found the serenity at Sweetwater to have been very appealing. Self-reliance and a do-it-yourself mentality had been instilled in him as a child, but he realized he'd also been raised with the conflicting messages of 'just-buy-a-new-one', 'we-can-pay-someone-to-do-that', and 'throw-that-away'.

A breeze drifted through the window and the room began to cool.

Colton removed the washcloths and readjusted his pillow. Hoping to have some answers in the morning, he was ready to shut down his tired mind. As his body relaxed, he came to one final conclusion: he could no longer deny the discomfort he'd been feeling for the topic of climate change.

He remembered Saffron's words, *You can't get too attached to things in life. So much more is going to be taken from us, a hell of a lot actually, but no one seems to really believe it. Most people just push it out of their minds.*

Colton felt like the king of pushing-things-out-of-his-mind, and he suspected he wasn't alone.

There was a dissonance he sensed between what the news and media were increasingly reporting as occurring, compared to the deepest denial and disdain from people around him. More and more often at church there was talk about a different kind of Revelations, those passages mentioned in the Bible about the 'End Times'. However, Colton had begun noticing that many things happening in the world were lining up to match the warnings of the scientists, more so than the prophets.

It was an exhausting tug-of-war of the psyche, and there was so much he didn't know.

Saffron and the Alarmists could potentially be dead right, he thought as he finally drifted into sleep.

An inner voice whispered, *So, what're ya gonna do about it?*

He awoke on the Sabbath with his stomach in knots. He'd been dreaming about building his own house in a bright meadow, hammering nails into boards as several blue-eyed and strawberry-blonde children cavorted around his feet. The last thing he's seen in his mind's eye before the alarm sounded was Saffron's smiling face looking up towards his.

Under the shrill blaring of his clock, his thoughts immediately returned to Kaelynne and all his worries from the previous night came rushing back. Colton still felt unsure of where he stood. All he knew was that he would soon see Kaelynne at morning service.

You can't keep avoiding this, he thought angrily to himself, placing his pillow over his head to block the morning light. *You've got to make a choice, and soon.*

His worries continued during church service as he sat next to her. As predicted, she gave him grief about where he'd been and why he hadn't called her. Colton explained briefly about the storm and the wet phone, but left out most of his experiences from the day before.

During the sermon, the pastor told a parable about a serpent and Colton's sleep-deprived imagination took a sharp veer. All he could think of was how a snake must feel when its skin gets too tight, and how wonderful it must be to strip it off, revealing the new skin hiding underneath.

At lunch, talk centered mainly on the blackout. For the majority of houses in San Juan County, the power was still out. Miles of undeveloped dirt roads had been turned into muddy quagmires with the sudden and intense downpour, and downed poles were everywhere from the hurricane strength wind. It had been over twenty-four hours and the electric company wasn't making any promises about when repairs would be finished.

The temperature inside the Millers' house was in the high eighties. Colton felt sweaty and uncomfortable in his church clothes.

Sitting at his family's long dining room table, a plate of grilled steak, corn and potatoes before him, his head bowed in prayer as they gave thanks for their blessings, his mind sent a silent plea to Jesus asking Him to guide and direct him.

Kaelynne sat next to him yet again. Her long blonde hair was perfectly curled and cascaded down the back of her flowered sundress. She sat straight, her manicured hands clasped daintily in her lap, with much of her food untouched. She seemed to be doing her best to put on a happy face with his family, but he could tell from the slightly worried and confused look in her eyes that it was an act.

Her brother, Gage, sat across from them. He'd been a pretty good baseball player during high school and still had the confident look of a jock. His dark hair and brown eyes differed greatly from his fairer-skinned sister, but they both shared a regal haughtiness, as if they were descended from royalty.

Since their father owned Stockton Oil and Gas, with wells located throughout the Southwest and Texas, their family struggled much less than others in the community.

Colton hadn't had much to say to his best friend in church that day; in fact, he'd been uncharacteristically silent. Gage caught Colton's eye and raised an eyebrow in a quizzical, *What up, bro?* kind of way. Colton gave him a tight-lipped smile and a tiny shoulder shrug before looking away.

Luckily, the rest of his family had plenty to say.

Cricket kept complaining about her useless appliances, including her hair dryer and curling iron. Looking ill at ease and self-conscious, she would randomly reach to tuck away some imaginary stray lock and smooth it back into place.

Meagan was mortified about the possibility of missing some reality dating show that evening.

Asa went on and on, repeatedly, about his upcoming trip to North Dakota. He had multiple demands on what Gage and Colton needed to do at work in his absence.

Colton kept his attention on his father, assuring him that they'd handle everything for the one week he would be gone. He was grateful for his father's monopoly on the conversation. It was a welcome distraction, making his own personal discomfort less noticeable.

At the end of the meal, he gave the excuse that he wasn't feeling too well, blaming a hypothetical heatstroke from the previous day's fishing trip. Cricket suggested a cool bath. Asa took yet another opportunity to stress the importance of managing the business in his absence. Gage told him to rest up and that he'd see him in the morning.

At the door, Colton turned to Kaelynne, wrapped his arms around her in a hug and told her to enjoy the rest of her day. The look on her face suggested it was not a good probability.

"We can complain because rose bushes have thorns,
or rejoice because thorn bushes have roses."
- Abraham Lincoln

Chapter II: How Does Your Garden Grow

Saffron left her house at 5:15am with music and men on her mind.

She'd spent most of the day on Sunday binging on country western songs and popcorn, with some wine and moments of masturbation. By evening, she'd played with her hair several times, traipsed in different shoes, and whirled through her wardrobe of favorite festival clothes, donning slinky boho fashions she knew from experience were popular to the opposite sex; and, to more than a few lesbians.

After hours of two-stepping and crooning with an imaginary version of Colton, she'd collapsed into bed at midnight wearing nothing but a pair of turquoise cowgirl boots, pigtails and a smile.

On the packed dirt pathway to the greenhouses in the dim morning light, she sang under her breath, 'Times Past' by a local performer, Terri Lynn Davis. She'd listened to it repeatedly until the song felt lodged in her head.

"*I remember the first time we met / sun on our skin / toes in the sand*". The slide guitar and melodious vocals had made her picture a honky-tonk dance floor, with Colton leading and holding her hand. "*Feels like lo-o-ove.*" Half-strolling, half-skipping, she sang louder, "*River of time / be still my mind.*"

Briefly, she wondered if Colton liked rafting, then admonished herself to stop thinking about him for the umpteenth time.

Damn right, she thought irritably, *be still my mind! He has a girlfriend, for cry-eye-sake. Give it up!*

One of the greenhouses was dark and unoccupied, the other shone like an opal. Craving solitude over community, she headed towards the empty tunnel. Inside, she inhaled the rich, humid air; a stark contrast to the dryness of the desert. Filling her lungs, she danced down the empty aisles, stretching and warming her muscles amongst the plants and greenery.

She had two yoga classes to perform in Aztec later that day.

Dance was excellent for making her limber and, in her opinion, greenhouses were a great place to twirl and bend unabashedly. The stimulating scent of the herbs and vegetables, along with the moist dirt and worms, created an earthy smell which always made her feel more zen and peaceful.

Grounded, as her mother would say.

Thanks to Zia, Saffron had been around gardens and farms her entire life. They'd been both a playground and a schoolhouse to her.

One of her earliest memories involved hundreds of green caterpillars, inching along rows of towering tomato plants; a bona fide epidemic. She distinctly remembered picking the hornworms' plump bodies and dumping them unceremoniously into wriggling piles until the buckets were full. Her six-year-old-self had absolutely loved 'fighting the invasion' alongside her family and friends. She remembered everyone laughing and hugging her when she'd suggested giving the bugs to the chickens in order to 'complete the circle of life'.

She'd always loved the cyclical rhythm of growing her own food; first, seeds to sprouts, then maturation to harvest, and back to seeds to save for the following crop. The repetition never grew boring to her because she'd realized at a young age that each year brought something new, something to learn. Like the caterpillars, another season could bring more challenges to overcome, as well as happy memories that could last a lifetime.

Nature held a quiet and powerful energy she revered; everything pointed to an order to the world; everything served a purpose. Plants never struggled to become what they were; they innately took the gifts around them, water, soil and air, and used them to transform into food, oxygen, and often, beauty.

In fact, her love affair with working in the dirt had been one of the reasons she'd left Ayden. Traveling from one congested city to another, one asphalt jungle to the next, had made her heartsick for the great outdoors.

Done with dancing, Saffron kneeled behind a row of beans, corn and squash, the Three Sisters, and put on her gardening gloves. She heard her best friend, Lorelei, come inside, singing a sped-up, punk-rock version of '99 Red Balloons'. Saffron peered around to greet her, but Lorelei was in her own world, completely selling her somewhat-off-key performance to the not-so-empty greenhouse.

Her rich, dark brown hair was tied back with a red bandana. Sporting a matching red and black plaid shirt, she bore a strong resemblance to Rosie the Riveter, however, her fishnet stockings worn under black short shorts, coupled with knee-high rubber boots covered in grinning skulls and laughing ducks was pure Lorelei.

Rosie the Rockabilly Riveter, Saffron thought and almost giggled.

Lorelei's most stunning feature were her golden brown eyes. Everyone noticed them, even behind the chunky emo glasses she wore. As a child, her nickname had been Hoot, because her eyes almost glowed, exotic and speckled like an owl's, or a leopard's; a genetic gift from her Diné ancestry.

Saffron loved Lorelei's grandma who went by the name, Shimásání, meaning 'my maternal grandmother'. For most of her life, Shimásání had lived a traditional life on the reservation in an old hogan with little water, a wood and coal heater, and land as far as the eye could see. During the turbulent 1960's when racial tensions in Farmington had been exceedingly high, she'd been raped by a white man, and impregnated. The perpetrator was never held accountable.

Shimásání had cherished her daughter, Carla Peshlakai, nonetheless, transmuting her violent creation into a fierce love that extended to her granddaughter as well.

Lorelei's parents were best friends with Saffron's. Lorelei's dad, George Harper, was a witty, rail-thin man with a goatee and glasses who taught anthropology at the community college. Saffron had seen him drive off for work that morning in his electric Nissan Leaf; in its back window was a large sign proclaiming, 'I Am Powered By The Sun'.

Saffron could admit to feeling slightly envious.

"Good morning, Sunshine," she said to Lorelei after she'd finished crooning to the corn. "How was Pagosa?"

The Peshlakai-Harper family had spent the weekend in the mountains of Colorado, soaking in the hot springs, hiking, and foraging for wild berries and mushrooms.

"Amazing!" she answered gleefully, completely unruffled that her singing had had an audience. "I got to jam Saturday night at our campsite with some excellent musicians from Seattle. One of them, Tyler, was supremely delicious," she said with a salacious glint in her eyes. "I enjoyed eating him up."

Saffron was sure Tyler was telling a similar story to his friends today.

"No nookie for me," she said with a pout. "I sort of made a fool of myself with this guy I met." She suddenly remembered the lake. "Hey! Did you guys get hit by that storm?! I swear, it was something out of a disaster movie. A major supercell, or was it a derecho? I'm not sure. Did you see it?!?" She paused for theatrical emphasis. "I nearly died."

"No kidding?!? No, we didn't get rain at all," Lorelei replied. "What happened? What guy?"

Saffron relayed the details of her misadventures while she watered the squash plants, their handful of yellow blossoms bouncing with each splash while the young zucchinis and crooked necks glistened.

"Okay, okay, but what about the guy?" Lorelei interrupted after being assured that her friend was indeed okay.

"Really nice," she answered, picturing Colton in her mind. "I liked him. Sort of your typical Farmington guy, but really easy to talk to and totally easy on the eyes. I drank too much and came on to him."

Lorelei raised an eyebrow.

"Does he have HHC?" she asked with a shit-eating grin.

HHC was their code for the perfect guy- head, heart, and cock; all the things a woman truly needed to fall in love, and to stay in love.

Their code had out started as Triple H (head, heart and hung), but as the girls had gained sexual experience, they'd realized that size didn't matter if the guy was ultimately a selfish lover. The word 'cock' implied a playfulness and a confidence, a perversion and a naughtiness that could make sex superbly enjoyable. In their opinion, there was nothing sexier than a man with control of his thoughts and feelings, an ability to express himself, and a mutually satisfactory lovemaking style.

Saffron giggled and said, "Well, he totally shut me down, so no clue on the 'C' part, but yeah, he seemed to have a lot of 'H' and 'H'." Pouting, she added, "Sadly, he's taken."

"Bummer," Lorelei replied as she began clipping chayote and pattypan squashes into a milk crate. "Did you tell him about Ayden?"

The Pesklakai-Harper family had fostered numerous children over the years. Ayden had been one of them. He was like an older brother to her.

"I mentioned him," Saffron said, feeling vaguely uncomfortable. "I told him about seeing the country on our big tour."

Beans spiraled up the corn stalks with their insistent vines and a variety of heirloom pods peeked between the leaves. Saffron put her watering can down and began snapping deep purple hulls into a wicker basket.

"And anyway," she added, "Ayden's not my boyfriend."

"Boyfriend...childhood crush...fuck buddy. Whatevs," Lorelei responded teasingly.

Saffron again had to laugh. To say that her relationship with Ayden was complicated was an understatement. Trying to come up with an appropriate explanation had flummoxed her throughout her teenage years. She hadn't seen him in several months, but they still talked every few weeks or so. He was busy in Washington, DC, railing away at the 'inequalities inherent in our systems'.

He didn't like to talk politics and details over the phone because he worried about being wire tapped. Phone sex, however, was always on the menu; maybe because he thought the phone was tapped.

The last time he'd visited was in time for a folk music festival in Colorado. Most of the members from Sweetwater, including her parents, had attended. The two of them had stayed behind, fucking like bunnies in their absence.

She'd learned from him then that his activist group, Timebomb, was behind the recent campaign, 'How Will They Die?'.

All over the country, people were holding up signs like the anti-abortionists used to do with pictures of dead fetuses. This campaign however took pictures of prominent politicians, corporate biggiewigs and other 'elites', then shared stats on how they could die and the dates.

Wildfire, 2027. Hurricane, 2030. Heatstroke, 2036. Riot, 2038.

It had garnered national attention when some hackers shared pictures of these prominent individuals' children and grandchildren and put them on the posters instead...along with choosing to display them in front of their office buildings.

All those innocent faces, hair in curls, smiles wide with their whole lives before them, and similar causes of death and dates.

Starvation, 2042.

Many of the people in San Juan County hated it and thought it was in deplorable taste. Saffron agreed it was distasteful, but for an entirely different reason. She knew enough about climate destabilization to know that it was eerily accurate to how the coming decades were going to kill thousands upon thousands of people, perhaps millions around the world.

Her decision to settle down, to refocus on self-preservation and to take a break from the 'Revolution' had driven a wedge between her and Ayden. However, at the heart, they could never be divided. Whatever they were to each other, it was deep and beyond explanation.

Saffron's thoughts returned to Colton. She couldn't deny the inexplicable pull she'd felt towards him, like the simple truth of gravity. Her stomach knotted with emptiness, not for food, but from some unfulfilled need.

Most days she kept herself busy, trying to focus on living in the moment rather than despairing about the crumbling world around her. Sometimes, she longed to live in blissful ignorance of the future like so many of the people she observed around her.

For the few hours she'd spent with Colton, she had slipped easily into that bliss.

"For my part, whatever anguish of spirit it may cost,
I am willing to know the whole truth; to know the worst
and to provide for it."
- Patrick Henry

Chapter 12: G$$gle eARTh

Colton spent Tuesday evening alone in the eighty-six degree heat of his second-story room, feeling utterly drained. He lay facedown on his bed with a wet washcloth resting on the back of his neck in an attempt to cool off. Briefly, he considered sitting outside on the patio with his mother and sister, but rejected the idea. He was in no mood for company.

Unfortunately, his exhaustion was not solely due to his uncomfortable physical conditions.

Normally, he enjoyed overseeing the family business when Asa was gone. It was a glimpse of what his life would be like without his dad always looking over his shoulder. However, since Monday morning Colton had been on the run, struggling to work in the heat and juggle the demands of the business with no electricity. He'd done his best to keep up, but in addition to the moderate madness of his work responsibilities, he'd been subjected to a multitude of intense phone calls from Kaelynne over the past forty-eight hours.

They'd first spoken late Sunday evening. The oppressive heat must have been taking a toll because Kaelynne's temperament had been more like a harpy than usual. All the things she'd politely kept suppressed during church and Sunday lunch had erupted.

She'd been livid, demanding to know what was going on with him, telling him that he was acting weird, and she didn't appreciate that he hadn't called her on Saturday or that evening either. She'd even been furious he hadn't taken her out to a movie that night. Colton had reminded her about the blackout and his heatstroke. This statement backfired and she spiraled into complaints about how horrible and difficult everything was.

"How hard is it to make electricity?!" she had complained. "I can't even watch tv."

Finally, Colton had had enough. He admitted that night, gently but with conviction, that he was questioning their relationship.

The phone calls had continued unabated since then.

Each call began with her crying, telling him that she loved him, but then she would segue into bitterness and anger; she hated him; she couldn't believe she had wasted so much time on him; he was a loser that would never amount to anything in life; she should have listened to her friends and family. Finally, she would hang up on him.

Then, the conversation would repeat itself when she called back.

Colton felt trapped, like Bill Murray in Groundhog Day, reliving the same moment over and over again, never knowing how to make it right. All he could do was apologize, tell her that he cared for her, but that he couldn't marry her. They needed to go their separate ways.

So far he had avoided spending a lot of time with Gage. They both had a ton to do at the office and their phones didn't always work well in the remote oilfield patches. When they had talked, Colton was apologetic, but evasive. He'd assured Gage that he wasn't cheating, but that he'd realized he wanted something different in his life. He had told him that Kaelynne would find an amazing man to love and care for her like she deserved, but that it just couldn't be him any longer. Gage had given him dark, brooding looks, and advice to keep thinking about what he was doing.

Now, sitting alone in the heat of his room after the last call, the phone dead in his hand with her last disconnection, Colton felt wrung out like a dish towel. He stripped naked trying to cool off. Having had enough sadness and drama for the night, he put his phone on Airplane mode. The decision to break up with her still felt like the right thing to do, regardless of whether or not he ever developed a relationship with Saffron.

He knew there was nothing he could do to alleviate Kaelynne's pain. Time would have to do that for her.

Turning on his tablet which still had most of its battery life, he pulled up various social networking sites, searching for Saffron's profile but it never popped up. Without much thought, he changed direction and searched instead for 'climate change', adding the words 'current facts'. A good number of the early searches that popped up downplayed the effects, but in today's world, Colton understood that simply meant those particular sites had figured out how to maximize exposure.

Getting priority billing on a search engine didn't necessarily equal truth.

Deeper down the list, he found articles that repeated terms such as tipping points, runaway global warming, carbon parts per million and overall global temperature increase. He learned that the planet had made several changes over its millions of years of existence. The last time the planet was an average of six degrees colder, there'd been an Ice Age; the last time it was six degrees hotter, a massive extinction event.

What made this time different according to the researchers was the sheer, unprecedented speed with which the planet was now changing. Instead of taking thousands of years to shift, the Earth had gotten almost three degrees hotter in a little over a hundred years, coinciding perfectly with the invention of trains, cars, and power plants.

According to the science, the world was not currently witnessing a natural climate shift, but a destabilization, which was unduly due to human consumption and over-population.

The birth of the Fossil Fuel Age had begun the death of the planet.

Colton felt sucker-punched. His fingers went to click the pages away when he stopped himself.

You look this beast dead-on in the eyes, he thought angrily. *Being in the dark is no longer an option!* Finally, he reckoned with himself, *Don't you want to know what's coming?*

Back on the websites, he learned that ice at Antartica was in an irreversible decline and had been for over a decade. Icebergs were shedding off of it like fleas off a dog. At the northern pole, vegetation was growing in spots which had been under ice for thousands of years; permafrost was receding at an alarming rate, releasing trapped methane gases which were predicted to speed up the warming trend even faster; many scientists were worried about ancient pathogens coming back to life after melting out of the ice sheets. Droughts were expected to be more frequent and prolonged, with more huge rain dumps periodically swamping and flooding the land. Crops and agriculture were going to be profoundly affected. Food supplies were going to be a problem for many.

Living in Farmington with its large population of Mormons, Colton was familiar with the term 'food security' as they were advised to keep up to five years' worth of food in case of emergencies. It made sense to Colton to be prepared, but he wondered how many millions were completely unprepared?

What will people do when things get worse around the country? Around the planet?

It was inside an article on extinction he first saw the words 'Phase 4', the phrase Saffron had briefly mentioned on the boat. It stated that the Earth's carbon levels had been steady between 250 and 300 ppm for tens of thousands of years, basically the entire span of civilized society, but had spiked tremendously in the last few decades.

This was the first time in history Homo sapiens were living at these new levels.

Carbon levels were now nearing 450ppm which was the beginning of Phase 2 in the climate shift. At this point in time, the shift appeared to be irreversible. The article warned that if we surpassed Phase 3, 500 ppm, then the likelihood humans were going to be able to slow it down or reverse the shift would get statistically less probable.

Phase 4 would see a temperature increase of 6 degrees Fahrenheit. It was predicted the majority of all species would die. Human populations would be gutted worldwide.

The projected timeframe? As early as 2044. He would be less than fifty years old.

If the carbon ppm went over 600, the entire planet could potentially die if the oceans acidified too drastically. Reduced algae + dead plankton = reduced oxygen = death. Phase 6 was the endgame, worse than total global nuclear war.

One author, Lawrence Wollersheim, wrote "once we lose meaningful control over escalating global warming, there is no way to reverse the fatal consequences that humanity will endure for centuries or thousands of years, if we even survive." But the article was quick to state that well before that point governments were going to go bankrupt because the destruction to infrastructure would be nearly impossible to repair; rising ocean levels, massive storms and extreme fires were going to exceed government budgets worldwide. People were predicted to migrate en masse. Many experts said war and terrorist attacks were extremely likely to increase.

Almost every person Colton knew had firearms. Lots of people in the region taught their kids to hunt and shoot at a young age. It was a part of the culture. A question formed in Colton's mind, *Would the guns be used to provide for their families and communities? Would people come together like the folks in Sweetwater, or would neighbor turn against neighbor?*

It was a sobering thought that made his blood run cold.

Am I going to experience bloodshed in my lifetime, in my own backyard?

He quickly pushed the idea from his mind.

The last thing he read was a quote which said, "Your inaction and/ or your seeking personal comfort or escape from your moral, ethical, and spiritual obligation to act is in fact, by omission, a form of contributing to the end of civilization and humanity as we know it."

After two hours online reading these dire predictions, Colton wasn't sure if he felt numb, sick, or if the panic inside him had short-circuited his brain. All he knew was that there was only one person in the world he wanted to talk to. Clicking off everything he'd been searching through, he felt a modicum of relief to close the door on the new influx of information before going back to his search engine and typing in 'Saffron LeMay'.

An entry for her popped up on a yoga website in Aztec. Out of curiosity, he opened it and learned the schedule for her classes which she taught twice on Mondays and again on Friday mornings. Disappointingly, the website didn't have any pictures of her.

He added 'phone number' to the search after her name and got the White Pages directory. There was still no match for Saffron, so he changed it to 'Jack LeMay'; there he found her (505) landline digits. For a moment, he held his breath. The urge to call her intensified.

He disabled Airplane mode and called. The phone rang four times as the palms of his hands began to perspire. On the fifth ring, a woman's voice responded "Hello? LeMay residence. How may I help you?" There was loud music in the background and the sound of people laughing.

"Um, hi. This is Colton Miller. I'm looking for Saffron."

"Oh! Hi Colton! So nice of you to call. This's Zia. Roni's around here somewhere. I'll go get her." The phone was set down with a small clatter and he could hear a faint "Roni! Telephone!" being yelled over the sound of the music. He thought it was The Pretenders.

"Hello?" came Saffron's lyrical girlish voice.

Colton quivered, thinking he'd just heard the two sexiest syllables ever spoken on the planet.

"Oh, hey," he said, licking his dry lips. "It's...it's CJ. Um, Colton. How are you?"

"Hi!!!"

Her excited voice sent Colton over the moon. She sounded genuinely happy he'd called. The music in the background, however, was still really loud. He heard Chrissie Hynes listing all the things she was going to use to get attention.

The thought of what Saffron could do with her arms, legs, fingers and imagination made him slightly erect.

"Hold on," she said, "Mom's gonna hang up her phone."

He heard the sound of a line disconnecting and the noise decreased significantly.

"Much better," she said in her sweet, upbeat way. "Hey! How are you, hero?"

"I-hope-it's-okay-I-called," Colton said in a rush before consciously steadying himself. Sighing, he added, "It's been a crazy couple of days and I've been wanting to talk to you. How have you been?"

"So far, so good," she responded. "Are you still without power?"

"Yeah." All the things he wanted to say knotted tightly inside him. He hadn't called a girl like this in a long while. Nervously, he continued, "It's hot as Hades. The heat and dead outlets are making my mother and sister *crazy*. Plus, my work's so much harder. But, aside from that," he said, eager to say something positive. "I've kind of liked the quiet."

It's helping me think.

"I was just getting ready to head outside and jam," Saffron said brightly. "You timed it just right to get a hold of me. You missed a killer fish fry Saturday night. The trout was delicious!"

Colton pictured her curled in the comfy cushions of the sofa, her face lit up with the animated way she had of talking.

"I'm sorry I missed that." He paused and thought of saying, *'I can't stop thinking about you.'* before plunging ahead. "Are you free to meet up with me tomorrow? My world's a little messy right now, but I'm no longer seeing Kaelynne. If you still want to get to know me better, I'd love to invite you to dinner. A proper date."

Saffron was quiet. Colton noticed his heart pounding in his chest. When her soft voice came back on the line, it stopped.

"I'd like that a lot," she said, then added, "Wow, you have had a crazy couple of days."

He let out a deep breath he hadn't realized he'd been holding.

"It's been awful," he said, rubbing his eyes, "but it's the right thing to do. I should have done it awhile ago." He felt some of his sadness bubble back to the surface, but he didn't give time for it. "Where would you like to go? Somewhere in Durango?"

"Here would be fine," she said. "I finish up at the farmers market around 6:30. If you don't mind me being a little sweaty, you can pick me up from there and we can go to the Thai place downtown. Oh! And I think they have live music playing at the brewery, but," she hesitated. "Um, only if you don't mind driving me back home afterwards?"

Colton's face erupted in his first smile in days.

"That sounds perfect," he said with relief. "I'll see you around 6:00. You can put me to work for a little while."

Saffron laughed and said she would like that, then they both said good night and hung up.

Darkness was descending upon the world and his room was changing to shadows. He found himself unable to relax and fall asleep. It'd only been three days since he'd met her, but visions of her had been dancing on the back of his eyelids ever since.

Twisting and turning, he became aware that his scrotum ached, his penis, literally throbbing for attention. Curling his hand around his hardening shaft, he pictured her wet skin and clinging clothes after the storm. He thought of the earthy scent of her silky, alabaster skin. Biting his bottom lip, he remembered the feel of her curves in his arms and the deepening of her breath when she'd leaned in to kiss him.

Moaning quietly, he imagined that he'd taken her initial invitation to stay, and made love to her in the dome room above. He dreamt of being pressed against her, surrounded by her fairie-like essence; her spun gold hair spilling in a fan upon her pillow; her eyes, daring him to please her.

Colton's stroking intensified. In a rhythm matching his thrusting hips, his fist and fingers whirled and clenched along his length. Pleasure surged through his entire body like all the lights of Las Vegas turning on at once. His nipples tightened as the sweat on his body cooled and his arousal climbed.

My God, I want her, he thought.

There'd been a fire in her eyes, a spark which had kindled a flame within himself. He felt it burning, his passion erupting and flowing like Vesuvian lava onto his hand and taut belly. Dazzling lights flashed in his mind as he shuddered in pure ecstasy; relief and joy spreading across every part of him.

He couldn't wait to see her.

"Get up tomorrow early in the morning,
and earlier than you did today,
and do the best that you can.
Always stay near me, for tomorrow
I will have much to do and more than I ever had,
and tomorrow blood will leave my body
above the breast."
- Joan of Arc

Chapter 13: Farmers Market

Saffron had started her morning with an announcement by Mr. Cocker, the resident rooster, that a new day had arrived. The previous night's phone call had been her very first thought, bringing both a giggle and a smile to her sleepy face.

If you still want to get to know me better, I'd love to invite you to dinner. A proper date.

The memory had sent her vivid imagination off into a sexy fantasyland with all of the naughty things she wanted to do to him. Beginning her day with a satisfying orgasm, she'd had high hopes it was going to be a great day.

Instead, she stood behind the Sweetwater produce table, hot, sticky and tired. The summer sun blazed onto the asphalt parking lot near a strip mall and a line of towering cottonwood trees; their cool shadows taunted the farmers under their sun hats and umbrellas.

Working at the market was usually one of Saffron's favorite things to do in the summertime; and occasionally, one of her least favorite.

She loved the freshness of the newly-picked produce strewn across multiple tables; the aliveness of homegrown fruits and vegetables in a rainbow of colors, God's own natural palette. She loved the subtle smell of earth which had followed from the fields and greenhouses; the smell of sun-warmed tomatoes, bursting with juice under their taut red skins; and, the scent of sweet peaches tempting her to the tables of the orchard owners, her mouth watering in a Pavlovian reflex.

Baskets overflowed with green beans, ready to dump into the plastic or reusable cloth bags for the transport home to kitchens around town. The lettuces, chards and kales were still firm with the hydrostatic pressure of water in their chambers, not wilted and sad like a desiccating worm on a sidewalk. Hopefully, they'd be eaten before they succumbed to that state in the cold dark of people's refrigerators.

This was the height of nutritional density, when each purple plum and elongated yellow squash held the most potential, the most lifeforce, and it thrilled her in a way she couldn't explain to be able to share the literal fruits of her labor with others. Which, ironically, is what made this her least favorite day sometimes.

The 'others' she was so keen to share with weren't always in tune with Saffron's belief system. Whereas she grew up knowing the value of good food and the truth she was largely responsible for her own health, she still lived in the land of fast food, television and sugar addicts.

Typically on market day, there would be a handful of people who merely strolled by, glancing at the goods, and moving on without purchase. Occasionally, some lugged their oxygen tanks behind them or moved on legs swollen with edema, backs bent with the burden of unwanted weight. Often, there'd be a dullness in their eyes, the pain barely masked, many of them hopelessly ill-humored.

Saffron had inherited her mother's desire to heal people.

She wanted to tell each and every one of them how their diets were poisoning them; that the factories and companies manufacturing their Frankenfood were only interested in developing their addiction and brand loyalty, not in helping their bodies to blossom on a cellular level; that the rush of released insulin they experienced with almost every meal was causing even more fat to be stored, even within organs like their livers; that those overburdened livers and chemical overexposure were causing toxins to build up in each and every fat cell in their bodies, making them expand and leak inflammatory chemicals into their interstitial tissues; ultimately, making them heavier than they wanted to be.

And it was all preventable.

These were not conversations most people were open to hearing. The programming from decades of endless commercials had done its job well. The claws of processed foods were firmly buried into the pleasure centers of their brains so they were blinded to the healing properties of the foods before them. Saffron could almost hear their thoughts, *Yuck. It's all vegetables. Let's go get a milkshake across the street.*

Some of these people would scoff at the prices, drive off, and a block away turn into a drive-through for half-off vats of soda, not realizing that their $2.50 mega-drink purchase was going to cost them hundreds, if not thousands, of dollars in prescription drugs and doctors' visits down the road.

It hurt Saffron's heart, every time.

This day's crowd of patrons was impressive in the sheer number of people milling about the square of parking lot, and by the massive amounts of food being purchased. It had been an amazing two hours of sales. Sweetwater's farmstand table was still laden with fresh produce, but the crates in the back of the sunny yellow truck had already been depleted.

It looked like they would run out well before the 6:30 closing time.

Across the county, the power outage had been extreme. Many homes had their electricity restored that afternoon, but the damage had been done; foods in fridges and freezers had spoiled as temperatures had been cruel and unusual for July. The rainy monsoon season had so far eluded the Four Corners; the weather had been hot, dry and cloudless until the skies had unleashed its massive downpour.

Multiple vendors had bemoaned the loss and damage to their unprotected fields. Zia had given her sympathy with sincerity, and told Saffron and Lorelei that Sweetwater should consider adding another greenhouse.

Superstorms were one of the hazards Earthlings now had to contend with.

The after-work crowd began arriving and many of the other vendors' tables were getting bare. As Saffron scanned the crowd, she noticed more and more irritation and tension on the faces around her.

She overheard two women arguing loudly above the normal conversations of the market. Turning, she saw a large woman in baggy purple shorts and a floral sleeveless shirt, using a death grip to hold onto the green-leafed end of a large red onion, as another plump woman with close-cropped, greying hair, wearing an extra-large Snoopy t-shirt, clenched the purple bulb part. Each was pulling the onion closer to themselves which only brought the two into closer proximity to each other, and as neither had the intention of letting go, the intensity of their exchange began to grow.

"I had it first!" Snoopy Shirt's voice rose above the crowd, her indignation apparent for all to see. "What kind of person goes and grabs something another person is already holding?!"

"You did not! I had it first," hissed Purple Pants. "Go get yourself another one."

Snoopy Shirt's face blotched into reddened patches then bloomed into a scarlet mask of anger on her sagging, jowled face.

"There aren't any more," she barked loudly. "This whole damn town is running out of fucking food. So get your fucking hands off of my fucking onion, or I'm gonna fucking hurt you!"

Saffron didn't know if her shrill, swear-word-laden statement was true or not, but regardless, it set in motion a palpable shift. The crowd reacted subtly at first. People turned towards whatever table was nearest them, reaching across people to grab whatever was left. Those removed from the tables began jostling the others in their attempt to get closer and not be shut out. She heard multiple voices rising, increasing in volume.

Standing in front of Sweetwater's table, an older man wearing overalls and a well-used, greasy cowboy hat, held out a crumpled wad of dollars and announced he was buying everything they had.

This caused several folks standing behind him to push forward, their brows knotted in frustration, demanding they get what they'd come for. Zia stepped in front of Saffron and Lorelei and began trying to calm everyone down, telling them there'd be enough to go around and she was sure they could work this out peacefully.

Saffron never saw the gun. There was only the deafening sound of the powerful leaden missile erupting from somewhere across the lot, then the screams and crash as the cowboy customer collapsed onto the table in front of them. Her mother pushed back into her with a shudder. Zia's body stiffened and Saffron heard her say with a wheeze, "We've got this."

Stiff one moment, then limp as a ragdoll the next.

The crowd disintegrated; everyone racing, backs bent, heads down, to escape the vulnerability of their sudden circumstances, driven by the basic, primal instinct to flee and be safe.

Saffron clumsily held onto her mother, falling to her knees onto the asphalt and cushioning Zia's fall with her own body. Her view was obstructed by the fabric of the table skirt so she was blind to what was occurring on the other side.

Lorelei was behind them both, trying to maneuver them up and away from the area.

Someone yelled "Drop it!" and then two more shots rang out,

sounding like two different guns. More screams sounded, followed a heartbeat later by the blessed words, "It's okay! Everyone. It's over."

Saffron immediately yelled, "We need help! 9-1-1! Someone call 9-1-1!"

Quickly, she scooted out from under Zia and got her lying on the ground. Once in this position, she could see blood darkening the right side of Zia's shirt, just above her breast. Lorelei saw it too and took off her bandana to press hard on the wound.

Zia's eyes were shut and her face was slack. Saffron spoke her name loudly, asking if she could hear her. There was no response. She checked for breathing and found it to be shallow, but present.

Lorelei kept pressure on Zia's chest. They'd both been trained in emergency response by Saffron's father, but this was personal, and real. Saffron turned to meet Lorelei's wide-open, golden eyes; her pupils were tiny dots in watery amber circles. They each held a steady gaze without saying a word; shock on the surface, a sense of purpose underneath.

Saffron tried hard to remember some of her father's lessons. It'd been a few years since he'd taught the group medical techniques for scenarios such as this. She'd been fifteen and hadn't entirely embraced the moment, thinking her dad to be overly macabre and melodramatic. She used her hands to check Zia's back for blood and an exit wound, doubting there was one since she'd been standing so close to Zia when it had happened. Her hands came back clean.

"No exit wound," she said. "The bullet's still in there."

"Lung puncture is possible," Lorelei responded. "Hopefully, no other damage to her arteries."

"Turn her over onto her right," Saffron said numbly, "so her lung won't collapse."

Soon, she became aware of police sirens approaching; the station was only a few blocks away. People were trying to help the cowboy on the table. Saffron was unable to discern much from her angle, but she could see a woman's delicate features contort into a mask of horror as she turned herself quickly away from whatever had been done to the immobile man. Saffron thought the woman worked at the Thai place she was supposed to go to that night with Colton.

Suddenly she became aware of blood dripping from the table onto her bare, outstretched legs. Recoiling, she shifted her body and averted her attention back to her mother. She was about to strip off her own shirt for an additional compress when the paramedics materialized beside her. Lorelei gave an account as they were both moved aside so the medics could administer first responsive care. Another team assessed the man on their table. Saffron heard them pronounce him as DOA.

She saw another body lying on the ground across the market, the gunman, surrounded by police and EMTs. As she watched their efforts, she noticed Colton sprinting from the nearby parking lot. He hadn't seen her yet, but he was charging ahead, scanning the crowd for her. When his eyes locked on to hers, it sent a flash throughout her body. He continued racing towards her.

She gave him a meager wave before turning back to her mother and the medics. One called for a gurney as the other administered a decompression to her thorax with a long needle. Zia's face clenched, but she stayed still and eyes closed. As they put her mother on oxygen, Saffron began to breathe better herself. She felt shaky and nauseated from the adrenaline in her system.

Get it together and deal with it, she chastised herself. *Now!*

Colton came around the table and stood behind her, taking it all in, the auburn-haired woman on the ground and Saffron's blood-splattered legs.

"What happened? Are you alright? Is, is she," he stammered, "is she going to be okay?"

The gurney arrived and the paramedics asked them to step further back. Saffron ended up leaning against Colton, his strength a welcome force since her legs threatened to become unsteady. He wrapped his arms around her.

Alongside the gurney, on the way to the waiting ambulance, one of the medics told them they were taking Zia to Farmington if they wanted to follow. Colton offered to drive them in his truck.

"Take her," Lorelei said, "But first, can we use your phone? We've got to call her dad." Squeezing Saffron's hand, she added, "She'll be okay, Roni. I'll be there as soon as I talk to the police and get our stuff loaded." She came in close, kissed her cheek and whispered, "Everything's going to be alright."

In a state of disbelief, Saffron let Colton lead her to his truck as the sirens screamed and faded towards their journey to Farmington. His cellphone was in her hand and it was ringing.

"Hello? Daddy?"

"Although the world is full of suffering,
it is also full of the overcoming of it."
- Helen Keller

Chapter 14: Counting Blessings

This was the first time Saffron had ever been inside a hospital; her birth had been at home with a midwife; her father's medic training and her mother's healing techniques had taken care of most illnesses and injuries she'd had as a child; even her tubal ligation procedure had been as an outpatient.

Hospitals were essentially foreign territory to the entire LeMay family, as well as to most of the other Sweetwater inhabitants. As a rule, self-care was their main healthcare; good diets and herbal remedies handled almost everything life threw at them. Bodywork helped when they hurt. For Zia's sake however, everyone planned to visit throughout the day to keep her company.

She had been moved early that morning from the intensive care unit following the previous night's surgery to repair the damage to her chest and right upper lung.

The bullet's trajectory had been like a pinball machine, first grazing the shoulder of its intended victim, a disabled mechanic who had tried to run with an armful of zucchinis. (A vigilante in the crowd had decided to dole out their own justice.) When the bullet was done with the Zucchini Thief's deltoid, it'd penetrated the aorta of the man at their table. On the last leg of the bullet's murderous journey, deviated by its travels through the cowboy's anatomy, it had landed in Zia's body. Fortunately for her, its speed had been tempered, stopping before reaching her spine. Had it continued, she may have been paralyzed, or dead.

Jack, Saffron and all of their friends had expressed gratitude for small favors.

After the room transfer, two nurses had come to assist her with therapeutic walking in order to keep her lungs expanded. She had smiled weakly, telling them she was going to be okay ("I've got this, babycakes") as she sauntered down the hall humming a song. Saffron couldn't be sure but she'd thought it had been 'These Boots Were Made For Walking'.

The nurses had come back, shaking their heads, saying it was the first time anyone had ever undergone that particular surgery and had then danced afterwards. Zia had balked and denied she'd *really* been dancing. The nurses had been adamant; she was the first one they'd ever seen sashaying down the corridors after that experience. Before the nurses had left, they promised to return in two hours to 'promenade' her again.

Once in bed, Zia had requested Reiki, closed her eyes, and fallen into what appeared to be a deep sleep. Saffron suspected she was merely meditating.

Her color was paler than usual; the red of her hair, the most vibrant thing in the monochromatic room. There was an IV in her arm, oxygen tubes in her nose, and an electrode contraption on her finger to monitor her body's vital functions. A bedside monitor carefully recorded her slow and steady beats.

Jack sat in the chair to Zia's right, Saffron to her left. Each held a hand, their eyes closed, lips moving in silent prayer. The air smelled of sage smoke from a smudge stick left smoldering on the window sill.

Saffron had always loved energy work. As she channeled universal lifeforce, she felt the opening of a secret door inside her; a feeling of both freedom and a connection to everything, tapping into the divine wisdom and love that was naturally around. She allowed this invisible energy to enter through the top of her head, the crown chakra, before it dissipated from her strangely warm hands into Zia, as God took care of the necessary healing. Saffron felt surrounded by white light.

Colton entered carrying a cowboy hat in one hand and a large vase of beautiful flowers in the other. The orange irises, mixed with green and purple flowers, reminded Saffron of her front garden. She wondered if he had thought so too.

"Good morning," he whispered. "They told me at the front desk she'd been moved. How is she?" he asked worriedly.

Hearing Colton's voice and seeing him near elevated Saffron's sense of peace up an octave. She took a deep breath, released it as a sigh, and smiled.

Colton's return smile felt generous and from the heart, touching Saffron profoundly. She felt her energy wanting to unite with his, and pictured pink light surrounding him.

"She's recovering," Jack whispered, "They say she'll be fine. The nurses will be here in an hour to get her moving."

"She looks peaceful," Colton responded.

"I've known her for almost thirty years," Jack said quietly, gazing down at his reposed wife who was breathing slowly and shallowly, "and I kind of know how her mind works. She's a fighter, enjoying a nice power nap. Right now she's probably working to heal her body, mend her tissues, repair damaged cells, who knows, maybe she's doing everything in her power to reboot with an upgrade to her system. It wouldn't surprise me if she's multi-tasking and enjoying some astral projection time, maybe checking out Fiji."

He stroked his wife's fingers, tracing the lines on her palm, his eyes dreaming in a far-off expression like he was willing his mind to peer deeper into hers, to engage with her on that spiritual plane.

Mom would try to transmute the darkness of her injured body into something beautiful, Saffron thought with a grin.

"Knock knock." Carla, George and Lorelei filed into the room. Jack shook George's hand in greeting, saying "Thanks for coming, Professor" before embracing him in an encouraging hug. Carla, an attractive woman with glossy black hair, honeyed skin and eyes of dark bronze, held a basket of oranges, apples and bananas which she placed on a nearby table.

Saffron got up and hugged Lorelei, who was dressed semi-appropriately in candy-striped overalls and Doc Martin boots. After a good, long squeeze, she took Colton's hand and introduced him to the Peshlakai-Harper family.

Carla went to sit next to Zia and took her hand.

Zia opened her green eyes.

"Good morning, Darlings," she said in a hushed yet musical voice as she beamed at her loved ones surrounding her. "Today is a good day."

The burst of laughter in the room seemed to take Colton by surprise, but his look of bewilderment was soon replaced by his wide grin; the happiness they exuded catching him in the net.

Everyone began the download of information.

First and foremost, Zia would recover. The hospital predicted she'd be out in a week. Zia scoffed and adamantly said, "Three days. Max." The initial shooter, the one who'd overreacted to the mechanic's vegetable theft, had been a veteran, recently home from the Middle East and suffering from PTSD. The citizen who had stopped the shooter (non-lethal shots to the leg and arm) was a retired penal officer from the jail with an open carry license. The poor cowboy who had died was named Louis Straussman. His funeral was going to be on Sunday.

For the first time, the room turned somber.

Luck or angels had spared their family that same fate.

Their storytelling was interrupted by a nurse who wanted to take Zia on another walk. Everyone stayed behind when she left.

Jack complimented both girls for their quick response techniques.

George suggested Sweetwater perform more practice drills for worst-case scenarios like riots, fires and EMPs.

"What's an EMP?" Colton inquired.

"It's an electromagnetic pulse," Saffron said, 'like a bomb. If one goes off, it'll destroy all electronic devices. No more working cars either unless you've got one built before the '80's, back before they put computers in them." The timber of her voice shifted into a more serious tone. "The craziest thing about an EMP," she confided, "is it may actually be our best chance for survival. Currently, nothing else we're doing is working."

Jack cleared his throat to interrupt.

"Sorry Saffy," he said, "but we're not going down the rabbit hole at the moment. Okay, George, that sounds like a great idea. Let's work in some target practice, too. Check the Big Board and find some time for workshops over the next two months while we still have a lot of daylight."

"In the meantime," Carla added, "it's going to be a full moon on Saturday. We should do some good mojo work for Zia."

"That's brilliant," Saffron exclaimed, recovering from her father's rebuff and excited by an idea which had popped into her head. "Would it be okay if I took Colton to the house on the reservation this weekend? I can do some moon work, and we can do some foraging, and bring back some plant magic. Please, please, pretty please," she begged before catching a glimpse of Lorelei's face from the corner of her eye; she appeared a bit crestfallen, her eyes downcast at her scuffed boots on the linoleum tile.

Oh, Hoot, my girl, she thought remorsefully, *I'm sorry.*

When Ayden and Saffron had been screwing like rabbits, Lorelei had often complained about feeling like a third wheel. When they had run off with the band for nearly two years, it had strained their friendship considerably. Saffron had been working to build it back up ever since her return. From the dejected look on Lorelei's face, she feared there was still work left to be done.

"I could hear all of you from down the hall," Zia chastised as the nurse guided her back into the room. "I think it sounds like a great idea. I'm just sorry I can't join you. Roni, will you take my crystals with you and recharge them in the moonlight?"

"Of course, Mom," she said, as her mother gingerly climbed onto the hospital bed. "Do you want me to bring back anything in particular?"

"Well, you can scout out the prickly pear harvest," Zia suggested. "They probably won't be ready until August, but they were early last year, maybe they're fully ripe now too. Check and see."

Saffron turned to Colton. "My mom makes the best prickly pear kombucha on the planet."

"This year," her mother responded, "I want to make syrup for margaritas. *Lots* of margaritas. After this, I think I deserve it."

Her comment brought the laughter back into the room although Saffron noted that Lorelei's laugh did not quite remove the aura of sadness away from her.

Leaning close to Colton's ear, she asked, "Do you want to go with me on Saturday? You don't have to if you don't want to, or if you're busy." Her heart froze as she waited for his response.

"Yea," he responded quickly, "I-I'd like that very much."

Saffron sensed a warmth surrounding her. Looking up, she saw her mother, palm raised towards her, sending her a silent blessing. Saffy blew her mother a kiss in return.

"Because of denial and your lack of understanding,
you and those closest to you will receive the likely reward
of suffering more and longer."
- Lawrence Wollersheim

Chapter 15: Final Breakup

Colton pulled into the parking lot at Miller Gas Supplies early in the morning to see he wasn't the first one to arrive. Parked in the spots closest to the door were two shiny vehicles; Gage's large Toyota FJ and Kaelynne's racy BMW. For a few seconds, he seriously considered backing out and heading home, or escaping to TJ's Diner for a leisurely breakfast.

Briefly, he considered relocating to another country.

Since yesterday, he'd been avoiding Kaelynne's calls and deleting her messages. He wasn't entirely surprised by the ambush he was about to receive. The Stockton family was used to getting their way.

Resolving to be the better man and face up to his new reality, he climbed out of his truck and went inside the office.

He found them in the conference room.

Kaelynne's face was drawn, showing evidence of recent crying; puffy eyes, minimal make-up and reddened cheeks; her blonde hair hung straight down. She did not look up when he entered, but merely stared at her hands clasped in front of her on the table, tapping her foot and ignoring him completely.

Gage, on the other hand, smoldered. He paced the room like a panther in a cage, his dark eyes blazing, looking ready to pounce and shred at the first opportunity.

On the table was a copy of the TALON, the local Aztec newspaper, with the headline, 'Riot in Market', and a picture of Zia on a gurney...with Colton clearly in the background.

Colton, with his arms around Saffron.

He couldn't remember a photographer. It had been an intense moment, a blur. Likely, someone had taken the shot with their phone and had sent it into the paper as a submission. Regardless, the evidence was before him, and it was time to pay the piper.

"What do you have to say, Colt?" Gage asked through clenched teeth. "Who is she?"

Colton did not like lying. He never had. If a person neglected to ask the right question then he could sometimes keep certain things private but, when asked a direct question, he found it very difficult to avoid telling the truth.

He felt Gage's glare dig into his back as he turned his attention towards Kaelynne.

The fluorescent lights cast a sickly green hue to her skin as if the envy inside her had been made visible. She sat, staring at the newspaper out of the corner of her eyes, her nostrils flaring; the relentless *tap tap tap* of her foot, the sole testament of her inner rage.

"I just met her," Colton said. "Last weekend during the superstorm, her kayak went under and I helped her."

A look of scorn metastasized across Kaelynne's rigid, half-turned face.

Boy, he thought nervously, *she's really not going to like what I have to say next...and neither will her brother.*

Having his back turned on Gage suddenly seemed like a foolish idea.

"And," he continued with a dry mouth, "I was at the farmers market because we were supposed to have our first date."

Immediately, she spun around to stare him squarely in the face, fury swirling in the depths of her blue eyes.

"I'm sorry you found out this way, Kae," he said quietly.

"Kae-lynne!!!" she screeched, all of her anger and bitterness encapsulated in those two shrilly spoken syllables.

Gage rushed him and pinned him against the wall, his dark eyes burrowing furiously into his.

Colton could see Kaelynne from the corner of his eye. She'd stood up but was not making any sign of interceding. He turned his focus back around as Gage began yelling obscenities into his face, spittle flying from his lips. Then just as quickly, he pushed off, releasing Colton before slamming an office chair to the floor with a loud clatter.

"You-are-a-son-of-a-bitch!!!" Gage growled. "What the hell're you thinkin'?! Huh?! We've all been expecting you to propose soon an-an-and," he spluttered angrily, "you're out making first dates?!"

His eyes burned with vehemence; white-knuckled, his hands gripped the edge of the conference table as if to prevent himself from throwing more objects, or punches.

Colton suspected he'd come very close to coldcocking his best friend.

Kaelynne began crying as she collapsed into a chair, defeated and lost looking.

"B-both of you, please listen," he pleaded, his voice breaking with remorse. "I-I didn't mean to hurt anyone. I'm not sure if I can explain it, but...things just weren't lining up for me somehow. I don't know."

How on earth am I going to explain this?

"I'm looking at my life differently," he said. "I see the mess the world is in, and I can't help thinking that there's got to be more than this. We can't keep doing what we've been doing. In all honesty, I'm probably going to quit my job too."

The words were out of his mouth before he realized what he was saying. He'd been rambling. Regardless, the words felt true.

"Have you lost your mind! You can't quit! It's the family business. You...you've," Gage stammered, "you've got obligations!"

His rage seemed momentarily displaced by bewilderment. He was wide-eyed, possibly conjuring a vision of the punishment Asa was likely to inflict.

"Wait until your father hears about this," he said with a degree of delight in his voice.

Dad IS going to kill me, Colton realized. *Mom will too.* His heart stopped hammering and sunk like a stone in his chest. *Why am I doing this?*

The answer came to him quickly.

Because I'm not happy, and now I may actually get to be.

It was time. Time to move forward and let go of the past.

"K-Kaelynne." His voice broke saying her name. "You were my first love. I'm sorry I've hurt you." Swallowing the lump in his throat, he added, "But I feel like a rat in a wheel, spinning and spinning, playing my role like a puppet. It's not just you. It's everything."

Kaelynne stared into the corner of the ceiling, a look of resignation creeping into her eyes. She sat perfectly still, in silent reproach. Gage turned to the coffeemaker, giving them the facade of privacy.

"How can I explain it?" Colton continued. "I-I want to get my hands dirty with something besides grease. I want to make things, to create something! To enjoy life while making a difference in it." He began to pace. "I want deep, meaningful conversations that push me to rethink all I've learned before," he said passionately. "To question things! To see the whole picture of the world and how everything is connected!"

"What're you talking about," Kaelynne asked with disdain. Her lip curled in a sneer of distaste like she had sucked on a lemon.

Colton looked closely at the young woman whom he had cared for, whom he'd thought he loved. She was a beautiful girl who frequently turned heads with her long blonde hair, clear skin, and trim figure. That beauty was nowhere to be seen at the moment. She'd been transformed into a spiteful shrew whose twisted mouth and beady eyes radiated hateful judgments upon him.

He firmly stood his ground under her withering gaze.

"I don't want safe," he said. "I don't want easy. I don't want the status quo. And for now, it means I don't want you. I'm sorry."

His voice had dropped to a whisper as he uttered those last two words. The previous words had choked out of him, unbidden, and had blasted into Kaelynne like a smart bomb.

She shook with anger and indignation. Her bloodshot eyes narrowed into daggers.

"Well," she said chillingly, "that's it then."

The air in the room whooshed like a vortex as she stormed out of the building, leaving a vacuum in her wake.

Neither Gage nor Colton spoke for over half a minute.

Colton broke the silence by saying, "I'm sorry, bro."

"Don't!" Gage warned. "Don't call me bro. We are *not* brothers."

His glare sliced like a knife into Colton's heart. Turning his back, Gage left without another word.

The room was deathly quiet in their absence; the only sounds were the slamming of the outside door, the whirring of the air conditioner, and a low-pitched *buzzzzzz*-ing sound coming from the fluorescent lights. Without thinking, he flicked the switch, and instantly felt some relief to his state of mind simply by the absence of the harsh light and irritating hum. He opened the vertical blinds and let the sun shine into the room as he let out a deep breath.

The deed was done. It had been ugly, more brutal than he had imagined. He'd lost more than he'd planned on, but there was no turning back. The journey into a different way of life was just beginning.

Colton felt exhausted from too little sleep, drained by too much confrontation, and overwhelmed by too many thoughts spinning through his head: Gage. Kaelynne. Saffron. The end of civilization as the world had known it.

The smell of coffee wafted his way.

Numbly, he walked over to get himself a cup, mostly out of habit. Inhaling the rich aroma of the Columbian coffee, his overwrought mind had the strange epiphany that the power outage had left a profound mark on him. Things he normally took for granted, that most people took for granted, had been stripped away in a flash; lights, television, appliances; even coffee had been hard to get during the blackout.

Everyone had had to adapt overnight.

Sitting down, he sipped his coffee and thought about its origins; in different continents around the world, coffee beans were picked and packaged for the haul across oceans inside giant tankers full of fuel. After shipping, warehousing and grocery stores, each requiring their share of energy demands, the product ended up in his coffeemaker which was itself powered by the coal-burning plant to the west of town; plumes of smoke and ash billowed from it at all hours of the day. He could imagine the dial of the electric meter for the office building whirling constantly as each and every kilowatt was consumed and recorded.

Before meeting Saffron, he had never considered the multitude of ways the world depended on fossil fuels. The coffee tasted bitter on his tongue.

His eyes focused on the paper lying beside him on the table. He peered closely at the picture. In it, he was standing with his right arm around Saffron's shoulders and his left hand holding hers, clasped between her breasts, her head upon his chest. The intimacy between them looked like second nature, like they'd known each other forever.

Colton's mouth was a thin line of worry. His eyebrows, furrowed with concern. His cowboy hat cast a shadow across his face, instilling a dangerous vibe to his features.

I look like I would die for her, he thought.

While he looked protective, Saffron looked comforted; still in shock, yet in control at the same time. The one thing he could not see reflected in her countenance was fear.

The article gave the rundown on the riot's particulars which had occurred before he'd arrived on scene. He skimmed through until he saw a quote from Lorelei whom the journalist had identified as 'another Sweetwater member in relation to the victim, Zia LeMay'.

"*We reacted fast,*" Lorelei had said. "*In today's day and age, you have to be ready for anything.*"

Colton gazed at the image of the two of them embracing and thought, *There's a woman I can trust with my life.*

With the door to his past slammed irrevocably closed, and the future an unknown factor, Colton hoped he was up to the challenge of living this new life.

"Even in the mud and scum of things,
something always, always sings."
- Ralph Waldo Emerson

Chapter 16: Night Calls

The house was strange without Zia in it, like a puppet lying dormant on a stage with no puppeteer to instill life into it. It had only been two days since the shooting and Jack was spending another night at the hospital on the tiny couch that masqueraded as a bed.

Saffron could hear people playing music in the pavilion. The bluesy twanging of metal guitar strings and the stomping of bare feet produced a driving, urgent beat which made her want to dance. When she was done packing, she planned on joining them for a handcrafted beer and a howl at the nearly full moon. She had already grabbed gear out of The Bunker, along with most of the food she planned on taking. All she had left to do was pick her clothes for the overnight stay.

What on earth am I going to wear, she thought as she stared into her closet. Her eyes passed over her lingerie drawer. *Or more importantly, what do I want to take off?*

For the hundredth time that day, her mind was again picturing the night to come; imaginings of romantic flirtations with many of her thoughts bordering on pornographic.

She simply could not get Colton out of her mind.

During her morning yoga class, she had had difficulty staying focused. No matter how many deep breaths she took or mantras she had uttered, her thoughts had drifted to him and the coming night. Anticipation and nervousness had kept her from fully engaging in the exercise. The class participants had presumed her lackadaisical performance was due to her mother's condition. Everyone had been very supportive and conciliatory, but Saffron was still embarrassed. It wasn't like her to get oogley about a boy.

When she had first invited him to go with her, it had seemed like the most natural thing in the world. Now, she felt jittery, like it was the night before her wedding.

We've never even had our proper first date, she realized.

She only knew that she wanted to be with him.

The telephone rang, startling her out of her thoughts.

"Hello? Saffron speaking."

"Hey, Dudette! Lorelei called and told me about your mom. How's she doing?" Ayden's smooth voice honeyed through the phone line. "Do you need me?"

Saffron's heart jumped into her throat. She hadn't heard from him in weeks. With a guilty twinge, she realized she wasn't ready to share the news about Colton, nor her feelings about him.

"No, no, she's going to be fine," she said. "We're hoping she'll be home before Tuesday. How are you?"

"Up to no good, as usual," he said with his characteristically casual charisma, "but I haven't been arrested in a month, so maybe I'm slacking. Lorelei said you're going to take a new boy toy to the Rez."

Lorelei, she thought with annoyance, *I'm going to kick your butt.*

Bristling, she replied, "He's not a boy toy!"

"Oh," Ayden said cautiously, her angry tone taking him off guard. "Well, excuse me, what is he then?"

"Honestly," Saffron sighed. "I'm not sure, but he's nice, and yes, I'm taking him out to the reservation with me tomorrow."

"With a full moon," he said chuckling "he'll be your boy toy by nightfall."

She bristled again but before she could respond, Ayden changed the topic.

"Hey, did you know we hit 450 today? I just read the stats online," he said. "Happy Phase 2 Day! Fuck 'em if you've got 'em."

The air went out of Saffron's lungs. She'd known it was coming, but to hear it confirmed was a gut punch.

When they were younger, they'd been taught that hitting 450 ppm of carbon was a big deal, a major mile marker. Unfortunately, it was later predicted that the climate had already breached so many tipping points that stopping at 450 was never going to occur. The planet was going to cruise right past that milestone and keep inching higher. The 450 number became almost meaningless. Still, it was a measurement they both understood, and feared.

It had continued to have meaning for them.

"N-no," she stammered. "I didn't know. I've been a little busy."

"Well, don't get your panties in a bunch," he purred. "If anyone is going to survive and thrive, it's you, my little vixen."

For once, his naughty pet names and sexual innuendo struck the wrong chord but she didn't feel like fighting about it.

"Listen, I'm in the middle of packing," she said. "I'll give you a call next week, okay? What number can I reach you?"

"Well, here's the thing," Ayden said slyly, "I'm going underground for awhile. We've got big plans with TB." He coughed when he said TB, trying to obscure any hint, trace, or mention of the word, Timebomb.

Pesky wire taps, Saffron thought and almost laughed out loud.

"You know? For the Phase 2 announcement?" he continued. 'If things go as planned, you may see me before the cum dries on your sleeping bag. And speaking of cum, I've got a whole load of it waiting for you."

Saffron could see him in her mind, his lanky, tattooed body lying on a couch or unmade bed somewhere, comfortably splayed and reaching for the zipper of his jeans, eager to hear her dirty talk and her breath accelerating in masturbation. For once, the image caused her to feel irritation instead of lust.

"Jesus, Ayden," she said. "I'm sorry, I'm not really in the mood. I've got to go." She still had the heart to add, "Stay out of trouble."

"Shit," Ayden said incredulously, "who is this guy? It's not like you to turn down a rub down. Should I be worried?"

"There's nothing to be worried about," she said, her irritation ramping up to anger. "You and I are friends, friends with horrible boundary issues which I'm rectifying tonight! No more phone sex. No more sex, period, for the foreseeable future. I'm going out with Colton and hopefully it'll turn into something beautiful, and pure, and lasting!"

The phone line went quiet. She could only hear herself breathe for several seconds.

"Ayden?" she said tentatively.

"I'm here," he said dully. "Well, he's a lucky guy, I hope he knows that. You deserve the best. And who knows?" His voice transformed into that of the Frontman, the confident lead singer. "It could all fall apart tomorrow. I'll see you when I see you." The phone line disconnected in her ear.

Saffron sat still, questioning what had come over her.

They had been lovers since she was sixteen. Together, they'd experienced teenage angst and rebellion, sharing a blinding anger at the world they'd been born into, a world which was threatening to rise up and destroy them. Like fugitives, they had escaped to see as much of the world as they could. Like artists, they had stood on stage and shared their thoughts. Like activists, they'd tried to make as big of an impact as they were capable of making. As they'd played in cities across America and Canada, they had attended as many protests as they could along the way.

Saffron and Ayden had been Outsiders together.

Even though the internet was full of information on climate change, ready to be read and studied, the majority of people, consciously or unconsciously, kept themselves from knowing the full truth. Thanks to the efforts of the fossil fuel magnates, there were still people who argued vehemently and erroneously against it even existing, although they had recently changed tactics and had started telling people that it was natural; the planet did this regularly; it was no big deal; just the will of God.

Sometimes, she felt pity for how badly people were going to be blindsided by the intense changes that were coming in the near future. Learning the details at a young age had nearly flattened her. She had felt soul-crushingly alone at times, and then Ayden had come along.

Together, they'd felt trapped inside a senseless machine which was intent on obliterating them.

When things got too negative, one of the best remedies Saffron had discovered was to turn her focus between her legs. Sex was a cure-all. It helped get her out of her head and elevated the senses, flooding her body with feel-good hormones. Sex was a drug and it had made the days bearable, drowning the din inside her cranium.

There were days when the connection and devotion between her and Ayden had been beyond expression resulting in heart-melding sex. Then there would be times, typically drunken, when their sexual experiences would push them both to their limits, testing the boundaries of submission and dominance. She'd begun to yearn for the Tantric sex moments, the kind of sex which would send her into the cosmos with explosive orgasms; the kind of lovemaking that brought them closer, linking them on a spiritual plane; the kind of sex you have when you love someone.

Ayden however had gotten more hardcore, both in sex and in his music, which had turned darker, more angry. The crowds had loved it.

Their band, Last Generation, had sung to a number of disenfranchised youth; to those who knew they were doomed as well as those who merely sensed it, like a cancer hiding in the recesses of the body, ready to multiply and devour the host at some future opportunity.

For Saffron, this lifestyle had stopped being the right energy, the right path. The pain and anger had started to wear thin, especially when she opened her eyes to what life could potentially offer her in the here and now. She became hungry to experience everything rather than numb herself to what she was feeling. Peace of mind had come more often with meditation and less often when playing in the band, or fucking.

The day Saffron announced she was leaving the tour for Santa Fe to study yoga, Ayden had torn her apart, accusing her of being a dirty hippie like their friends and parents. He'd called her a traitor for leaving the fight to bring awareness of climate change to the masses. The argument had been brutal.

He had taken the remaining trio and had changed the band name to WokeAF, becoming even more radical. By the time Saffron had resumed her life at Sweetwater, he'd stopped music completely and had joined Timebomb, a more zealous and extreme version of the Occupy Movement; anarchists with a cause.

However, the bond between them was still there, possibly created by the act of first love or else during a soul-connecting fuck; either way, they still shared a link.

In some ways, their relationship had finally shifted into a healthier one. They both accepted and understood to some degree the life paths they were each taking, but the anesthesia of their sexual chemistry had continued as friends with benefits; casual, tension-releasing jerk-off sessions over the phone whenever possible; replays of sexual encounters they'd had with others; and, a heightened, more graphic level of sexual vocabulary between them even in everyday conversations.

We love each other, Saffron sadly realized, *but we use each other.*

And what of her feelings for Colton?

Hopefully it'll turn into something beautiful, and pure, and lasting?

It had felt true when she had said it.

Saffron walked out on the deck to breathe the warm night air and collect her thoughts.

Under the expansive twinkling of stars, she realized that if she truly intended to live her life appreciating all the blessings on this planet, then she was pretty sure that meant having her heart expanded too; maybe, through a committed, loving relationship; perhaps, one like her parents.

In her heart of hearts, Saffron realized she wanted that more than anything else in her life; needed it; deserved it. For with it, she reasoned, the hardships of the future might be easier to face.

Because it could all fall apart tomorrow.

"Resistance is what you add to pain
to make it last longer and hurt more."
- Errol Strider

Chapter 17: Showdown at Noon

Bright sunlight shone through the dark cherry slats of the blinds and landed in stripes upon the thick beige carpet. Colton peeled his eyelids open, peering groggily around. His sheets had twisted around him in a restless display of the poor sleep he'd received. Vacillating between articles on climate change, replays of the fight with Kaelynne and Gage, combined with thoughts of his first night alone with Saffron had not made for an easy night.

The rest of the room was neat and orderly as he'd been raised to keep it. Growing up, he used to think the phrase, 'Don't mess with Texas', had been invented for his mother.

His furniture matched the blinds. The walls matched the carpeting. Red and hunter green curtains complimented the plaid bedspread. Overall, it was attractive and comfortable, yet he realized it was like a fine hotel room, one that looked rich and inviting, yet generic and impersonal at the same time.

He'd never considered it depressing before, but it felt that way to him at the moment.

There was no denying the discomfort in his bones. Worry of what was happening on the planet, coupled with fears of his parents' reactions, and dread that Saffron would reject him mixed into a bitter cocktail of doom.

The urge to cancel the trip briefly fluttered into his consciousness.

Come on, Colt, don't chicken out, he scolded himself. *I'm not the quitting type.*

Trying something new was never easy for him; in truth, most people tended to avoid change like an involuntary reflex which had to be overcome. Even animals could hate a shift in their routine. When he'd first gotten his horse, HoneyLemon, she'd stubbornly resisted being loaded into her trailer, fighting all attempts to get her inside the enclosed space. It had taken patience and bunches of carrots to cajole her. The reward for facing her fears was that the two of them could now go out in the boonies and ride together, free to explore and be wild.

Colton thought about his own life. There was no denying his existence today was a comfortable one, even with the stress of a struggling business. The Millers had everything they needed or wanted. However, as he spent more time researching the facts of scientists around the globe, the more aware he became it was also a way of living which was leading to his own demise.

The evidence was far from pretty, if not downright ugly.

The more he learned, the more he wanted to turn away, but he reminded himself that ignoring it would not stop it from happening. To close his eyes to global warming was akin to an ostrich sticking its head in the sand while a stampede rushed around it. Disregarding the information wouldn't make him less vulnerable. Realistically, if he continued to deny what was happening, it could actually increase the likelihood he would become a victim someday.

Colton didn't know what the future held for him, but he knew he couldn't keep living the way he had in the past; he could no longer live in ignorance; he would have to change.

How he would do that was unclear, but pursuing Saffron was a major part of his plan.

His stomach grumbled loudly.

Fighting against inertia, he made himself get up and out of bed. Opening the blinds to the bright sunlight, he resolved to face the unknown with courage, and that included facing his parents to tell them where his head was at; standing up for himself and his decisions, whatever the consequences.

As he went to gather his clothes, his eyes wandered along the lines of his old oak dresser. It had been built by Grandpa Miller when he'd been born. Alton had blessed each of his grandchildren with one-of-a-kind pieces which he'd lovingly created for them.

Colton remembered standing in his grandpa's workshop, the sweet smell of wood shavings and sawdust peppering the air, the sound of saw teeth gnawing through planks and posts. He remembered the look of satisfaction and pride on his grandpa's face when he had seen a project through unto completion.

The memory made him smile.

Once dressed, he packed his rucksack with his nicest jeans, an extra pair of cargo shorts, a Waylon Jennings t-shirt and a flannel shirt and vest for when it cooled at night. As he grabbed an extra pair of clean underwear, his worry about the evening ahead started to creep back into his psyche.

He stuffed his anxiety down into his gut and stuffed his belongings into the bag.

In the kitchen, his mom was putting dirty dishes into the sink. His sister was in the pantry looking for an after-lunch treat. The room smelled robustly of meat and bean chili, making his mouth water.

"Well, look who finally decided to wake up," Cricket teased. "I was going to head upstairs to get you after I got done cleanin'. Are you sick? I feel like I haven't seen you in a week."

Colton had been avoiding the house and by extension, conversation with his family, for several days.

"No, I'm not sick," he replied. "It's just been a really intense week."

The chili was sitting in a large pot on the stove, ready to serve to Asa when he arrived home. With lunch in hand, Colton shoveled a big spoonful into his mouth before sitting down at the table. Swallowing both his food and his anxiety, he bravely admitted, "Well, I guess it's time to tell you that Kaelynne and I broke up."

Meaghan peered out of the pantry with a handful of Oreos and a mouthful of chocolate goo. "Oooo di sswhat?!?" She stood dumbfounded as small cookie crumbles fell to the floor from her open mouth.

"Colton James Miller!" Cricket scolded loudly. "What on earth is going on around here? Why are my babies' relationships fallin' apart?" She came to the table to sit beside him, forcing him to look her in the eyes. "The world has gone crazy."

"I'm sorry, Mom," he said sincerely. He really wanted her to understand but knew it would be hard. Cricket and Asa had been teenage sweethearts who had married immediately after high school. As far as he knew, they had only ever loved each other.

"I care about Kaelynne," he said, "but I don't love her, Mom. I'm sorry. I don't want to marry her and it wasn't fair to keep stringing her along." He hesitated only briefly before plunging ahead. "Plus, I've met someone else."

"Figures," his sister said contemptuously and stuffed another cookie into her mouth.

"I can't help it," he responded, looking at his mother pleadingly, willing her to comprehend his feelings. "I really like her. She's smart, and beautiful, and hardworking. And her family is really nice too. Her mother was the woman who got shot during the riot at the farmers market. I went to see her on Thursday at the hospital."

"How long has this been going on?" his mother asked, clearly taken by surprise; eyes wide, her mouth hung open as if she'd just heard the news he'd been drafted into the military, or been probed by aliens. "Why haven't I heard about this before now?"

Frankly, Colton was astounded the town and church gossipers hadn't already tattled on him.

"It's not been long," he answered, his hands perspiring. "I just met Saffron last Saturday on the lake. I rescued her during the storm when her boat tipped over and we've been talking ever since." With the big secret out, Colton finally started to relax. He wiped his sweaty hands on his jeans and felt some tension leave his shoulders. "She's amazing, Mom," he said, smiling. "I think you'll like her."

"We-e-e-ell, I don' know 'bout that," she said, her Texas twang getting thicker by the second. "This all seems kinda sudden. Are you sure about this? I mean, good heavens, you and Kaelynne were practically engaged!"

"Yes, I know, Mom," he said gently. "All the more reason to end it now."

The need for his mother to understand suddenly overtook him.

"Nothing's the same," he said. "It's like a whole new world! I feel so alive with Saffron, so inspired to travel and do good things. In fact Mom, I was thinking about Grandpa Miller's woodworking. Do we still have his old tools? I want to take up furniture making and carpentry just like him."

The door to the garage opened. Asa entered carrying his overnight bag and the mail which he put on the counter before looking at his family.

Cricket was on the verge of tears.

Colton glanced down into his bowl, having lost his desire to eat.

"What's going on," his father asked, walking towards the stove. "How is everyone?"

"Your so-o-on," Cricket drawled, looking relieved that her husband was home to talk some sense into her youngest child, "has just informed us he broke up with Kaelynne, and…he's seein' another wo-o-oman."

"Really?" Asa said, noisily dropping the ladle into the pot of chili. "Who is she?"

"Her name is Saffron LeMay," Colton said, his stomach clenching. "She's a yoga instructor in Aztec and she lives and works at the Sweetwater farm at Navajo Dam."

He suddenly realized he feared his parents' response, their probable judgment. Frustration surged through him, but then he remembered his resolve to face the unknown with courage. Taking a leap of faith, he asserted, "I'm going camping with her tonight near Shiprock."

"Oh," his mother interceded, her lips pressed firmly together with displeasure. "You are, are you?"

"Sweetwater?!" Asa repeated as he sat down at the head of the table. "That hippie place? Good lord, son."

His expression was hard for Colton to make out. There was obvious incredulity that a liberal, hippie type would be of any interest to the fruit of his loins. He also detected Asa's usual undercurrent of anger and resentment towards 'treehuggers' whom he blamed as the reason for his struggling business.

How am I ever going to explain what's happening to the planet? Colton wondered. *I have no idea how to make him understand.*

"What can you possibly see in a girl like that," his father asked tactlessly before taking his first spoonful.

"That's not fair," Colton responded hotly. "You're always preaching we need to treat others as we would have them treat us. You know, 'this is My commandment, that you love one another, just as I have loved you.' John 15:12."

Cricket got up silently and moved to the kitchen sink, noisily rinsing and jostling the dishes from lunch before putting them in the dishwasher. His father harrumphed and put another large spoonful of chili into his mouth.

Colton continued undaunted.

"Saffron's amazing, Dad." He felt a ghost of a smile travel across his face as he said her name. "We've got more in common than you can imagine. She's strong-minded, with a good heart. Plus, she loves the outdoors and isn't scared to work hard."

He stood up to get a glass of water, filling it from the spigot in the refrigerator, busily trying to avoid his parents' expressions as he continued rambling.

"She's silly, and smart," he gushed. "Totally beautiful, yet humble. Saffron takes life in stride and works to make it better."

He stopped and looked directly at them.

"Honestly," he finished, "she's the most astonishing and capable person I've ever met in my life."

He heard himself speak his inner truth out loud and was blinded by the realization, *I'm falling pretty hard for her.*

Both Asa and Cricket were silent.

Meaghan burst from the pantry, her face contorted with anguish and stuffed cheeks.

"Ah caah ta ani mo diss," she sputtered as she left the kitchen towards her room upstairs.

The hush continued until Colton said, "I-I'll be back sometime tomorrow."

Cricket threw her hands and her dishrag up into the air. "Well, I never expected this from you!" She turned from Colton to Asa, who was hungrily eating his lunch. "Asa! Do somethin'…explain to your son that he's making a mistake." Before his father could swallow and respond, she whipped back around. "Colton James, I want you to make amends to Kaelynne immediately. I'm sure she'll take you back if you try hard enough. Go eat some crow and make it right."

"I'm sorry, Mom," he said, grasping her hand. "I don't love her. I need a change. I think I'll feel better if I'm out trying to make a difference in this world."

There are serious issues going on today, and I want to be a part of the solutions, he thought, but didn't say out loud.

Instead, he said, "I've been thinking about living a simpler life… working with my hands and making things. And, I need the chance to be with this girl, because a world without her in it is currently too much for me to bear. Please Mom, give her a chance."

Cricket was quiet, looking deeply into her son's eyes. It was clear this was not what she had wanted or pictured for her baby.

Colton gazed back, desperate for approval.

She closed her eyes and took a deep breath before speaking.

He suspected she was talking to God, asking for advice like she often did.

"Well, son," she said hesitatingly, "I may not understand all you're talkin' about, but I believe in all of my children's ability to do good in this world." She gave him a feeble, yet warm smile. "Your path is your path and I respect you for speakin' up." she said, squeezing his hand before letting go.

Colton felt his heart lighten and switched his gaze to his father.

Asa swallowed slowly, silently, pausing to sip his water as if he was pondering how to respond, or purposefully trying to make Colton sweat.

His continued silence was working on Colton's last good nerve.

Taking a deep breath, he said, "You taught me to be a good man, Dad. I'm only trying to achieve that goal."

"Well," Asa said, wiping his mouth with a napkin, "like your mother said, I don't understand what you're talking about, but if you truly don't want to marry Kaelynne, then don't."

There was more Colton wanted to say, especially about how he was feeling about the future, but part of him deflated. He'd won a small victory but the war itself was far from over. At the moment, he didn't have the energy to fight another battle.

Standing up quietly, he took his dishes to the sink, kissing his mother on the top of her head as he walked by.

"Thanks," he said gratefully. "I'll be back tomorrow. Don't worry."

"Hope has two beautiful daughters;
their names are Anger and Courage;
Anger at the way things are, and Courage to see
that they do not remain the way they are."
- St. Augustine

Chapter 18: Hot Date in the Hyundai

Colton arrived in Sweetwater mid-afternoon. Parking under a sail shade, he spotted Saffron in the chicken yard. She was unmistakable, her golden hair shimmering in the sunlight, wearing a light grey tank top and a curve-hugging red skirt. He approached her, unnoticed, as she spread scratch for the flock of hens which cavorted around her like tiny, hungry dinosaurs.

"*Bawkbawk, bawkbawk,*" she spoke unabashedly in chicken-speak.

"Do you always talk to chickens?" he asked with amusement.

She quickly turned around and burst into a luminous smile which melted his heart.

"I talk to all the animals," she said. Tilting her head to the side and raising an eyebrow, she added, "You should try it sometime."

"Oh," he asked with a chuckle, "do they talk back?"

"Sometimes," she said, closing the gate to the pen. "Tesla here thinks you smell very nice."

Colton felt something nudge his butt and whipped around to see the snout of an enormous Great Pyrenees sniffing his backside.

"Oh! Hello!"

Tesla the Dog gruffed a greeting then went back to the comfort of the shade.

Music drifted through the air from the direction of the greenhouses. He caught the scent of peaches and noticed some people standing at a makeshift table, canning the sweet fruits in oversized pots on camp stoves.

"I'm ready to go," she said, touching his arm and leading him towards his truck. "I hope you don't mind, but I prefer taking my car."

"No problem," he agreed. "I don't mind. Let me grab my stuff."

Near his truck, she bent towards a garden bed and picked a fistful of sprawling green shoots and took a small bite.

"Um," he said dubiously, "isn't that a weed? Stuff like that grows everywhere around here."

"It's purslane," she said, offering it to him. "A weed you can eat. I'm gonna add it to our salad tonight. I hope you enjoy it. I'm planning something fun, and I've been looking forward to cooking with you all day." She bounced up and down like a kid on Christmas. With a wink, she added, "I hope you're ready for an adventure, cowboy."

Colton felt his skin flush.

A voice in his brain hollered, *Yippie ki-yay!*

Gulping, he managed to take the succulent green pearls from her hand and pop them into his mouth; they were bright and crunchy like a citrusy bell pepper.

"Oh, God," Saffron said suddenly, her face stricken with fear. "Okay, don't panic. This isn't a total deal-breaker, um, just pretty close to it." Opening her blue eyes like a Disneyland Princess, her bottom lip quivering, she pleaded, "Please, for the love of God and all that's holy, please tell me you like to cook." She stood plaintively waiting for his answer, melodramatically crossing her fingers and biting her lip; the ones he so wanted to kiss.

With you, he thought, *I'd do almost anything.*

"Yes, ma'am," he said cordially. "Up to a point I can, but I'm willing to learn more."

"Whew," she said, looking relieved. "That is an excellent answer!"

In minutes, they were on the road, headed for their destination near Shiprock; a house owned by Lorelei's grandmother on the Navajo reservation. Saffron had spoken to Zia that morning and confirmed that her prognosis was still good; the hospital had tentatively agreed to release her in a couple of days if she continued to improve.

"She told us to have a good time," Saffron said with a glint in her eyes. "She said she likes your energy."

"Well," Colton said, unsure of how to respond, "I-I guess it's good to know I'm putting out good vibes."

She left the air conditioning off ("It wastes more gas," she explained), so they drove with the windows down, the breeze flying through their hair. It wasn't easy to talk over the roar of the wind so they listened to music instead, a folksy, bluegrass band called The Lil Smokies. Colton hadn't heard them before but the feverish fiddle and banjo playing got his feet to tapping.

He began to relax, absorbing the sunshine, the view and the music, letting the feeling of freedom overcome him.

Drought had kissed the area harshly over the last few years. Some of the stalwart vegetation had lost their battle to survive. Once in awhile he saw blackened patches; either the BLM, Bureau of Land Management, had done a controlled burn, or else lightning had touched down to do a little house-keeping on Nature's behalf.

The greenness of spring had gone and was replaced by the stubbornness of the remaining flora; the land, bathed in muted greens, olived greens, silvered and saged greens. These were not the colors found in most places around the globe; the bright, vivacious greens bursting with life and abundant water. Instead, these were the colors of tenacity with the occasional, miraculous blessing of a desert flower; the simple audaciousness of yellow, orange and purple.

Watching the passing scenery, he thought of how he couldn't imagine living in a big city with its congestion and wall-to-wall humanity. Living in the southwest, one could experience heart-opening vistas; the roads twisting, turning, rising and falling, many of them following paths originally cut by wagon wheels a hundred and fifty years earlier.

Look at what's happened since then, he mused.

His grandfather had told him numerous stories about what the area had been like in the past; the trading posts, the apple orchards, the lawlessness, as well as the folks that had fought back against it. This wild land had been settled by pioneers who had had to use their wits and might to eke out an existence back in a time when your handshake and your word meant something.

The Hyundai headed up a hill towards the expanse of blue sky as if in flight, cresting at the top with a wide-eyed view of the endless stretch of open ground. In the distance were the LaPlata mountains, part of the vast Rocky Mountain range. Grandpa Miller had told him about them as well; for Indigenous peoples, these mountains were sleeping deities to be respected and revered; holy mountains.

Colton tended to agree.

His thoughts returned to the coming night. Literally and figuratively, he was heading into new territory. He gazed at the emptiness surrounding him with fresh eyes. The wildness of the place was only interrupted by the finger of road and the defiance of the oil and gas apparatuses they passed along the way.

His stomach knotted. He had not yet told her what he and his family did for a living.

What if she hates me? he wondered.

That thought was followed by the more terrifying one, *What if she laughs when I tell her I'm a virgin?*

"What a week, huh?" Saffron said, interrupting his worries.

"That, my friend, is an understatement," he said in agreement.

"Okay," she said, pausing to remove a piece of hair that had flown into her mouth. "Let's list the top three shittiest things that happened to us this week. After that, we'll share the top three best things. Okay, I'll start." She raised her fingers one by one as she ticked them off. "First, I almost drowned in a nightmare storm and lost my kayak. My mother was shot and could have died. Hell, I could have died, twice this week! And," she deliberated before finishing with, "I pissed off my best friend...I think."

She turned her eyes from the road in front of her to look at him, "Okay, your turn."

"Well, let's see," he said, raising his eyebrow and looking upwards in mock contemplation. "This week, you say? Well, my best friend is definitely pissed at me, plus I got to be the jerk who broke someone's heart." He paused for a moment before making the decision to be brave. "And, it's a tie for the third worst thing," he said. "It's either that I spent hours reading about climate change until I wanted to climb out of my skin, or it's that I missed out on a kiss from an amazing woman."

The Hyundai noticeably slowed and began moving over to the emergency lane. Saffron pulled to a stop, put the car in park and looked at him.

"You did what?" she asked, her voice squealing. "And regret missing what?"

Her face was too cute for words; her blue eyes wide and her cherry lips in a tiny, open-mouthed O.

Colton suspected it was rare for her to be at a loss for words, so he sat and purposefully drew out the moment.

"Seriously!?!" Saffron said with incredulity. "Did you read about the oceans heating up, changing the currents and how the jet stream is jacked? That's why the winter storms are so much worse up north. In the next few years, it's predicted we'll see our first Category 6 hurricanes. They're predicted to flatten the coastlines."

Her face and voice dropped before adding, "I just learned yesterday we hit Phase 2. Carbon parts per million is at 450." She seemed to collapse into herself, fighting back a tsunami of emotion before letting it go with a sob.

"Y-you've no idea how hard it's been to be Noah," she said, "to have studied the scope of the coming disaster, and been surrounded by people who either think you're crazy, or worse in some ways, feel so overwhelmed by the truth, they hide from it and do nothing."

"Roni," Colton said hesitantly, "I have to tell you somethin' and I don't know how you're gonna take it." His Adam's apple bobbed up and down as he swallowed his fear. "My family and I work in the oil and gas industry. I-I'm sorry," he choked. "If you want to take me back to Sweetwater, I'll understand."

Blinking away the glistening tears in her eyes, she reached out to take his hand.

"Most people around here are, pussycat," she comforted. "I don't blame you. And for the record, I don't believe anyone is truly innocent. Well, maybe the Aborigines and the Amish, the Mennonites too, those folks totally get a pass. But let's be honest, no one living a modern lifestyle today is clean. We're all involved in this mess, which ultimately makes us each other's murderers since our choices are killing us." Quietly, she added, "I've known this for a long, long time.

"At first, it made me angry and punk rock helped. I wanted to fight and rage against injustice, to feel separated from those I blamed for fucking everything up. But," her face softened, "as you start to wake up, the mirror goes up too, and you start taking a good look at yourself. For instance, I'm behind the wheel of a gas-fueled engine right now. Sure, it gets thirty-eight miles per gallon, but it's still a contributor. And I haven't checked, but chances are, my clothes and shoes came on a huge tanker across the ocean from another country. It helps that most of my possessions are second-hand.

"The point is," she paused, giving his hand a squeeze and looking deeply into his eyes. "You pick your battles. Now that you know some of the truth, you can decide to do what you can. Try to live up to your ethics, but don't beat yourself up. Climatologists say we're only going to fix this problem from the top down anyway, that bottom up changes aren't going to be enough.

"But you do what you can, everyday," she said, "and pray that the top people in charge, the ones with influence, will make the changes necessary to save us. Shifting and prepping now are key, so yeah, if you want my advice, you should probably start considering your next career. The era of fossil fuels will end before you know it."

Her seriousness and depth of emotion moved him, as Colton felt the anxiety from his 'dirty secret' leaving his body. Ironically, it created room for his anxiousness about the future to grow. "I read a quote that said 'procrastination is merely punishing a future version of yourself', and because we didn't make changes thirty or forty years ago, the sacrifices we're going to need to make soon are going to be enormous."

Saffron nodded her head knowingly.

"God, I don't know how I feel about learning this stuff," he said shakily. "Sort of like the ground has shifted under my feet."

"Well," she chuckled, "don't be too surprised if that literally happens at some point. As the ice melts at the poles, the pressure on the tectonic plates is changing. Chances are, this could be a brave new world before we know it...with a fuck ton of dead people."

She exhaled loudly, her tongue hanging like a panting dog, breathing out the melancholy of her words.

Colton was suddenly aware of how hot it'd gotten in the car; sweat dripped down his back. He noticed small circles of perspiration staining her shirt under her breasts.

As though reading his mind, Saffron wiped her brow and squared her shoulders.

"As for missing a kiss," she teased, "you'll have to wait a bit longer. If I start kissing you now, I might want to jump you and it's way too hot."

Colton's skin was on fire as he murmured the words, "I'm a patient man."

Hopefully I won't disappoint her, he prayed.

"I just thought of something," she said. "Can we hold off on the top best things from our week?" She gave his hand one last caress before easing back onto the road. "It's not over and I think the best is yet to come."

Tomorrow's fate was unclear, but from Colton's point of view, it already was a brave new world.

"Beauty radiates within me. There is Beauty before me.
There is Beauty behind me. There is Beauty below me.
There is Beauty above me.
There is Beauty all around me.
There is Beauty again. Hózhó Náhásdlįį.
There is Beauty again."
- Diné prayer from Navajo Beauty Way ceremony

Chapter 19: Little House On The Rez

Dry land spread out in every direction, unobstructed and uninhabited. The only sign of civilization was the dirt road in front of them.

Colton gazed out the side mirror at Shiprock's famous monolithic mass rising up from the desert floor and towering in the sky. To the Navajo Nation, the sacred outcropping was the remains of the great winged bird which had carried the First People to the area; for scientists, it was the cratered core of an extinct volcano which had erupted over twenty-seven million years earlier. Regardless of its origin and history, there was something captivating about it.

Colton finally lost sight of the majestic mound in the rearview as Saffron drove north around a craggy bluff. After a few bumpy miles along a rock wall next to miles of yuccas, junipers and chamisas, a pallet fence appeared leading towards a stand of trees. The driveway split into a circle surrounding a large corral. A magnificent cottonwood stood in its center, its thick boughs spread wide, its roots undoubtedly tapped into a hidden aquifer below.

The mesa rose forty feet above them, curving around the homestead and providing a protective and private cove.

Saffron parked under a gnarled piñon tree, the house obscured by a storage shed.

"Welcome to Grandmother's house," she said excitedly. "We built it when I was little, before we bought the land in Navajo Dam. Shímísaní's old one was falling down. I still remember making the bricks and stacking them with Lorelei and her mom...and my mom of course."

She smiled at the memory before a shadow passed over her features, her lips tightening, her eyes losing their luster. Colton presumed she was thinking about Zia's trauma. He watched her take a deep breath and release it.

"It was pretty cool," she said, the light returning to her face, "watching a house grow from the ground up, from beginning to end. I remember my mom telling Carla that if women could do that with their bare hands, then they could do anything. I never forgot that.

"We always have a wonderful time here," she said.

"Well, it's nice and quiet," Colton responded, looking around and stretching his legs.

This's prime riding country, he thought, wishing he'd brought his horses.

"Now, Lorelei's grandma lives in Kirtland," she said, grabbing her guitar and a bag of supplies from the back seat. "She allows us to come out here sometimes to get away from things and ground ourselves when we need to." Slamming the car door shut with her hip, she added, "We call it Sweetland."

Colton carried the cooler towards the empty adobe house. It was the same shade of sandy beige as the earth around it, which made sense considering how it was made. Its windows were shuttered and weeds ruled the yard, giving it an unpretentious and forlorn feel; a mere shelter to withstand the elements.

Not very promising, he thought to himself, then changed his mind when he entered.

Inside, the dark home was surprisingly cool, both in temperature and design. Sturdy log beams called vigas crossed the ceiling above whitewashed walls like an old pioneer homestead. The hushed air was still scented from an old fire in the wood stove. In the dim light, Colton spotted small recessed openings called nichos with displays of Puebloan pottery and native statue figurines nestled inside.

Saffron opened the two front shutters and let the light shine in.

Near the door was a red leather couch with a large Navajo rug hanging above it and another on the floor below. Dust lightly obscured the polished gleam of the reclaimed wood planking. In the center of the room was a long dining table fit for a feast. The kitchen in back had handwoven native baskets along with copper and cast iron pans hanging from the walls. The furniture was simple and rustic, however, some had ornate details carved into them in the style of Mexican artisans. Colton admired the filigrees and scrolls cut into the honeyed wood of an armoire.

Saffron grasped its metal latches and opened it, revealing dishware and linens stored inside. She placed some of the dry good groceries on an empty shelf. Taking the cooler from Colton, she went to the back wall where an old fashioned ice box was built into the adobe. She tucked away the perishables and loaded the bottom tray with ice before bending towards a small, book-sized door near the floor.

Colton wondered what it was.

A mouse door, he briefly pondered, then inexplicably thought, *Or maybe it's for fairies?* Either idea was ridiculous and made him almost laugh out loud.

"We built this house into the mesa behind it," Saffron explained as cold air flowed into the house from the tiny opening. "This pipe is buried underground and should cool us off even more. My house works the same way."

On the right side of the room were two doors. The one in the back, off the kitchen, held a claw foot bathtub and a vintage washbasin table complete with a ceramic pitcher on its lower shelf. Above it hung an old mirror, minor imperfections marring its reflection. Everything in the room looked antique except for one thing.

"It's a composting toilet," Saffron told him after seeing Colton's questioning face. "It's easy to get used to. Also, there's an outhouse out back." She opened a closet and placed the clean white towels inside onto the empty rods.

In the darkness of the second room, she pulled the curtains and released the shutters. Light poured into the cozy room revealing a rocking chair, dresser and a queen-sized bed with four poster legs nearly touching the ceiling.

"If you'll bring the water jugs inside, I'll make up the bed," she said as she emptied the dresser of its linens, pillows and bedspread. "The house has a well but we usually treat it as a dry cabin. I brought some blankets too if we decide to sleep out under the stars."

Colton's nervousness had returned as soon as he'd seen the one bed. The prospect of lying naked with her in the desert night made his heart race uncontrollably. He was grateful for the opportunity to duck outside, armed with a task. She'd packed four containers of water which he took inside with two trips.

The house felt nice and comfortable when he shut the door behind him.

"Put those in the kitchen, please," she hollered from the bedroom.

Next to the sink was a ceramic jug with a spigot. Colton filled it, then remembered the shallow washbasin and pitcher in the bathroom and filled them as well. He wasn't sure about the toilet so he left it alone until further instructions.

On the next trip, he brought their overnight bags from the trunk. At the bedroom door, he saw her placing candles into blue Mason jars and dusting off an old kerosene lamp. The bed had been made with a golden yellow cover which was brightened by the late afternoon light. Dust motes spun in a sun patch around her feet like magical supplicants.

"Oh, thank you," she said. "Put the bags over there by the dresser please. You can unpack if you want, but we're only here until tomorrow."

Saffron took something out of her purse that looked like an overly large cigar; a sage bundle for smudging.

Colton knew what it was but had never seen one used before.

"What does that do?" he asked.

"Well, for one, it smells nice," she said, casting the sage smoke over her head and down her body. "It's supposed to clear out old energy, any lingering negative forces or nasty spirit that's gotten in while the house was empty. I don't know," she said somewhat self-consciously, "it just *feels* better after you do it. I can't explain it."

Wandering from room to room, she wafted the rich earthy scent into the corners.

"I also like to ask permission to be here," she added. "I don't like presuming I have a right to be on this land. I tell any listening ancient ones that I come in peace and I'll respect this place while I'm here." When she finished with the house, she turned back to him. "Don't laugh," she demanded, as she moved the sage smoke over his head and back.

"Oh," he reassured her, watching her intent and earnest face. "I wouldn't dream of laughing at you."

Oddly, his anxiety did feel like it was lifting, his body becoming more relaxed. Breathing a deep sigh and letting it out, he realized he had no reason to be nervous. He was exactly where he wanted to be, and it was good.

"What else can I do to help?"

"Next, we'll head outside and get the fire going," she said. "I'm cooking you dinner tonight, al fresco."

Behind the house was an outdoor area with a fire-pit, a rustic bench swing, and several Adirondack chairs covered with burlap sacks. Saffron removed the sacks from two chairs and placed them on the ground nearby with a rock on top to keep them from blowing away. Nearby was a metal garbage can filled with charcoal briquettes. She placed some in the fire-pit and lit them with a box of matches.

"There," she said, dusting her hands off vigorously. "We'll let those heat up and you can help me with dinner."

Inside, she handed him a bottle of chilled white wine she'd been keeping in a thermal tote. "Might as well have some while it's cold."

Colton opened it then took two short glasses out of the armoire, dusting them off with a dish towel he found inside. "Do you want any of this?" He gestured towards the food items she'd placed inside.

"Yes, please," she said. "I want the raspberry vinegar, red onion, garlic and cayenne pepper. There should also be some walnut oil, too. Oh! And the corn meal and canned cream corn."

"Wow, okay," he said intrigued. "What're we havin'?"

"Tonight, ma cherie," Saffron responded in a sultry French accent, "for your dining pleaz-zure, I am preparing wood-fired trout wrapped in corn husks, a salad with piñon nuts, feta and pears, and my speciality, the tour de force, a moist cornbread cooked in the fire outside." Saffron's sexy rendition ended and in her normal voice she said, "I usually add green chiles to it, is that okay?"

"Um," Colton said salivating, "that sounds delicious." He handed her a glass of wine and they clinked them together with a combined "Cheers."

Saffron, donning an avocado green apron, handed him one with red chili peppers on it. Trying not to disappoint, he followed her lead, cutting up vegetables and fruit, taking down bowls and pans when needed, and rinsing them off in the sink.

She poured the batter for the cornbread into a greased Dutch oven which had three small feet and a flat lid. When she was done, she handed him the heavy pot and asked, "Can you put this outside in the coals? Six underneath and fourteen on top. Here are some tongs. We can wrap the fish next and get the fresh peaches and cake ready to bake outside too. Muchos gracias!"

Fresh peaches and cake?! Colton's desire for her was mounting.

By 6:15, the table under the canopy of an elm was laden with mouthwatering food. Saffron brought out an old portable CD player and they ate listening to the haunting melodies of Neko Case.

Colton had never heard her before, but he loved the spaghetti western sensibilities of her songs and her plaintively sweet vocals.

The hammer clicks in place / The world's gonna pay / Right down in the face of God and his saints / Who claims their soul's not for sale / I'm a dying breed that still believes / Hunted by American dreams.

"I think I've found one of my three best moments of the week," she said, gazing at him over the rim of her glass.

"Yes, ma'am," he agreed wholeheartedly, "easily one of the top three best things."

"The next time we come out here," she said, "we'll need to bring our horses. I love riding out here."

The next time. The words sent chills up Colton's spine.

"I thought the same thing when we drove up to the house," he said with surprise. "I'd love that. I'd also love a look around here, if you'll show me." He stood up and began clearing the table for her. "Can we go for a walk?"

"Great idea," she said. "I'll grab some water bottles and stuff for the top of the mesa. I can't wait for you to see the view. This place has the best sunsets on the planet."

Before they left, Saffron grabbed a Pendleton blanket and one of the reusable grocery bags from the car to take with them. Behind the house was a small hill that abutted the adobe home. There were stairs cut into the earth, leading up to and continuing along the rocky bluff. As they climbed, she took individual solar lights from the bag and placed them on stakes, jutting up from intermittent points along the trail. By the time they reached the top, the bag was empty and she folded it up, setting it under a rock for later.

They were standing on a large plateau that stretched out before them. To the north, the mountains filled the horizon. To the east, ten yards away, was an intricate design of rocks spiraled around a walking path; a labyrinth. Immediately to their left was a recessed pit with the remains of charred wood. Circling around it were a few large stones, like a miniature Stonehenge, to lean against when the fire-pit was in use. However, it was the stunning scenery that dominated Colton's attention. The flat mesa was dappled with desert plants. It rose above the valley floor with an open stretch of acreage in every direction.

Colton gazed at the wild beauty of the high desert, enjoying its quiet and ancient atmosphere. The sun was already deepening towards the western horizon, hovering over the mountains and mesas, with puffy patches of clouds spilling across the brilliant blue of the sky.

Taking in the view, he consciously took in a deep breath, down to his toes, grounding his feet on the dusty soil. For a brief moment, he felt like the King of the World.

"Keep your eyes out for prickly pears," she said. "If they're ripe, we can pick them in the morning."

Saffron offered her hand and Colton took it, linking together to begin their hike into uncharted territory.

"Just to live as a human being is a religious and sacred act. The true atheist is not that person who no longer believes in the existence of an anthropomorphic God, but the true atheist is that person who refuses to recognize the sacredness of existence, from the very breath of our bodies to the rhythmic ballet of the constellations, and the mystery within those expressions."
- Reverend William Edelen from Spirit

Chapter 20: Moonclad

The walk worked its magic as serenity settled over Colton while they hiked through the scrub. Large clouds provided intermittent cooling relief from the sun's glare. On the distant plains, the clouds' dark shadows danced across the desert floor like ancient myths. Saffron pointed at some and recited stories of the native legends she knew; First Man, First Woman, Monsterslayer and Coyote.

Colton told her they all looked like amoebas, except for one that distinctly looked like SpongeBob SquarePants.

Before it got dark, they returned to the house for supplies. Colton carried as much kindling and logs as he could in a burlap bag he found, leaving Saffron behind to pack a picnic basket. Inside the fire-pit, he arranged dried tumbleweed, and built a teepee of wood around it. The fire started easily; outdoor survival skills had been another gift from his grandfather.

Grandpa would have loved this place, he thought as the distinctly southwestern aroma of burning piñon wood drifted into the dusky sky.

Grandpa Miller had been on his mind a lot lately. There was so much he wished he could ask him, things he wanted to know, things that maybe he *ought* to know. His grandfather had been a rancher's son, a Marine, and an oil and gas man. He'd been a confident and loving person who took responsibility seriously, but didn't let it interfere with his appreciation for beauty in the world.

Colton suspected his grandfather would have seen stories in the cloud shapes, too.

In comparison, Colton's father was all work, no play. If Asa wasn't focused on business, then you'd likely find him in a recliner, watching sports or the news, complaining how messed up everything in the world was. At age fifty-two, he was already taking blood pressure medication.

For the first time in his life, Colton felt pity for him. He didn't want to, but he did.

There's got to be more to life than that, he thought, *and maybe, here it is.*

The light was beginning to yellow and lengthen, slanting across the land and coloring it like a painter's brushstroke as the sun prepared to set.

Over one shoulder the moon was rising, and over the other stood Shiprock, both sentinels to the powers of erosion and cosmic time. Alone on the mesa, Colton felt a profound sense of awe, a feeling of reverence. Bowing his head, he prayed Asa would wake up one day and realize there was a wide wonderful world out there he was hiding from.

In the kitchen, Saffron packed a bottle of cabernet along with dates, almonds and fresh bread into a handwoven hamper. She added a sage bundle, her mother's crystals (rose and clear quartz, amethyst, hematite, citrine, and turquoise), a lighter with a bare-breasted mermaid on it, and lastly, the pièce de résistance, a compact one-hitter box containing some of Colorado's finest sativas.

She helped herself to a hit of cannabis, feeling armed and ready for a good time.

At the door, she considered bringing her guitar, then realized she only wanted to wrap her arms around Colton, and choose the CD player instead.

Behind the house, she got her first glimpse of the full moon rising over the horizon, and remembered the reason she was at Sweetland in the first place; for Zia and a bit of moon magic. Tonight, she'd planned to express her gratitude to the Universe, to God or whatever powers that be, thankful her mother had not perished in a senseless act of violence.

She imagined Zia lying in the hospital, holding her dad's hand while they watched an asinine television show out of sheer boredom, or maybe curiosity; the LeMay household didn't watch much tv. More than likely, she reasoned, they were each reading, enjoying their quiet companionship.

It opened her heart thinking of their love for each other, and for her love of them both.

Her thoughts suddenly turned to Colton and she realized she didn't feel ready to express her feelings in front of him, to share something as personal as prayer and energy work.

If she wanted privacy for serious mojo, then this was the place and time.

Ansty to get back to the mesa and already feeling the effects of the weed, Saffron opted against a lengthy and sacred meditation, choosing instead to do a quickie version.

Einstein proved Time is relative, she rationalized, *and God should know my intent, so let's skip the foreplay and get to it!*

Turning to face the moon, she removed her sandals, letting her bare feet sink deliciously into the soft sand. Centering herself in mountain pose, she closed her eyes and quieted her mind. Picturing the Reiki symbol to send healing energy across space and time, she made motions with her hands, 'drawing' in the air in front of her, and repeating the names for the corresponding symbols.

Saffron's hands warmed and a sensation of light surrounded her, like a door opening, love pouring into her from above. She gently allowed that love and light to fill her, then felt it extend effortlessly out from her hands, across the miles to her mother's bed; her prayer and intention for a positive outcome rolling away from her like a wave on the ocean.

Before she finished, she envisioned the healing energy expanding towards everyone on the planet, enveloping them in true peace. She even sent it to her 'enemies', those she blamed for the global emergency, which wasn't easy; she maintained the intention for only a minute before stopping.

A rare summer breeze brushed along her skin and she shivered. Opening her eyes, she felt calm as well as eager for the night ahead. The light had turned golden. She would have to hurry to catch the sunset. Supplies in hand, she climbed each and every step of the trail with increasing anticipation.

Colton watched her approaching from his position facing west. The sun was coloring the clouds, providing a stunning backdrop for the heavenly vision striding towards him. Saffron's hair was aglow and her skirt swished lightly with each delicate footstep. Clenched tightly to her chest was a picnic basket with a clunky CD player perched precariously on top.

With a smile, he thought, *I might need to buy her some new tech.*

Walking towards her, he reached out to relieve her of her burden.

"Thank you, kind sir," she said with a mock curtsy and a wide grin, her bright white teeth showing. "I brought some goodies, too," she said playfully, opening up the basket and handing him the wine.

As he poured, she took a cigarette-shaped one-hitter, filled it with weed, lit it, inhaled, held her breath, then let the sweet smoke curl out from her rosy lips.

"I thought you didn't drink or smoke that often?" Colton teased before raising his hands and quickly adding, "Hey, I'm not judging you or anything."

Saffron appeared to seriously contemplate his remark before saying, "That is patently true. I have definitely been heavy on the alcohol this week." She inhaled deeply from the pipe a second time. "I guess it's been a tougher, more stressful week than most." Pouting her Kewpie-doll lips, she batted her eyelashes, released the smoke, and offered him the pipe. "Do you want some?"

Colton decided to come clean and tell her the truth…at least, one of his truths.

"I-I've never smoked before," he admitted reluctantly.

"You don't have to if you don't want to," she said, shrugging her shoulders. "This type helps to have all sorts of amazing thoughts and ideas, usually about the interconnectedness of everything. Some strains make you relaxed and sleepy which is good for stressed-out, anxious people, but I like the strains that open up my mind for awhile."

Colton took the offered pipe and filled it as he'd seen her do. He lit it, inhaled deeply, then exploded in a coughing fit.

"Don't worry," she said, laughing at him in her good-natured way, "that happens all the time. Just take it slow. One more time will be plenty."

The second hit was smoother than the first. He breathed out a large amount of smoke and passed it back to her. After her third puff, she put it away and reached over him for her glass of wine.

She smells like lavender, he thought, enjoying her scent as his body melted into a warm, peaceful feeling.

All was still except for the soft crackles of the firewood; the rest was the quiet of innocent, unmarred land. As the sun descended towards the horizon, the bountiful clouds orgasmed into brilliant colors, forms and textures like a scene out of 'Gone with the Wind'.

"Now in Technicolor!" Saffron exclaimed with a flourish towards the picturesque sky.

Colton laughed harder than the joke warranted.

It felt incredible to be with her, resting against the smooth stones without a care in the world, enjoying the blessed feeling of idleness. Turning, he saw the Moon looming behind them, hauntingly beautiful, a witness to the passing of its sister, the Sun.

As they watched, holding hands like longtime lovers, the sunset pinked to coral before reddening to rose, like an exotic bird of paradise during mating season. The tapestry of clouds began to dim and darken into the divine hues of violet, orange and indigo, until the evening's last light collapsed into the curve of the earth.

"Well," Saffron said, a look of total satisfaction on her cherubic face, "that was sexy as hell. I may need a cigarette."

Again, Colton laughed out loud. Never before had he met a girl as open and as free as her. Momentarily released and unbound from the shackles of his own worries, he felt like flying to the stars which were blinking in a dizzying panorama in the heavens above.

"You," he said courageously, "you are the sexy one."

He locked his eyes upon hers, overcome by the compulsion to kiss her. Inhaling her intoxicating scent, he leaned in.

Clasping her small hands behind his head, she crushed her petite body into his with a passion that rocked him; a hunger. Saffron wasn't holding anything back. Immediately, Colton's body reacted to her desire, a force that came off of her in waves as the kiss lengthened. Her hands began an exploration to the flesh below his clothes.

Pulling back abruptly, his heart beating like a jackhammer in his chest, he willed himself to practice control and to hold back the flood.

"W-wait," he stammered, "let me catch my breath." Chuckling nervously, he added, "Whew, that was a first kiss for the ages."

Saffron had been far, far away.

That first kiss had transported her into the vast reaches of her imagination. She'd felt surrounded by light, as if their auras had melded. Simply inhaling the smell of his skin (*Ah, pheromones!* one portion of her brain had chimed in) had made her vulva clench and moisten.

And his lips! The soft skin of them, surrounded by the scratchiness of his late afternoon face, had driven her wild. She'd wanted to devour him, as well as offer all she had, in that first kiss.

Now, as Colton pulled back, Saffron felt herself go from floating in the substance of the universe to drowning in doubt and unrequited hunger.

"W-what's wrong?" she asked, her mind coming back into focus from the dizzying rush of endorphins and weed.

"Nothing," he replied unconvincingly. He shifted uneasily, adjusting himself in the confines of his jeans. He looked uncomfortable and ready to make excuses, but then he seemed to change his mind, resolve crossing his face as he straightened his shoulders and faced her.

"Okay," he said, "I've got one last revelation for you. I promise, this's my last secret." Turning his eyes from hers onto the flames, Colton took a deep breath. "I-I've only been serious with one girl before," he said haltingly, "and we never had...sexual intercourse. I-I'm a virgin."

Saffron took a breath and focused on reigning in her unfulfilled libido, holding back the tide. She wasn't used to practicing restraint when it came to sex. Typically, when an opportunity presented itself, she would let her appetites run wild.

She watched his profile as the firelight danced on his cheekbones and downturned eyes. He was so beautiful, yet he looked so sad as he stared blindly into the fire. She caressed his cheek and he responded by turning his eyes back to her, so vulnerable and expectant; strong, but not impervious to pain.

Her desire for him was undeniable, undeterred by his admission, though it did shift.

It was as if she'd found a unique rock, only to learn it was crystalline inside; a geode; a treasure hidden beneath its surface. Saffron's sexual energy deepened, transforming into a gentle warmth and understanding.

Colton watched her intently, his breath held. Her cupid-bow smile and compassionate eyes were all the acceptance he needed, until he heard her words.

"I said I wanted to get to know you," she said quietly, "and I meant it. You don't have to keep secrets from me." She took his hand into hers. "I'm sorry, it never occurred to me I was moving too fast for you. Let me be clear, there's absolutely no pressure. We can take our time and savor the moment."

Relief flooded throughout Colton's entire body and he finally relaxed.

With the departure of the sun, the desert had blued under the reflective force of the moon's mirror. It dazzled. Colton was momentarily lost in the beauty around him. Gazing into the heart of the fire, he watched its colors dance from the logs and spit sparks, trailing spirals into the night sky. Even the stars conspired to complete the tableau; they sparkled, pulsed and twinkled as if to say *We are watching over you, lovely creatures, so full of life. We see you.*

A fundamentally pure thought arose in him, *We're all connected, all God's children, all the same.* It was followed by the age-old question, *So why are we killing one another?* Colton shuddered, his thoughts shifting back to the grim possibility of extinction. *What will the world look like when we're all gone?*

"Wow," he said, shaking himself back into the present moment. "I think I might be high."

Saffron's gay laughter echoed across the mesa.

"I've been watching you bliss out, staring into space," she said giggling. "I'd say you're definitely stoned, good and proper."

"And," he admitted, "I think I'm ready." He was suddenly overwhelmed by the inherent truth of his words. "I'd like you to be my first," he said. "Tonight...in this place."

He leaned in for another kiss.

"Okay, Casanova," she said thickly, placing her hands on his chest. "Thanks for your consent, but I said we're going to take our time and I meant it. We've got all night. Let's start with some music. I brought The Accidentals. Oh," she said, bouncing on the tips of her toes, "one more thing, I truly love to dance, it's kind of like my favorite thing, so I hope it won't be a problem for you."

She pushed play and ethereal vocals and stringed instruments reverberated into the darkness.

"Then, Señor CJ...mi amigo, " she said with a Spanish lilt and raised eyebrow, "we'll see where we go from there."

Blowing him a kiss, she sashayed to the other side of the fire, slowly moving to the beat. Her outstretched arms curved sinuously up to the starlit sky, as she whirled and bathed in the moonlight like a pagan priestess of old. Her eyes were closed; her long hair, a diaphanous halo as she spun.

Colton watched her body flow with every nuance and rhythm of the music, like a conductor bringing to life the intentions of dead maestros. The song and her dancing urged him to follow.

He was no longer content with being an observer.

With a gulp of wine, he stood to face the fire and his own inner drummer. Giving in to the moment, he circled and stomped like he hadn't a worry in the world. Removing his shirt, he felt the coolness on his exposed skin when he turned away from the flames, delighting in the primal act of dancing at night around a campfire.

Watching Colton's half naked body, his muscles relaxing and contracting as he danced for the sheer joy of it, Saffron's desire for him escalated. His taut abdominal muscles and chest hair were distracting as her thoughts returned to all the things she wanted to do to him. Regardless of his sexual experience, there was no doubt she wanted him.

Briefly, she wondered what his skin would taste like.

Take your time, she reminded herself. *Enjoy the Now.*

Her shadow disappeared in and out of the fire as she circled it, teasing her, the desert night calling. She slipped deeper into it, leaving the warmth behind. Her shadow self led the way, matching her dancing move for move. She was entranced by the vividness of its stark contrast, the bright moon casting her frame in a perfect, black silhouette.

My dark twin, she thought, smiling as she danced alone with herself; she felt transcendent; in harmony with the music, the moment, and the land.

"I told you," she called ecstatically, her arms raised to the moon. "All matter and life is made from vibrating quantum strings. Can't you feel it!?!" The hem of her skirt rose up and twirled around her. "God bless the ultimate orchestra!!!"

Her loud voice echoed out into the emptiness around them, heard only by hidden animals and eavesdropping spirits.

Colton felt a quiver of arousal coursing through his body.

She never ceased to amaze him; her intensity, her intellect, her vivaciousness. Yet she scared him a little too; the thrills, the speed, the anticipation. She was like a roller coaster in motion, or a bucking bronco, only much more benevolent.

Saffron exuded lifeforce from every pore in her body.

The song ended and she turned to look at him over her shoulder. She was glowing and a little out of breath. The cool blue light fell gently on the ripeness of her creamy white shoulders and cascaded down her back.

Colton's heart rose up into his throat as she gazed at him.

Who's ever looked at me like that, he asked himself.

No one else, his inner voice answered.

The next song was slower, calmer. Saffron drew back to the fire, her sandals padding softly in the sandy soil. When she got close, she bypassed him and went straight to the picnic basket, busying herself with her mother's crystals. She placed them in a circular pattern on top of a nearby flat stone, the moon reflecting off their shiny surfaces like tiny inner lights.

He knelt beside her on the blanket, getting up the nerve to kiss her again when she asked if it was okay if she prayed for a minute.

"No, no," he said, "of course not." He remembered her promise to Zia. "Go straight ahead."

Saffron sat back on her heels, hands open and upturned on her lap, her eyes closed. She felt ready for deeper prayer work. The quickie wasn't going to cut it. Zia deserved the best of her, and maybe the world did too.

If Colton can be brave and reveal his true self, she realized, *then so can I.*

When she felt centered, she rose with a lit smudge stick, its strongly herbal scent blending with the smoke of the fire.

"Thank you God," she spoke quietly and clearly, "for sparing my mother. Thank you for the healing power of your love. We're blessed and give gratitude for all we have. Our prayers are with the families of those who lost their lives this week, in the storm and in the riot. Please give them strength.

"I, too, ask for the continued strength to fight back the darkness in this world. I ask that I may be a Light that shows others the way, the natural and harmonious way, in line with the consciousness of Christ and the planet." Bowing her head, she said, "I pray for a return of the health and wellbeing of our bodies, to the waters, lands and air around us. As we cleanse ourselves and the world of toxins and pollutants, may we purify our minds and souls, too."

Recalling her earlier Reiki experience, she added, "I send my love out to every being in the four directions, north, east, south, and west. I commit myself to bringing peace, love and unity to the people You have created. I AM a steward of the earth, for the beautiful garden You provided for us and that Mankind has abused time and time again. I will die to protect it if necessary. Please God, continue to guide me as your agent of positive change. Amen."

She remained standing in peaceful repose, breathing slowly, her arms outstretched and her head tilted towards the heavens in communion. A light breeze swirled around the campfire, making it hiss and pop. The flames rose higher with the increase of oxygen.

"Do you really mean that," Colton whispered, rubbing his bare arms which had erupted in goosebumps.

"Yes," she said serenely. "I offered myself to God and the angels a long time ago, to be a part of the mission to save the Earth and its inhabitants." Her face fell and her eyebrows furrowed. "Unfortunately, most people don't understand the circumstances we're in, and those who do are still pretty lost about what's to be done about it."

She paused to take a sip of wine, her mouth suddenly as dry as the Sahara.

"People who deny climate destabilization is happening," she said, "do so because they're either overwhelmed, misinformed, or simply because they profit from not acting. However, for those that accept the reality of the scientific evidence, there are also three ways to respond. One can accept the truth and still do nothing, because the changes we need to make seem so severe. Or, we can fixate only on helping our own families to survive like the survivalists and preppers do."

With bitterness in her voice, she added, "There are several billionaires and multi-millionaires building shelters, true bunkers, in remote parts of the world to protect their families during the later stages."

Rather than helping us divert disaster, goddamn it!

Inhaling deeply, she pushed her negative thoughts and emotions down into the earth, her gaze moving back towards the moon.

"But, for those of us that hear the call," she said resolutely, "for those who decide to be courageous, to take on the enormity of the problem, we choose to do anything and everything in our power to stop the shift, and hopefully, reverse it before Phase 3, the Hot Mess, when the effects will increase exponentially, an irreversible downward slide towards extinction."

Colton's mouth was bone dry.

He couldn't think of anything to say.

"I know this sounds bleak and melodramatic," she continued. "I've been attending marches and writing letters to influential people and politicians since I was a kid. I've got multiple lists of the world's billionaires, the highest paid CEO's of the largest corporations, and the names of thousands of elected officials. Every year on my birthday, I send some of them requests to take action before it's too late. I once took a topless selfie with the words 'Help us, Elon Musk. You're our only hope' written in lipstick on my tits and sent it to Tesla headquarters."

Her smile was back but it was somber, the fatalistic humor of the terminally ill.

"Oddly," she said, "I never got a response."

Colton couldn't imagine not responding to such a request.

"However," she said, "I do believe that if more people spoke up, the tide would change and we can turn this world around. For now, I push my boulder up the mountain and pray for others to join me before we race like a runaway train into a nightmarish hell."

She'd been speaking in a cavalier tone, but her words caused Colton's throat to constrict and his stomach to recoil in horror. He felt his euphoric feelings from earlier start to collapse within his chest.

Saffron seemed to notice the despair taking hold of him and quickly rushed to his side, placing her warm hands onto his chilled skin.

"I'm so, so sorry," she said emphatically. "We can change the subject. The world isn't ending tonight, and you and I are pleasantly stoned. If we go down this road right now, we're in for a very unpleasant evening. Marijuana doesn't do well with negative emotions."

"It's just...so intense," Colton responded.

Saffron hugged him and laid her cheek upon his chest as she soothed him.

"I know," she comforted. "It's going to be okay. We can discuss the particulars tomorrow and in the days that come, but tonight, our job is to emit joy, to be in the present moment, and to appreciate the beauty surrounding us." She laid a gentle kiss against his bare chest. "For now, let's express our gratitude for the life that's been given us."

The CD ended and the silence was a gift.

Colton tilted her chin, finding her lips eager and ready to explore his. This second kiss was deeper, with Colton leading. He wrapped his arms around the small of her back, urging her to feel the immense emotions inside him. She felt strong, yet invitingly soft. Her breathing deepened seductively.

His passion was building, ready to consume.

"I want you...all of you," he panted, "if you'll let me."

"Are you sure?" she asked. "I don't want to pressure you."

"I think," he began, peering with amazement at the woman in his arms, at her pale skin, luscious lips, and worried eyes; it was a face Colton wanted to look at until the end of time.

"I think I've been waiting for you...and now that I've found you, I'm ready. Show me the way, my rebel," he said, giving her a playful tap on the curve of her alluring ass.

"Yee-haw!" she said loudly. "Giddy up, cowboy!"

"I remembered that the real world was wide,
and that a varied field of hopes and fears,
of sensations and excitements, awaited those who had the
courage to go forth into its expanse,
to seek real knowledge of life amidst its perils."
- Charlotte Brontë from Jane Eyre

Chapter 21: Ascension

Quickly, they snuffed out the campfire after sharing one last puff on the one-hitter. Laughing and acting silly, howling and blowing kisses to the moon, they headed back to the cozy adobe house; the solar lights, aided by moonglow, making for a safe trek down the rocky stairs.

Saffron was proud she'd only stopped once for a brief make-out session, and hadn't stripped him of the rest of his clothes before they made it home.

Colton excused himself to the outhouse, admitting he wasn't in the mood for a composting toilet lesson.

"You're right," she admitted. "It might be a bit of a buzzkill."

When he returned, soft music was playing, the iconic poetry of Norah Jones aptly setting the mood. She'd just finished placing lit candles throughout the living room, their wavering light warming the wood of the tables and flicking shadows along the walls.

"Can you please light some candles in the bedroom," she asked, passing him the mermaid lighter. "I just need a minute," she said before entering the bathroom with a small bag in her hand.

Once alone, her thoughts of the intimacy to come led to an impromptu dance of joy and an internal squeal.

Eeeeee!!! she thought. *I really, really, REALLY like him!*

She was suddenly overcome by a desire to make Colton's first time a truly memorable event. Then, in true marijuana fashion, she had the random thoughts, *Wow, I'm like the perfect balance of horny and giddy,* as well as, *Man, that was some good weed.*

When she entered the candle glow of the bedroom, she was delighted to see Colton had read her mind and removed his clothes; he was bent over the mattress, naked ass in the air, pulling down the sheets of the bed.

Hmm, she thought lasciviously, dialing in on the curve of his back and his beckoning butt cheeks. *Now, that's what I call hospitality!*

Unintentionally, she uttered an appreciative and audible noise in admiration of his firm backside; a yummy sound. Colton heard her and turned around. The sight of his fully exposed frontside caused certain parts of Saffron's anatomy to demonstrate appreciation as well; a dewdrop of moisture slicked her. She shifted her feet, rubbing her thighs and labia together, clenching and swelling with anticipation.

It's his first time, she thought, deciding to give him a full show. *Let's do this right!*

Colton had been nervous until the moment he saw her petite form standing in the doorway. She was dressed in a silky, dove grey slip, the color perfectly complimenting the apricot locks of her hair which fell lightly past her collarbones. Her skin glowed like porcelain china under the candlelight. Her delicately painted blue toes curled and uncurled slowly as her legs rocked slightly from side to side.

Like a heroine from a Hitchcock film, her eyes, enticingly kohled in a retro cat's eye look, penetrated into his own; her lips curled in a cat-with-mouse grin.

With the dreamy vocals and soft piano playing lightly in the background, she began dancing coquettishly to the music, a burlesque flair in her movements. Baring each shoulder, she seemed to relish in the power of her young body and the perfection of the song. Demurely crisscrossing her arms over her breasts, she teased him, extending the seconds before the final reveal. Peering over her right shoulder, she leaned against the door jamb, giving him an unrestricted view of her heart-shaped behind as her nightgown puddled at her feet.

Between her shoulders was a tattoo of koi fish intertwined in the Yin/Yang symbol.

Colton stood rigid as a statue, his heart missing a beat or two.

His eagerness to touch her, to join with her, was a ten alarm fire inside of him.

When his eyes came up to meet hers, she winked and turned provocatively around to face him. Her arms and neck were lightly sun-kissed; her nipples, a pale pink like a rose; her pubic hair, reddish brown. When his gaze finally arrived back to her face, she stared at him daringly with a sultry fire, her lips lightly parted.

He could almost hear a purr emanating from her essence.

Her eyes slowly slipped down his own body, hungrily, reciprocally.

Being exposed to her wandering gaze excited him in a surprising way; the voyeur, remade to the one admired.

Saffron had wanted this moment from the first day she had met him.

One week ago, this stranger had been her savior, a man she might not have met during her normal routine and daily existence. Fate had brought them together.

Starting at his strong shoulders and muscular arms, the same ones which had held her in her most vulnerable moments, her eyes traveled across his light chest hair and hardened nipples to his firm abs, then traced the route of fine hairs down until focusing on his penis which was uncircumcised and very erect.

Houston, we have confirmation of HHC, her stoner-girl brain thought, making her smile and almost giggle. *Head, heart and hella nice cock!*

As she continued to stare, getting more turned on by the second, she had another thought, *God, I'm soooo glad I wasn't rescued by a hairy old dude!*

Now, that thought did make her laugh out loud.

Colton quickly covered himself. His face turned ashen, a look of disbelief upon it that she could possibly be laughing at him while...he... was...naked! He looked sucker-punched, like his heart was imploding inside his chest.

What have I done?!? she thought, realizing the depth of her mistake.

"Oh my goodness! I'm so, so sorry," she gushed, quickly crossing the room to wrap her arms around him. "That wasn't what it looked like!"

She began planting small kisses up and down his body as she apologized.

"You're so beautiful." *Kiss.* "I'm just high," *Kiss,* "and I made myself laugh," *Kiss,* "thinking how lucky I am," *Kiss,* "that I wasn't rescued," *Kiss,* "by a Wookie." *Kiss,* "I'm so sorry." *Nibble.* "Let me make it up to you." *Bite.*

At some point, her apology had shifted from repentance towards exploration. She heard Colton gasp as she lightly bit the flesh above his left collarbone, her exhaled breath hot against his sweaty skin.

She loved the taste of him; just a hint of salt mixed in with the desert and moon energies humming along the surface. His soft chest hairs tickled her lips, bringing her to the edge of distraction.

Fully distracted, Colton stood with the heat of her gloriously silky skin touching his body in various spots along his length, awakening every square inch. He felt electrified by her mouth and hands and their occasional brush against his nipples. His cannabis-infused brain sunk under the flood of new sensations.

With a final kiss on his right pelvic bone, he opened his eyes to see the candlelit goddess kneeling before him.

In a half-whisper, he said, "I trust you." Then, playfully, he put his arms around her, lifting her onto the bed and holding himself above her, inches from her delighted face.

"But, can you trust me," he asked, slipping his hand down to cup her, delicately fingering her warm opening and gazing into her blue eyes; they closed, a look of bliss on her face as her hips arched appreciatively towards him.

"So, I'm forgiven?" she asked with a Cheshire grin and another giggle before her breath was suddenly stolen from her.

Colton's fingers penetrated and deftly began playing her, working with a rhythmic precision. There was no resistance, only acceptance, her body open and responsive to his manipulations. His other hand gently embraced the back of her head as he pressed his mouth to hers in a passionate kiss.

It was unbelievable to him that only a week ago, this creature, a siren, had been delivered into his world and into his arms. She was almost otherworldly, a Celtic angel who pulsed with pleasure, wetting his fingers. He drove her over the edge as he kept his lips connected with hers. She moaned into his mouth as he swallowed her scream.

Feeling her quivering below him, no holds barred, wracked with satisfaction, was one of the most erotic experiences he'd ever had. Kaelynne, he realized in a flash, had never let herself completely release the way Saffron had.

The full potential of the moment was beginning to dawn on him.

What more can this girl teach me?

Saffron's spirit was on the ceiling. She felt expansive, cradled by the cosmos and Colton simultaneously. She could feel her back arching higher and higher, rocking harder and harder against his hand, as a mind-altering orgasm exploded within her. When her soul finally came back from the ether to reunite with her brain stem, her body coalesced around her once again, returning to solid matter.

Her vision came back into focus.

"Damn," she said lustfully and a little out of breath. "Where'd a virgin learn to do that?!" Her head collapsed into the pillows, a cheek-hurting smile plastered across her face. "Holy shit," she rasped.

"Well," Colton admitted, "if you spend years denying yourself actual sex, you get pretty good at doing other things."

Saffron briefly fantasized how thrilling it would be to have his warm tongue and hot breath on her, licking and sucking, her fingers tangled into his hair as she fed herself to him. The image caused her to shudder with an aftershock.

Houston, we're entering Full-On Vixen Mode!

Her naughty inner voice thought of saying something like, *'So, what'll it be, Mr. Denial? Would you like a nice blowjob to start our evening, maybe a little 69 action, or shall we go straight to sliding that beautiful cock inside of me?'*

If Colton were more like Ayden, she wouldn't have hesitated, but she realized this moment meant more than just sex to her, and to him.

It wasn't just play.

It shouldn't only be about fucking.

From the thunderous, raging storm to this tantalizing union, the time she'd spent with him felt like magic.

It could and should be, she realized, *more meaningful...deeper.*

"I'm open," she said, "to doing 'all the things', if you are. No more secrets between us. No guilt, no shame. I'll do whatever you're comfortable with."

"I'm all yours," he replied in a low and guttural voice. "You may do whatever you'd like. Lady's choice."

Saffron bit her lower lip, considering, before grasping his erection with her right hand. She slowly worked the smooth skin over the hard shaft. Her left hand caressed his firm behind, kneading it lightly, pushing him down towards her.

Yes, she thought, watching his hazel eyes glaze over, then close, as he gave in to her touching. *Mine.*

She stopped and pushed him off and over onto his back. Colton yielded easily to her guidance. Starting at his chest, she flicked his nipples with her tongue while resuming her play with his penis; stroking his cock with her fingers and pressing it against the warmth of her soft belly. The palm of her hand could feel the heat from his expanded blood flow, beating in unison with his heart. She spread herself around his leg and pressed her heat and dampness upon his thigh.

Colton's breath sped up and his hips began to shake, urging himself into the tightness of her grip. His face turned into the pillow, eyes shut.

Her mouth descended along his abdomen, giving more kisses, exploring his skin. Hovering above his pelvis, she viewed the naked man beneath her. His penis was rock hard as the soft folds slid up and down in her hand, revealing the hidden tip like a flower opening. Saliva pooled against her tongue as she lovingly let her relaxed throat take him as deeply as she could into her eager mouth.

Drifting in ecstasy, Saffron worked him in and out, enjoying the firm yet velvet smoothness of him. Her tongue curled and licked the underside as she increased suction. Her fingers swirled along the slick shaft before lowering to the tightness in his testicles. She swallowed him again, and again, speeding up, drawing him in, suctioning harder, encouraging him to fill her. She was lost in the taste of him, moaning with need, humping his leg with abandon.

Colton was completely undone; his whole being, focused into a single point, fully centered in her avid cocksucking and her unabashed desire to take him. He tried to hold out, to disengage, but she was relentless. As she artfully worked him, the friction building, he spilled into her throat as she accepted him without reservation.

A primal cry of release ripped out of him and reverberated around the room.

Nimbly and wordlessly, she straddled him and slipped his still erect penis inside her. His head snapped back into the pillow, his neck arching, as a gasp tore from his throat. Reflexively, he grabbed her thighs, pressing deeper within her.

He was still reeling from his orgasm.

The heat, wetness and tightness that enveloped him as she began expertly riding him was beyond anything he'd ever imagined. A door opened up within, freeing him from all insecurities and doubt. His physical body was bursting with pleasure while his inner being radiated light and joy...and then he remembered.

"W-wait," he said, starting to pull away. "What about protection?"

"Don't worry," she said, "I won't get pregnant, and I've always been careful in the past. I just want you so badly."

With those words, she continued working herself up and down, rotating, grinding, her strong vaginal muscles stimulating his erection back to full recovery.

She closed her eyes and let go, panting, whimpering, thoroughly enjoying the feeling of fullness within her and the delight in every nerve ending in her body.

The small candlelit bedroom dropped away. Saffron pictured the four poster bed covered in silk scarves in the center of a marble-lined palace room. Like a concubine from Egypt or India, she imagined herself masterfully pleasuring her lover. Surrounded by opulence and gold in her mind, she envisioned their bodies anointed with oils as she made love to him.

When she opened her eyes, she found his already on hers. Licking her lips and fondling her breasts, Saffron's gaze never wavered from Colton's face as she watched him, watching her.

Slowly, she raised herself up and paused, the head of his penis barely inside her, then glided down until she held his full length buried deeply within. Her head rolled up towards the wood beamed ceiling while they moaned in unison. Three more times she performed this tease, holding him captive, stealing his breath, his eyes held tight in ecstasy, until she could no longer hold back. She had to have him. She began bouncing and gyrating, working him, using him, as the intensity of her pleasure rose up into a crescendo. Suddenly, she was shattered by pure bliss. Vibrating, she exploded around him, saying "Yes! Yes! Yes!" over and over and over again.

Colton was in another realm. He could feel her spasming, shuddering, clamping down on him as she came. His own ejaculate poured out, seemingly never-endlessly. He buried himself in the kiss she offered him while down below she began moving yet again.

He had to have more.

With a swift move, aided by years of experience in roping and tying calves, he flipped her over onto her back, still joined together. Now, it was his turn to thrust.

A lusty growl escaped her throat.

Together, their urgency multiplied, their breathing in sync, the romantic music accompanying their lovemaking like a guiding force.

Saffron was completely in her element, relishing in her sexual skills and in the responses they generated from Colton. He was her willing, able and very appreciative partner. The happiness and ecstasy she saw reflected in his eyes was the strongest aphrodisiac she'd ever experienced. She thought she could go on forever touching his skin and making his fantasies come true, even the ones he had no idea he harbored.

She greeted orgasm after orgasm, marveling at their perfection as each one built deeply within before blending into an enticing combination of body, mind and spirit.

Each stroke, each moan, each penetration was a revelation.

This was what she loved best in life, the feeling of connection; giving of herself and giving in to the myriad potentials of the Universe; simple Oneness.

She came for the final time, shuddering and gasping, her nerve endings screaming out for mercy. Euphorically, she lit up with a white glow. Her breathing ceased, cut off by the climax inside her, until her autonomic nervous system finally kicked in, raggedly drawing oxygen deeply into her lungs before she accidentally passed out.

La petite mort.

Colton fell onto his elbows and buried himself in her hair, collapsing upon her as he bucked helplessly, driven again to the pinnacle of release. A kaleidoscope of colors erupted behind his closed eyelids. His nipples hardened almost to a point of pain that shared the line with pleasure. As his scrotum drew in tightly, it pulled the thread of tissue that stretched the entire length from scrotum to tip, pulsing as it feverishly attempted to eject more semen.

He clung to her, letting the warm ripples of satisfaction ebb and flow throughout his body like the tide caressing the sand.

This, he thought with amazement, *was a first time for the ages!*

"W-wow," he panted, blood returning to his brain so he could speak. "I-I don't know what else to say." His smile was so wide it was hurting his face.

"I have an idea," she said silkily. "How does peaches and cake sound to you…naked…under the stars?" Kissing the tip of his nose, she purred, "And then, we'll see what comes to mind."

Colton truly had no words, just an overwhelming sense of joy and gratitude.

Part of him had worried he'd feel shame or remorse for breaking his vow about sex before marriage, but he only felt a profound sense of peace. He knew he was a bit naive, but he suspected the gift he'd just received, the blessed union they'd shared, was probably rare to most people's experiences.

More than rare, his instincts told him. It had felt…*divine.*

He was ready, then and there, to give her everything he could in order to have moments like this become a part of his life forever.

Heart and soul, he would give to her.

She's the one! he thought with amazement.

No matter what else transpired in his life, come what may, he would never regret his first time.

"I told him. And as I walked on I was lonely no longer.
I was a guide, a pathfinder, an original settler."
- F. Scott Fitzgerald from The Great Gatsby

Chapter 22: Pillow Talk

Morning light dappled the bedroom with the sunrise's halcyon touch.

Saffron awoke to Colton's warmth upon her bare skin, his chest beneath her head in the rhythm of restful slumber. His heartbeat resounded in her ear, full of life.

Sighing contentedly, she inhaled his 'addictive pheromones' and smiled.

Memories of the previous night's lovemaking rushed back; the kissing, the touching, the happiness. For Colton's first time, Saffron had given her all, marrying heart-opening tenderness with heart-pounding fierceness; play and passion uniting in uninhibited acts of mutual caring.

The sacred level of intimacy had almost shattered her.

Totally Tantric, she thought sleepily. With amazement, she realized, *He's the one! HHC to the nth degree!!!*

Floating on the clouds, she drifted blissfully until becoming aware of a darker emotion swimming beneath the surface; an uneasiness in her core. Briefly, she wondered if the unpleasant feeling came from a forgotten dream, but it didn't ring true.

What's going on? she wondered. *Why do I feel like I'm about to cry?*

Saffron was surprised by a bitter voice inside her saying, *The more you love, the more you'll lose.*

It was a horrible, dejected voice; her deepest fear laid bare.

Suddenly, she realized she *did* have more to lose. Falling for Colton gave her even more reason to fight against the coming apocalypse and create a future worth living.

But there's still so much he doesn't understand, her sad, still voice reminded. *And, until he does...I'm on my own.*

Images flashed through her mind of the catastrophic events and injustices to humanity which were predicted to occur across the globe.

War, famine, disaster, disease; the four horsemen in full regalia.

In the next twenty to thirty years, no one on earth would be able to deny the existence of climate destabilization. The changes were going to be grotesquely obvious to even the most diehard denier.

Saffron had been living with this knowledge locked inside her for years, going through each and every day with a low level sense of impotence and impending doom, knowing deep in her heart not nearly enough was being done to rectify what was wrong.

Tightly squeezing her eyes, she fought back unwelcome tears.

It'd been awhile since she'd opened Pandora's Box of Panic. Typically, she overcame her worries by holding in her heart the intention for only the highest good to manifest; choosing to live each day by being present, both eyes open, consciously taking what life had to offer and swallowing it down, as if she could assimilate the fabric of the universe into the molecular structure of her DNA.

If it were possible, she would eat the moon.

This morning however, thinking of the decimation to come, she wished everything would disappear, leaving her and Colton in peace. Unfortunately, she knew the likelihood of the world staying peaceful for long was getting slimmer by the day. Like a cornered animal, she felt torn between running or hiding, her instincts pacing restlessly inside her.

What good's hiding gonna do anyway, dummy, she asked herself sarcastically, *when the whole damn world's in jeopardy?*

On the tailcoat of that thought, the full gravity of the week's events slammed into her.

First came memories of the storm. Saffron shuddered, remembering the dark, wind-tossed waves. She'd been so vulnerable; too far from shore; too deep for a foothold to stand on. In other circumstances, in another timeline, she could've easily drowned, cut off prematurely from everything she loved in the world, never again to have moments like the one from the previous night.

Life's fragility and fickleness made her think of the insanity of the riot as she rapidly replayed the gunshots, screams, and blood.

My God, she realized like a slap, *my mother ACTUALLY took a bullet for me!*

Her heart raced, her nude skin chilled to the bone.

If it can happen once, a dark voice said presciently, *it can happen again.*

With an image in her mind of Colton, lying bleeding in her arms, her tears finally spilled down her cheeks.

"Wha-what's wrong?" he asked groggily, sounding like he wasn't sure he wanted to hear the answer.

"I-I'm sorry," she sniffled, her voice sounding scratchy and hoarse, a ghost of her normal manner. "I-I don't know what's come over me."

Tensing her muscles, she steeled her body up against his.

"I'm stronger than this," she said angrily. "I-I can't cry! I gotta be able to face all the shit life's gonna throw at me, wi-with-without breaking down!!!" Through clenched teeth, she stated, "I can't be weak!"

The floodgates ignored her words and opened as she burst out crying in full surrender. Holding on for dear life, she wrapped her arms tightly around Colton.

Once again, he was there to steady her.

"It's okay, Roni," he said reassuringly, stroking her hair. "Being strong doesn't mean you never cry." Gently, he kissed the top of her head. "You're the most incredible woman I've ever met in my life. You're smart, and brave. I see that in you. But, crying's a part of being human. It shows how big your heart is. And, having heart's just as important as strength, maybe more so."

Saffron felt surprised by the tidal wave of emotion washing over her.

Luckily, Colton's soothing had the desired effects. She snuggled against him, gaining control, pushing her worries back into the dark where she repressed the bleak thoughts of her psyche.

Breathing deeply, she thought of her morning mantra, *This moment is a gift.*

"Thank you," she said calmly. "It's just really hard sometimes... knowing what I know. I want to save everyone so badly, but I have no earthly idea how to do it." A loud sigh escaped her. "Feeling powerless doesn't sit well with me."

"Ha!" Colton said, surprising her by laughing.

"Well then," he said teasingly, "you've had one hell of a week. First the storm, then your mom. That's a lot for anyone to handle." He gave her a comforting hug. "Don't be too hard on yourself," he said. "Just remember, you aren't alone."

Saffron's heart squeezed uncomfortably inside her chest.

If you love him, Saffy, said an inner voice which sounded a lot like her mother, *if you love him, then you have to tell him Everything.*

Again, she choked back tears, her throat burning.

Okay, she decided, *if he's gonna be my partner in the days ahead, then he's got to know what's coming.*

This time there was no holding back the tsunami.

"It's-just-that-I-really-really-like-you!" she released in a rapid stream. "Hell, I could love you...AND IT'S ALL FUUUUUCKED!" she screamed. "We're all gonna get fucked so, so hard! One way or another, in greater degrees for some than others, but no one's gonna go untouched by the changes that're coming, my friend. No one. People, animals, plants, insects...everything's going to start dying, prolifically, in our lifetime."

"D-do you really believe that?" Colton rasped.

"Oh, yeah, big time," she responded emphatically. "With the amount of shit we have to accomplish...with so few people helping out...and in the short amount of time we have left to respond? Oh, yeah, like fucked-in-the-ass-with-a-red-hot-poker-and-no-lube kind of fucked."

The cussing relieved some of Saffron's pent-up anxiety, like a pressure valve. She felt mildly steadier, less like she was going to keep on sobbing. Unfortunately, there were more truths to reveal.

Dejectedly, she shared her most pessimistic thought, "It'll take a miracle to save us."

"S-so," Colton stammered, "what do you think's going to happen?"

"Oh, a bunch of stuff," she said. "Economic collapse, for starters. Inflation out the wazoo. Major failures in infrastructure and agriculture. Plus, floods, rising seas and wildfires."

She stared at the ceiling, but her vision of the destruction to come was far out beyond the little house.

"There's going to be more heatwaves and mega-storms all around the world," she said. "Everyone's gonna hide in their air-conditioned homes, their fucking McMansions, most likely cooled by a fossil-fuel-based power plant, which will only make it worse, by the way, like a lobster turning up its own heat as it slowly and unknowingly cooks itself to death. Oh," she added sneeringly, "and let's not forget, more war. Potentially, lots more war. Maybe with drones.

"And, where there's war, instability and hopelessness," she said incongruently with the bubbly enthusiasm of a high school cheerleader or a game show assistant, "there's always more rape and human trafficking!" Sarcastically, she broke out into jazz hands. "So, yeah, it's gonna be a fucking party, especially for people with vaginas."

"Oh my god," Colton said, looking ill, "the most likely scenario is the worst case scenario? Total collapse around the world?!"

"Ha! I wish," she responded sharply. "I think I told you this before, that if there's a failure at that extreme of a level, like, if EMP's are used and modern civilization comes to a screeching halt, well, that nightmare scenario may be our best chance to survive, as horrific as it sounds. Currently, it's the only solution that'll drastically cut back on our oil and gas consumption the way the planet needs us to.

"Either way," she said morosely, "millions of people will die, but at least with a total collapse, the destabilization of the climate might stop."

This was the part of the equation which had always tripped Saffron's neurons; the notion that collapse, or entropy, was inevitable. It chafed at her, because it didn't feel true. Somewhere, she prayed people were coming to the same conclusions as her, that destruction did not have to come to pass.

It infuriated her to think humanity was allowing itself to slip towards dystopia instead of bringing more positive actions into the world. Deep in her soul, a more kind and ethical way still felt possible, but neither her left nor right hemisphere of her brain had yet come up with an answer.

Colton was silent, barely breathing, as if turned to stone.

"Unfortunately," she continued, sighing sadly, "the measures we've taken have been insufficient, with some solutions overturned too soon. Add in the fact we've not yet developed enough effective technologies to reverse the damages and, well...it doesn't look good. As of today, global warming is currently irreversible, and it's just going to speed up."

She paused, swallowing a gigantic lump in her throat, and said, "It breaks my heart to tell you this."

Her mouth was parched, musty with weed, wine, semen and secrets. Already, the topic of conversation was exhausting her. Saffron longed to change the subject, but an image formed in her mind of an hour glass, with sand running mercilessly out of it.

Rip off the goddamn bandaid, she yelled at herself. *Just do it!*

"Without major changes," she said, "and I mean *major*, it's likely over seventy-five percent of the planet will be extinct in a hundred years or less...and it's gonna be a more dangerous place."

"Boy," Colton responded queasily, "you're really cynical in the morning."

"What I'm cynical about," Saffron replied somberly, "is the ability of billions of people to collectively get their shit together in a fast enough manner to count. It's a simple fact of life that human beings move at a snail's pace. There's too much inertia in our systems. Bureaucratic red tape rules the day!" She laughed bitterly. "I mean, we aren't total Vogons, like those aliens in the book I gave you, but we're damn close when it comes to making massive changes like the ones we need to take."

"I've only gotten to page twenty-seven," Colton said, "but I know the creatures you're talking about. I can see the resemblance."

"And it's made worse," she continued, "by the bullshit coming from those who stand to profit from our ignorance." She rolled away from him, onto her back, and threw her hands up in exasperation. "Plus, most people are still asleep! It seems like folks are perfectly content to let everything degenerate and rot around them...their bodies, the planet, their minds, while they get lattes and stare at screens most of the day.

"Meanwhile," she said with disgust, "the *real* world...the one and only place we can actually live, crumbles and destructs around us."

"But, people have rallied before," Colton said optimistically. "Many times, they've had to band together when things got desperate, and in those hard times, they found strength they never knew they had. They got the job done. I know folks are messed up nowadays, it's a damn fact, but I believe that deep down, people are basically good. It's true we haven't always acted like it, but I think we have to have more faith."

Faith versus Fear, her inner voice repeated.

Saffron had come fully awake.

Who needs coffee when you're a raving lunatic, one part of her brain mentally chastised. She knew this was a lot to dump on him. She hadn't intended to do it this way, but she couldn't stop the words from pouring out.

Telling people that much of their lives was a series of selfish choices leading everyone to their ultimate demise was not a pleasant way to wake up.

But if people don't wake up now, she thought, *when we can still save the world, when will they?*

"I don't think I'm wrong," Colton continued with the conviction of a preacher. "People've had to make difficult choices throughout history, hard decisions based on what was best for everyone. It's like, the foundation of society! Human beings are absolutely capable of making sacrifices, just think about World War II. They rationed food and gas, grew victory gardens, and a whole bunch of other stuff to conserve resources as true, patriotic Americans.

"If people could do things like that before," he argued passionately, "then we can do it again…if it's what needs to be done."

Saffron appreciated his strength of character and belief in his fellow man. She too thought the human race was capable of moving mountains when necessary. Nonetheless, she looked piercingly deep into his eyes before speaking, not wanting to hurt him more, but needing him to understand the full scope of the problem.

"Yes, you're right CJ," she responded quietly, "but people back then at least *knew* there *was* a war. They had leaders who inspired them to unite for a common purpose, to come together and make sacrifices for the common good."

Scathingly, she said, "We've been living in an undeclared state of emergency for decades. It hasn't mattered who's been in the White House. Since the 70's, the critical nature of our situation has been mocked, ignored, or downplayed over and over and over again. The vast majority of people have no earthly idea the intensity of the changes that are coming, nor how quickly. They only have an inkling. Plus, millions more are purposely keeping their heads in the sand, enjoying their everyday little luxuries and routines like pampered poodles, ignoring that the sky is falling.

"So, you tell me," she said, "how're we to come together as a team, to fix this Hot Mess, when it's barely acknowledged as happening?"

This was truly her worst fear.

How would the miracle happen? How can I save the world?

Every cell in her body was screaming at her, demanding she act, willing her to do something.

And she was completely clueless on how to proceed.

Colton didn't speak.

Saffron watched his profile, letting him explore his thoughts and feelings. She remained quiet as the pain tore him up inside. Again, she felt remorseful for being so cavalier. Her own anger and resentment had hardened her, building walls inside her like scar tissue.

If you weren't scared, she wholeheartedly believed, *then you weren't educated enough, or paying attention.*

She knew for those new to the full spectrum of information it could cause feelings of helplessness and paralyzing fear; the deer-in-the-headlights response; fight or flight. In her experience, most people typically choose flight, back to sleep-walking through their regular lives with a measure or two of change but not the full-scale, life-altering variety necessary.

Having finally emptied out her Giant Download, she felt marginally lighter and her training kicked in; she had had years of developing coping skills, too.

Today is a good day, breathe in and center.

This moment is a gift, breathe out and ground.

Sat Nam, open to truth and wisdom.

Saffron felt herself gaining control and offered a prayer for herself, for Colton, and for the whole world.

Angels, Jesus, God, Goddess?...Whomever's out there, please, give us strength.

The silence was interrupted by the *knock knock knock* of a woodpecker beating his beak on a tree.

"Isn't there anything we can do?" Colton asked with anguish in his voice. Unspilled tears shimmered like stars in his eyes. "There has to be something we can do," he whispered.

"Lots of people have been trying," she responded gravely, "but nothing we're doing right now is slowing it down, let alone reversing it. I'm sorry. Unfortunately, that's the honest-to-God truth."

Colton stayed stoic for a heartbeat before releasing his torment. He grabbed Saffron, not hurting her, but on the edge of it.

"H-how could we've let this happen," he sobbed, his voice muffled by her shoulder.

"Oh, pussycat," she comforted, making quiet, shushing sounds and smoothing his hair. "No one knew ahead of time, and when we did know what we'd done, well, we were addicted to cars and electricity, plastic and junk food, not to mention our unhealthy obsession with wealth and materialism. We're such full-blown junkies that the gears of the machine are seriously hard to stop. Plus, the people with the vast majority of money and influence are keeping us right on track, straight towards our destruction."

Consume, consume, consume, she thought bitterly, *like a locust plague.*

"But, there has to be something we can do?!? I can't," Colton faltered before steadying himself. "I-I can't let this be my legacy. Hell, no! I was not raised to be a person who takes things lying down. When you make a mess, you clean it up. You take care of your family, your land, and you protect 'em!"

Curled on the bed with Colton, releasing the intense thoughts she held, was cathartic for Saffron. Having him be open, responsive to her, was the bonus she needed, a balm for her worries.

"I'm so sorry, CJ," she said. "I've got so few people that'll let me talk about this. My parents shut me down every time I get too dark and scared about the future. I guess, in many ways, they're probably right."

"Well," he said, "I'm glad you're talking about this."

He suddenly stopped cold, his eyes widening as a smile grew on his face.

"Well, um," he said chuckling, "maybe not *glad* exactly, but, we can't fight what we're too scared to face."

Saffron giggled and her heart swelled.

The light seemed to come back into the room.

"You're right," she said. "I seriously have to do better than this. I'm way too powerful a manifester to let my thoughts run wild with negatives. Together, we've got to do better at imagining we can fix this, that we'll find a way to survive and thrive, to prosper, maybe even evolve." She felt her energy field expanding. "Soon, we'll wake up and rise as stewards of the Earth."

"We'll be both saved and saviors," he added with conviction.

"Yes!" she exclaimed, her head collapsing onto Colton's chest from weariness.

Holding him in her arms was already so natural. She felt relief and a beautiful sense of familiarity. As she moved her fingers absentmindedly across his chest, delicately touching the light hairs, she looked up at his kind face. His eyes peered at hers with an immense longing. She kissed his lips, which were mildly salty from their combined tears.

"We still have time," she said. "Not a lot, but some. I'm sorry I'm so doomy and gloomy."

"It's okay," he said. "My mom used to tell us to expect the best and prepare for the worst. We've had bug-out bags in case of emergencies ever since the hurricane, with matches and other survivalist gear. There's another bag with ammunition and firearms stored near it...just in case." His voice deepened. "'Never again will the Miller family be caught unprepared,' my dad's preached." Sighing dismally, he added, "I can't imagine being less prepared than we are."

"Your mom's a smart lady," she said. "All of us need to dream of the world we want to see, and prepare ourselves for the worst case. Individuals *have* to keep making the best choices they can until the top people in charge take ownership for the role they play."

"Well," Colton said angrily, "this's horse shit. I'm not gonna to give in so easily. The world will have to come at me pretty hard and heavy to knock me down."

Saffron pictured him at a rodeo; a cowboy hat set purposefully on his head, a wild stallion beneath him, his leather gloves gripping the reins, waiting for the opening of the gate when he would be tested.

"There're still plenty of folks in this world," he said with a resolute, Texas drawl, "who know how to roll up their damn sleeves, git dirty, an' git shit done. I think you're underestimating people. So...what do you think, Little Miss Brainiac? In your mind, what's the *perfect* scenario? What *should* we be dreaming of? Give it to me!"

"You're right," she said, feeling stronger. "Law of Attraction 101, baby. Shine your light on what you want to attract, and tell the negative to go fuck itself."

The last remnant of dark cloud hanging over her seemed to blow away.

"Well," she said earnestly, "I'd love to see more churches involved, preaching universal love, you know? Less polarization and division, and more about how we're all related. They need to recognize the earth is a gift, too, which shouldn't be squandered, and that loving your neighbor as yourself means having a habitable planet for us all. I kind of think if Christian churches spoke up, as well as Muslim, Buddhist, Hindu, Jewish, and all the denominations in between, it would make a hu-u-u-u-uge difference! Every single congregation in America needs to demand it."

"Well," Colton said, not looking convinced. "I love my church, but admittedly, they aren't always the most welcoming to differing opinions. Sadly, they're framing the coming disaster as a punishment for sinners and a chance for only the righteous to ascend. I don't know how that's going to change."

"Me either," Saffron admitted sadly.

Undaunted, she added, "I also love to picture everyone driving around in clean cars. No more gas guzzlers. Plus, wind turbines and solar panels everywhere! Rain barrels, too. And, I wish more people would get back to gardening, with dirt under their fingernails like we used to. It'd be wonderful to see a new renaissance in agriculture. using old-time methods which are better for us and the planet as well as adding new tech like hydroponics.

"Honestly, it's only been a handful of generations since this knowledge has been lost. I think we can get it back."

She envisioned fields with tall corn and sprawling squashes, patches of tomatoes on trellises, and rows of vibrant chili peppers next to clumps of marigolds and sunflowers; honeybees merrily tending and toiling over it all.

"Just think how amazing it'd be to see gardens and greenhouses everywhere," she said excitedly. "In the inner cities and throughout the suburbs. Green, living roofs and painted-white ones, too, and more bermed houses for better temperature control. I don't know. Maybe we'll wrap the real energy hogs in straw bales." She paused and chewed her bottom lip. "I may not know all the answers, but I do know people need to get creative on how to heat and cool their homes naturally, without the help of power plants."

And, if they don't wanna do the work, she thought, *they'd better get up off their asses and convince their local governments to switch immediately to renewable energy.*

This was something her ex-Marine father would frequently complain about. Except, he had a tendency to say things like, *They'd better do it ASAP, or else things are gonna get FUBARed.*

Saffron almost snorted, remembering her mother's typical reply, *Yes, dear, it'll be quite the SNAFU.*

Military humor.

Unknowingly, she smiled and Colton smiled in return.

"And definitely," she said, "we should return to a more locally-based economy. San Juan County and places across the country need to become more self-sustaining, making and selling the stuff we need, in our own backyards, rather than shipping stuff in from all over the world. All that does is send our money out of our county, hell, out of the country, funneling it into the hands of millionaires in faraway places, to their offshore bank accounts in Panama. All it's doing is sucking away our financial security like a Hoover vacuum!

"And that reminds me, people've *got* to reduce their waste. Too much energy is devoted to making products we barely, if ever use, and then we simply toss it into the trash. We get rid of so much on a daily basis, it's obscene. What we need are more things that last!"

"So far," Colton said, "none of this sounds impossible."

"Last thing," Saffron said as the vision of a brighter future took hold, "we need to protect our oceans and focus on habitat restoration. Conservation is key, planting millions of new trees for carbon capture and increased oxygen production. I've been interested in a project like that for awhile."

At the moment, she only sent small donations to organizations which were involved in doing this important work.

"See," he said with a pleased grin, "there *are* things we can do."

"Yes, but to truly fix it," she warned, "we're going to have to go up against some very powerful people. This world is run by the wealthy, not the 99%. Oil and gas tycoons, bankers, CEO's, and don't forget the good old-fashioned oligarchs."

She had meant it to sound silly or lighthearted, but failed. None of this was funny.

"I don't think they want the world to change," she said sadly, "or else, it's possible, they're as ignorant of their actions and consequences like everyone else is."

Some of them, however, are guilty as sin, she thought to herself but didn't say out loud. She had long thought of these people as The Architects of Disaster.

"Well, I'm not goin' down without a fight," Colton twanged. "I'll personally go to DC and give 'em a piece of my mind if I have to."

His stomach interrupted and grumbled loudly.

"Hey, I've got an idea we can put into action right now," he said, getting out of bed and reaching for his underwear on the floor.

"How would you like some breakfast?" he asked. "I'm gonna cook and you can have time to yourself for yoga, or meditating, or whatever you want to do. Afterwards, we can pick those prickly pears. Then, maybe, you can let me ravish you again before going to visit your mom."

Saffron's heart chakra was about to explode. She kissed him appreciatively on the lips and said with a squeal, "Yes, please!"

If there was ever a competition for the best in the head, heart and cock category, she would nominate Colton James Miller without hesitation.

Triumphantly, the voice inside her said, *The more you love, the more you'll gain.*

"Do not be daunted by the enormity
of the world's grief. Do justly now.
Love mercy now. Walk humbly now.
You are not obligated to complete the work,
but neither are you free to abandon it."
- The Talmud

Chapter 23: Lazy Sunday Morning

Saffron took Colton's advice and went to the mesa for her morning exercise routine. Colton stayed behind to make a cowboy breakfast on the coals outside the kitchen. The act of cooking turned out to be a blessing, giving him time to work on his thoughts.

Colton pictured the world Saffron had described and thought it sounded challenging but also satisfying. He thought again about his woodworking skills and the different items he could make. There was already one special project he had in mind.

But, he thought, *getting others to adopt these ideas is gonna be tricky.*

The biggest problem he could see was his family's line of work. He was legitimately concerned how much backlash they were going to give him, and how they'd react to some of the changes to be made in a short period of time.

The prospect of talking with them about it made him nauseous.

Colton loved his family; they were really good people, hardworking, friendly, neighborly; qualities which were shared by most of the people he knew. The last thing he wanted was for everyone to be ambushed, taken by surprise, as their way of life started collapsing around them with sky-high temperatures turning into higher utility bills, worsening health, and threats to ranchers and farmers.

In his opinion, they deserved to be prepared for the future, not blindsided, as the proverbial rug was yanked from under their feet.

But, he pondered, flipping the bacon which sizzled in a cast iron pan, its pungent perfume making his mouth water, *how can I possibly convince them?*

The tea kettle whistled like a scream.

While Saffron's Darjeeling tea steeped, he sat in the Adirondack chair, contemplating how to make his 'argument'. Listening to the wind in the trees next to the ancient-looking adobe, his thoughts again turned to life in the past. He'd always loved history, which had a habit of repeating itself, like a rise and a fall, the breath of time.

The one constant in life was change.

Life in small towns, however, was inherently slow-moving by nature. Colton's upbringing had been stable and loving, surrounded by people whose families could trace their lineages in the area for decades to thousands of years depending on whether they were Indigenous, Spanish, or Anglo.

People around him had deep roots and relationships with each other and the land.

In some ways, he thought, *many here already live an eco-friendly lifestyle.*

Still, he predicted they were going to balk at any mention of change.

Letting go of oil and gas was going to be hard, but as he saw it, folks had had innumerable occupations over the centuries which simply didn't exist anymore; ice block delivery men; telegraph operators; riders of the Pony Express and the stable hands who'd helped them.

Throughout history, there was a long, long list of antiquated employment.

It couldn't have been easy, he reasoned, *for any of them to've seen their livelihoods replaced by new inventions and society's changing whims.*

Here and now, it seemed poised to happen again.

Colton had learned from the hurricane and flood that life was not static and could change on a dime. The supercell storm, and the damages it had wrought, only reinforced his conviction.

He desperately wanted his loved ones to know changes were happening in the environment whether they were paying attention or not, believed it or not, liked it or not.

It was real.

His grandfather had taught him no one could control all of the things that happened to them in life, but people could always decide how they wanted to react. He thought about his options; giving in to despair, turning his back and keeping quiet, or working for a more positive outcome, towards a happier and safer one.

Briefly, he wondered what Grandpa Miller would have done if he'd known more of the details and facts of climate change sooner, if he'd understood better how fossil fuels were turning the world into an oven, and how the tipping points were making it worse.

If he'd known the real story, he wondered with strained optimism, *would he've committed to doing what was difficult, but right, for the younger generations?*

Colton felt strongly about taking action, to do something important to help the future unfold closer to the vision Saffron had described, rather than a surreal nightmare. His ideas were still vague, but they were burrowing into his mind. The seed had been planted, and it wanted to grow into a plan to influence as many people as possible.

The smell of overcooked food brought him back to the moment, and to the ironic metamorphosis of his scrambled eggs into an omelet.

Sometimes, he thought with a bitter smile, *things don't turn out exactly as planned.*

Wanting to surprise Saffron, he used the small picnic basket and a thermos to bring the tea, breakfast, and leftover desert up the mesa. As he walked along the path, gazing out at the view, he remembered something she'd said on their first day together.

There's beauty and perfection in the little things in life, too.

He realized how right she was. While big actions were necessary at this time, so were the small ones. It was equally important to spend time in the present moment doing little, loving things for others and appreciating what was before you.

When he reached the top, he found her standing in the middle of the labyrinth, undressed, her back towards him, arms and torso stretching to the sky, toes barely touching the earth. Seeing her nude body, unabashedly basking in the sunshine, facing the expansive desert as if offering herself to the universe, Colton felt a cord strumming deeply within his center, in concert with his racing heart.

Certainty settled into his mind.

I'm going to marry this girl.

It was a dizzying thought; a simple truth; no doubt whatsoever.

He watched her for a moment, his free-spirited lover, etching the memory into his mind so he would never forget the precise moment he knew he was in love for the first time, and potentially, the last.

"Woman," he said when he could find his voice, "you could stop a man's heart and make him keel over dead." Shaking his head, he added, "I swear, I honestly think you're gonna kill me."

Saffron turned and faced him, grinning from ear to ear, her strawberry blonde locks hovering above her bare breasts.

"Aww, Colt," she drawled in a southern-belle fashion, "you say the niii-cest things."

She bent to pick up her sundress, ass in the air, and slowly slipped it over her head, sans panties; a reverse strip-tease.

"Damn," he said, whistling appreciatively. "How'd I get so lucky to find a girl with a strong heart, a sharp mind, and a body that makes a man sweat and go weak in the knees?"

"HHC, babycakes," she said, walking slowing towards him, a sylph, stepping over the stones of the path.

"Huh," he asked quizzically.

"Never mind," she said, barefoot and tippy-toed as she nuzzled him, her arms around his neck. "I'm the lucky one," she whispered, her lips hovering over his. "You're quite the catch, Colton James."

Hungrily, she kissed him, her soft lips and tongue exploring his, her breath hot and hitched.

His arousal climbing, Colton hardened.

"Whoa, whoa, whoa," he said, disengaging from the mounting passion of the kiss. "I've got to put a warning label on you, 'May Cause Temporary Blindness'."

"Aww, sweet-talker!" she giggled, seeming to relish in his attraction to her. "Okay, Buzzkill, let's eat first," she conceded, "but we're definitely playing later on."

Both of them were ravenous; breakfast was delicious and quickly consumed. After eating, they used the basket and thick gloves to forage around the rocky terrain, skirting the sage bushes, piñon trees and chamisas, looking for the purple cactus fruits.

Everywhere, lizards scurried from their sunbathing spots on tiny, blue-green legs, their striped tails swishing frantically.

For half an hour, they hiked, gathering the ripest ones and leaving the rest for Mother Nature, thanking each plant as Shimásání had taught her.

When they finally returned to the house, they immediately piled into bed and engaged in more lovemaking, this time with the bright light of day pooling into the room, allowing them to delight in the visual of each other's naked bodies.

Colton didn't think he would ever tire of watching Saffron's face when she orgasmed; the unadulterated abandon she exhibited during her multiple releases, shuddering and clenching around his engorged cock while her face transformed into the epitome of rapture.

When they were ready to leave Sweetland at high noon, the Hyundai was blisteringly hot. Saffron acquiesced and turned on the air conditioning to make the drive home more comfortable. Neither one could wipe the smile off their faces.

His cheeks were starting to hurt.

As they drove, however, his concerns came back to him, most of them dark and heavy, some hopeful. He decided to start with the positive.

"I came up with an idea this morning while I was cooking," he said, squeezing Saffron's hand. "I want to make a trip with you to DC. Sittin' back and doing nothing isn't resting too well with me. If you're going to fight, then I want to fight too." He entwined his fingers with hers and kissed the back of her hand. "Will you come with me? Help me dream up a plan?"

Tears welled in Saffron's eyes.

"God," she said irritably, "why am I so weepy?" She wiped her eyes with the back of her hand and said with a catch in her voice, "I-I'd like that very much."

"The problem is," he added hesitantly, narrowing his eyes at the passing landscape as if the answers existed outside himself, "I have no clue what I'm going to say to my parents. For them, the subject of global warming, well, it's not exactly something they want to hear. In fact, they're usually pretty hostile about it.

"For that reason alone," he said sadly, "I'm skeptical how we're going to be able to convince a whole bunch of folks to change, if we can't even convince the ones that love us?"

"Well," she said, her eyes on the road ahead, "maybe it's love that'll save us?"

She paused, taking a deep breath, filling her cheeks like Louis Armstrong, then blowing the air out in a whoosh.

"I don't know," she said, "Maybe we start with this, okay? What's important to your family? What do they care about?"

"Well, that's easy," he said. "Family's everything to the Millers. The whole world could be against us, but we always have each other's backs. The Bible is important too, and the church. I thought it was interesting what you said about getting more churches involved, although I'm not sure how we're going to get them to change."

"Getting the billionaires and millionaires to change is actually the number one priority for humanity. We need new laws and treaties plus the cooperation of the companies they own. Motivating churches is just one possible way to influence the 1%ers as well as the masses, quickly and peacefully."

Her lips thinned and her brows creased in frustration.

"What people truly don't seem to realize," she said, "is the future of our entire society is at risk. Or maybe they do…but buying more guns, prepping for Doomsday, and making as much money as they can, by any means necessary, isn't problem-solving. We can't keep focusing on the symptoms of a collapsing world. Instead we need to address the causes… greed, apathy and inertia."

They drove through Farmington's historic downtown, so similar to the strip in Aztec but larger and more congested. Mom and Pop shops, small businesses, and local entrepreneurs struggled to capture the attention and loyalty of a community who routinely spent the majority of their dollars at corporate Big Box stores and on the Internet.

"We need to wake people up to the fact we're entering dangerous times," she said, "but we can still do something about it. I can't stand people talking about the Rapture, that what's happening is pre-ordained. It falsely absolves them of responsibility, making them feel superior to others, like only they'll be saved and the rest damned. But, what's happening now can be fixed! I cannot believe Christ would want us treating this planet and each other with such flagrant disregard."

The words stung Colton to the bone. He'd been raised that his faith was the right faith. Even as a kid though, he'd wondered about the great people he met who'd had different beliefs, but who were still great people.

A God who would punish them for not adhering to one particular doctrine over another had always seemed pretty callous to him.

"All we've been doing," Saffron continued, "is bickering and letting the people with the most money control the conversation. Any expert who's denied what's happening has been bought and paid for by the fossil fuel barons. Just follow the money. Back in the 90's, they actually hired lobbyists from the tobacco industry to muddy the waters and cast doubt.

For decades, they've been frighteningly successful in deceiving so many."

The fire and fight was back in her eyes, but she quickly shook it off.

"Sorry," she said, softening her tone and facial features, "I don't want to be in a shitty mood. I just have a hard time managing my anger sometimes."

The light turned from red to green. Saffron turned towards the hospital.

"As for your parents," she said gently, squeezing his hand, "you can try framing the conversation this way- tell them you love them, you're concerned about the future, especially for the youngest members, and that to be fully prepared, truly ready, they need to examine this issue as if their lives depended on it, which they actually do."

It sounded like common sense to Colton, but he said doubtfully, "I'm still not sure how they're gonna respond."

"It's okay," she said, turning to briefly offer him an understanding smile. "Just be kind and compassionate. Most people's negative reactions come from fear. Shit, everyone's scared. Liberals, conservatives, they may seem scared for different reasons, but at the heart of it, the essence is always the same. We want to feel safe, and we want those inalienable rights of life, liberty and the pursuit of happiness. This crisis puts everything in jeopardy.

"Hell," she said with a self-deprecating laugh, "I'm Little Miss Optimism and I still struggle with my fears as you witnessed this morning."

A grasshopper splatted onto the windshield, leaving a greenish smear.

It made Colton think of an expression of Asa's: *Some days you're the bug, and some days, the windshield.*

"I see your point," he said, "but my family tends to be a little more black-and-white, how-is-this-going-to-effect-me-personally kind of people. They aren't bad, but they only trust a handful of folks, and like you said, those people are telling 'em that global warming is all horseshit or ordained by the Bible."

"Just act respectfully," she suggested softly. "Be civil and operate from love. We've got to have faith that approach will work. It's what's worked in the past."

The power of her grace overwhelmed him. Sometimes he forgot she was liberal; so many of her beliefs and attitudes reflected his own values. The message, drummed into him from television and social media, that conservatives and liberals were diametrically opposed, was appearing more and more paper thin.

More lies to keep people from uniting, he thought derisively.

His urge to problem-solve grew more intense.

"Okay, let's brainstorm," he said. "What can we do to wake people up and get 'em movin'?"

Outside his window, he saw passing cars and storefronts; hundreds of people going about their daily lives, oblivious to the mounting strain on the planet, or at the very least, too overwhelmed to do anything about it.

Most of them, totally unaware they all shared a universal problem.

Universal? Colton hesitated. *Why does that sound familiar,* he wondered, then remembered Saffron's words in the aftermath of the storm. *"It's a universal law. Plato even called music a moral law. He said it gave 'soul to the universe and wings to the mind'. No matter what language we speak, we typically have this love of music in common."*

In Colton's opinion, people could use more soul in their universe and wings on their minds.

Suddenly, his seed of an idea started to sprout.

"I got it!" he said excitedly. "You're such a beautiful singer! How 'bout you write and perform a song?"

"I-I'm sorry," she said snorting. "Don't get me wrong, I'm flattered, but which one am I, Bill or Ted, in this musical version of saving the world?"

"Come on," Colton said laughingly, continuing undaunted, "seriously, what should we be tellin' folks?" He gazed at her profile, at her red-kissed golden hair, her flawless skin, and steadfast stare out the window. "I know you've thought about how to fix this."

"Ah," she snickered bitterly, "The Trillion Dollar Question! Wait, do you think I can simply snap my fingers and figure out how to wake people up, just like that?" She snapped her fingers loudly. "Or maybe wiggle my nose and POOF, it's magically all better?" Her button nose twitched like Samantha from the television show Bewitched.

Colton had seen old episodes and had thought Elizabeth Montgomery was kind of sexy.

"Well, yeah," he said winking. "Something like that. Open up those pretty lips, and dazzle me with your brilliance."

"Oh Jesus," she said tiredly, like the weight of the world was upon her. "Colton, I truly don't have a clue what else we can do. We-we've been on the brink for so long."

Her face crumpled, as if her heart was pinching inside her chest.

He hated seeing her look defeated.

"Hey!" he said, feeling a rush of inspiration. "That's it! A 'Bring Us Back From The Brink' campaign for the millionaires and billionaires! You told me you've reached out to several of them over the years. Well, let's get others involved in the same mission and present our case to them. We can rally, make it national."

"Actually," she said, biting her lip as she parked her car, "that's not a bad idea."

Colton noticed a far-distant look in her eyes, her wheels spinning like she was trying to solve a difficult math equation in her head.

"It's crazy," she said, turning to him with a smile, "but I might know someone who can help. But for now, let's go see my mom."

"Lord, make me an instrument of Your peace.
Where there is hatred, let me sow love;
where there is injury, pardon;
where there is doubt, hope;
where there is darkness, light;
and where there is sadness, joy."
- St. Francis of Assisi

Chapter 24: It's Not All Roses

Zia's hospital room was finally empty of well-wishers. Jack perched precariously on the narrow bed with her, interlacing their fingers. She looked up to see Saffron and Colton entering the room, holding hands and smiling.

"Oh, there's my Roni-kins," she said. "How was the homestead?"

"Oh, it was heaven!" Saffron said ebulliently. "The sunset was insanely beautiful, and the moon too! I brought your crystals back, totally re-energized." She squeezed her father's hand and kissed her mother's cheek. "But more importantly, how are you?"

"Well," Zia responded irritably, "it appears getting shot in the chest isn't as cool as it sounds. It's taken way more energy than I'd anticipated. I'm ready to go home."

Zia heard the complaining tone in her voice and stopped herself from pouting. Truthfully, she was grateful for the care she was receiving, the medical professionals had saved her life, but she was looking forward to when the allopathic medicine stage would end and the holistic healing process would begin.

"Umm," Jack said, barely holding back a laugh, "your mom hates the food and is jonesing bad for some spirulina and saunas." His blue eyes sparkled. "And some 'herb' would probably help," he said with a singlehanded air quote maneuver.

"Hush," Zia said, giving his nipple a pinch.

Laughing, he clumsily extricated himself from the bed.

"When're you coming home?" Saffron asked.

"The doctors say she'll be released tomorrow," Jack responded, placing a kiss on top of Zia's head, "if her O2 count is good. And she'll have to continue physical therapy for about a month or so afterwards.

"Hey," he continued, reaching out to shake Colton's hand, "I'm heading down to the cafeteria to grab some food." Turning to wrap his arms around Saffron's shoulders, he asked, "Have you two eaten?"

"I could eat again," Colton said. "I'll go with you. What can we bring back for you, ladies? Anything in particular?"

"Oh yes, please," Saffron said, nodding her head vigorously. "Anything with chickpeas, you know, garbanzos? And if they don't have that, which they probably won't, a salad will be fine."

Zia, who truly was sick of the hospital's food selection, said dejectedly, "I guess one more day won't kill me. I'll have whatever you find."

"So," Saffron began, scooting her chair close after the men had left. "How are you? Really?"

"Well, it's been nice," Zia said, "having so many people come and check on me...although, I could have done without the drama."

Newspaper and television reporters, with their cameramen in tow, had descended upon the hospital to interview the victims of the riot. In general, Zia hated sensationalism, but with it being personal, the attention had felt intrusive, almost vampiric, and familiar.

Repressing a shudder, she softly said, "I think the shooting brought up trauma from the tragedy at the high school."

On December 7th, 2017, Aztec had been blindsided by a perverse attack. That day, the troubles of the outside world had crashed with a tympanic force into the heart of the town; just another school shooting in an apparently endless stream, but this time it had happened to their own.

Zia remembered it like a slap in the face, a stabbing in the gut, a raping of innocence.

In grief and solidarity, neighbors and strangers alike had bonded, no one untouched by the senselessness of the crime. Their vulnerability had been exposed to them like a raw nerve; their sense of safety, desecrated.

Quickly however, the townspeople had found resilience; strong rods of steel in their spines inherited from their pioneering ancestors, the homesteaders, merchants, tradesmen and ranchers who'd settled in the late 1880's. Like their kin, the people living in Aztec in 2017 had not bent in defeat to their suffering.

They had stood. They had held. They were #AztecStrong.

It had given Zia hope for the future.

In her opinion, true grit was one day going to be of Darwinian importance as extinction events began occurring with increasing regularity. People who could stand tall in the face of disaster, who knew how to come together, to support one another...these, Zia believed, would be the ones the future would favor.

Sadly, she knew there'd be those who would lose heart, succumbing to their fears, who would fight their neighbors, tooth and nail, if resources ever dwindled to dangerous levels.

Unfortunately, history had proven people could sometimes respond explosively.

When they finally realize the consequences of their actions, Zia wondered, *what will they do? Will they take responsibility, cleaning up the Hot Mess, creating a better world or…would they turn on each other?*

When the world finally falls, Zia thought, *would they bend?*

Time would tell.

She looked lovingly at her only child. On more than one occasion, she'd shared these thoughts with Saffron, driven with a mother's instinctual drive to protect and prepare their young.

During her pregnancy, she'd had dreams about her daughter; and premonitions. She had never shared the details of her visions with anyone, not knowing if they were real or the product of an active imagination, but the feeling that Saffron would be a force of good in the world was forever cemented in Zia's thinking.

To strengthen her child for whatever would come, she'd taught her several things over the years, including the edicts to love unconditionally, to appreciate everything, and to care for herself. In Zia's opinion, a life without love, joy, and health would be intolerable.

With them, anything could be survived.

"So," she murmured, "I'm happy they're gone and you're here."

She noticed the clock; in less than an hour a nurse would come to take her for another walk around the ward.

Like an invalid, she thought with annoyance.

"I'm going to be okay," she added. "I'm not used to being laid low. For once, I'm feeling my age and I don't like it." She gave an overly exaggerated pout, trying to lighten her mood, while gazing at her daughter's worried face. "This experience has been humbling, but don't worry, I'll get my head on right, once I get home."

"My head hasn't been on right either," Saffron admitted. "I totally lost it this morning, a complete meltdown. To Colton's credit, he didn't go running for the hills." She paused then said, "In fact, he asked me to take a trip with him to DC for climate support."

"Oh, honey," Zia said warmly, "that's wonderful."

"I just," Saffron began, her face falling, "I-I just can't help feeling overwhelmed, mama." Tears welled up in her eyes. "W-what if it doesn't work," she asked hoarsely, "and we fail?"

Zia didn't have to ask what she meant.

Looking deeply into her daughter's pain-ridden eyes, she thought, *It must be in the air.*

Everyone Zia had encountered lately seemed twitchy and on edge. She'd been having similar conversations about the planet, and society at large, over the past few days with the Sweetwater folks as well as some of her closest friends from the Unitarian Universalist church who had come to visit.

Everyone seemed to sense impending instability; everything felt like it was speeding up, as if the ripples of anxiety coursing through town were also vibrating throughout the Collective as well.

On the news that morning, she'd watched live footage of the horrors and havoc that were occurring in Florida. Two days earlier, when a tropical storm off the Atlantic coastline was upgraded to a hurricane, every major insurance company had imposed stiff rate hikes and new surcharges due to 'high exposure risks'.

Millions of people had had their home and rental insurance premiums quadruple, or more.

Not surprisingly, the change in coverage had not been received well. The public seemed to view the act as another gross example of wealth inequality; more greedy corporations favoring the rich. The Internet, as usual, fed the panic, swimming in conspiracy theories about bankruptcy and imminent financial collapse.

Then, overnight in Miami, an integral power station had blown; terrorism had not been ruled out. In the ensuing blackout, the most violent and costly rioting the country had ever seen had erupted. Dozens had been confirmed dead and hundreds more were injured. Even some celebrities and high class elites had gotten caught in the fray.

People in the media were buzzing with the brutal rape and killing of a well-known pop star and the disappearance of a wealthy heiress.

Adding to the volatile situation, Hurricane Cassandra was expected to land on top of the beleaguered city within hours. Things were predicted to go from bad to worse, and it was already pure chaos.

With all these thoughts running through her head, Zia's batteries felt drained. Once again she yearned for the sacred space of her home, but she couldn't leave yet. In the moment, making her child feel loved and supported was her number one priority. She mustered up her remaining inner strength.

"Darling," she said, her voice coming out strong and level, "every day you show up, that you do your work, living simply and reaching out to others, just being an example of what's possible, that's the opposite of failure." She squeezed Saffron's hand reassuringly. "The world's going to shift and change no matter what happens, and some of those changes are going to be positive, even in a shitstorm. Focus on that. Always on the good."

"I know, I know, I'm sorry," Saffron said with exasperation. "It's just that…CO2 levels hit 450…and, I feel so lost."

Zia's heart froze.

She'd reacted similarly when she'd received the news from Jack; her chest tightening, rendered immobile like a stone.

From my birth until now, Zia thought sullenly, *the world's witnessed an increase in atmospheric carbon of 327 to 450 ppm. Over a hundred points.*

And it totally pissed her off.

The world she had borne her daughter into was unlike any that previous generations had ever experienced, in a country where the masses were inadequately prepared.

A twinge of guilt coursed through her body. She fought back against the soul-ripping fear she'd made a mistake by damning her only child to an unforgiving world. She fought off the dark thought and switched her thinking immediately to more positive ones, allowing her unfettered and deep love for her daughter to fill the room.

If she could make Saffron's pain go away, she would. However, that was never going to be an option, so she could only respond by empowering Saffron to deal with whatever may come.

"I know, honey," she said gently, "but remember, you're so much more prepared than millions of other people, perhaps billions. Just imagine how scary it is, or will be, when the reality of the Hot Mess finally hits home."

When the fresh water runs out and the crops begin to fail.

Deep in her marrow, Zia sensed humanity was approaching a tipping point in consciousness.

"I-I've done my best over the years," she said, her voice cracking minutely, "trying to teach you all I can."

Every parent yearns to protect their babies. Knowing how shitty the world was going to become had spurred Zia to go above and beyond with her only child.

"All those chores," she said, "those lessons to prepare you for any scenario, we did that because we love you. You've got a nice toolkit of knowledge you'll be able to share with others." Zia smiled, her confidence returning. "I know in my gut you'll do amazing things."

"That's just it!" Saffron said in exasperation. "What amazing thing can I do to fix it all?!?"

"Oh, Saffy," Zia said, deflating, unable to wipe her daughter's worry away with a wave of her hand. "It's never going to be just one thing," she said. "It's going to be lots and lots of small things with some bigger ones thrown in for good measure.

"Go to DC," she recommended. "Be seen, try to be heard. Then come home and do what you know is right. Meditate, pray, make music, grow food and preserve it for winter. Simply help others and educate them whenever you can." *Be the Light, my love.* "That's all anyone can do."

"But I feel drawn to do so much more!" she said.

"I've always known this about you, Saffy," Zia said fondly, "you were old when you were born, an ancient soul. I trust, and I hope you will too, that when the time is right, you'll know exactly what to do."

She could see the pressure bearing down on Saffron and hoped she could lift some of the burden off of her. Repositioning herself on the bed, she looked her daughter straight in the eyes.

"Do you know how much grief I got from my family back in Chicago when I let you leave home at sixteen to see the world?" Zia asked. "None of them could wrap their heads around it." She snorted derisively. "Hah, they were never that understanding of my own choice to leave and 'drop out'," she said sarcastically, making air quotes. "But when you ventured off, they flipped out at a whole new level."

Saffron sniffled and let out a small laugh.

"Grandma gave me grief, too," she admitted. "In retrospect, I was probably a little rude. But, when I get an idea in my head…"

"It's hard to let it go," Zia finished saying. "I know. You inherited that trait from me. The point is, I was never worried. Well,…a little bit. But I had to have faith we raised you with enough self-reliance and tenacity to face the challenges in life. Plus, we were always a phone call away. I knew then, as I know now, you needed to spread those wings of yours, because child, they're as big as the room." She squeezed Saffron's hand and admitted, "Containing you was never going to be an option."

Outside the room, they heard the heart-wrenching sound of someone crying out in pain or distress. One of the nurses rushed past their room to help.

"However," Zia added, "even though you've always been ready to take on the world, we're only human which means we can never completely know what will come. You ask if we will succeed, or fail," she said as the sounds of suffering from the hall wound down. In the relative silence that followed, she answered truthfully, "I don't know."

Zia wanted to instill this message deep within her child and to everyone else on the planet if she had the chance. "We simply have to have faith, and hold ourselves accountable, doing our best to live each day as peacefully and harmoniously as we can. To leave each day a bit better by making more positive choices and less negative ones. Hopefully, others will follow our lead."

Saffron took a deep steadying breath, as if her footing was materializing back under her. She looked stronger.

"Okay, mama," she said. "I'll keep trying to be brave." She kissed Zia on the cheek. "I love you. I'm glad you're coming home tomorrow. I've missed you."

Jack and Colton walked back into the room. Both seemed relaxed and comfortable in each other's company. The remnants of a shared joke hung between them.

"Who's up for some sushi?" Jack asked.

"Hospital sushi?" Zia scoffed with disdain. "Now, that's what I call bravery."

"Come sit with me. No agenda, no censors.
Just you and me and our favorite songs.
Let's talk about how strange the world is,
and what the fuck we're actually doing here,
and then laugh until it doesn't scare us anymore."
- Brooke Hampton

Chapter 25: Sunday Night Jam

The air was golden, its dusky half-light infusing every face, leaf, and stone in Sweetwater with a magical glow as the sun lowered towards the ridge line of the bluffs. After another scorching day, the evening temperature had lowered to a drowsy warmth like a tepid bath. Bees buzzed drunkenly around the lavender flowers of the Russian sage bushes; their little legs, fat with pollen to take back to the hive before the sun set.

Contentedly, Colton lounged next to Saffron in the pavilion, full from the delicious, farm-to-table dinner he'd had in the large yurt.

Satiated, the whole group had gone outside to relax into a carefree idleness before night fully fell. Some sat in chairs under the sunshades, continuing their dinner time discussions. Alice Cardeñas, the resident pottery artist, was in the pasture doing tai chi with Marlowe and a few others. Lydia and Nick, the schoolteachers, were playing a game of frisbee near the entrance. Kristen and Clay were lazily swaying on a bench swing near the Kokopelli sculpture; they each shared a yawn before sharing a joint.

Weaving its way around the gathering of people was a petite grey and white tabby, purring and slinking from one hand to another, while Bucky the Cat rested regally on a plum tree branch, surveying his kingdom.

Colton watched Telsa the Butt-Sniffer and a border collie competing with one another, sprinting between Lydia and Nick with pure canine playfulness, hoping to catch the frisbee on an errant throw. In their favor, one out of four always seemed to go blessedly off course.

Relaxing in the late afternoon light, he took in the jovial energy around him; the entire Sweetwater crowd had been in a vibrant, celebratory mood, full of anticipation. He could only imagine what it would be like tomorrow when Zia truly returned.

His first day as a non-virgin had been an eventful one, full of new people, new friends, and some new thoughts and possibilities. At the hospital, Jack had been very responsive to Colton's interest in an apprenticeship in woodworking and carpentry. In fact, he'd looked really pleased by the idea, smiling warmly, shaking his hand and touching his shoulder. The experience had made Colton think of the good-hearted character, Charles Ingalls, from 'Little House on the Prairie'.

To his relief, Jack had made him feel welcome, and capable of anything.

Colton and Saffron sat next to each other around a blackened fire pit in the center of the pavilion. On top of the charcoaled remains was a troop of green army men, their weapons drawn, surrounding a large Godzilla, its claws raised triumphantly as if it'd been responsible for incinerating the landscape and toy soldiers. Saffron told him she suspected the 'art installation' was her best friend's handiwork.

"It fits her twisted sense of humor," she said.

Lorelei had been friendly during dinner, charming and lively, asking Colton questions, laughing and making him feel included. After dinner, she'd returned to her tiny house to grab her fiddle.

The sky over Navajo Dam inked from blue towards black. Venus appeared as the bright evening star to the east as the day's last light disappeared past the horizon. Onstage, solar lights twinkled; many others, hidden beside the paths and clustered under trees, shone like incandescent beacons for sprites and fairie-folk.

Lorelei came back and took a seat next to Saffron. John Perry sat down on a stool and began tuning his banjo. The rest of the group trickled into the circle, some with instruments in hand, others without.

Saffron's guitar, a well-worn and well-loved Gibson, had been resting at her feet in anticipation of the nighttime jam session. She took it out of its case and strummed, its strings perfectly in tune.

The group began to play a blend of old-fashioned, classic roots music; folk, bluegrass and country; a perfect mixture of yesteryear's traditionals and more modern-day Americana. The music was ethereal and mesmerizing one moment, frenetic and complex the next. Voices melted in harmony. Fingers deftly plucked strings as hands slapped thighs in rhythmic concert. The night air pulsed with the beat of their feet stomping on the sun-baked bricks.

Each person took turns calling out a song to play. In between selections, laughter and camaraderie intermingled, the joy of performance evident on each person's face. On Saffron's turn, she choose 'Gospel Train', a song she'd seen performed by a band called Front Country at a folk festival one summer. She told Colton it had become one of her favorites.

In a clear, strong voice, she sung, *"I woke up with heaven on my mind / I woke up with heaven on my mi-i-i-ind / Lord, I dreamed of a train, of a glory bound trai-ai-ain / I wonder, will my children be on that train?"*

The night air stilled in an attempt to listen.

Colton found it impossible to take his eyes off of her. Goosebumps rose on his forearms as the hard-driving, gospel-inspired, blues-infused song poured over him. Slowly however, a droning sound intruded, building from a tiny whine to a loud roar.

Not far above Sweetwater, a small airplane, its running lights blinking in the darkness, flew over the property before circling back and buzzing them a second time. The sound of its whirling propellers overwhelmed the band of musicians, disrupting their play as they stopped to watch it fly back down the valley towards the dam.

John Perry craned his head with the rest of the gang and said in his dead-pan way, "I don't know if anyone else's thinking this, but low flying planes never worked out well in Hitchcock movies."

"It is a tad bit ominous," George Harper said, observing the plane's disappearing taillights.

"O-o-ominous?" John Perry spluttered, his eyes wide behind his glasses. "It's downright unnerving!" Suddenly he jumped up, frog-legged, his banjo held high to shield his head, and made a run for his dome house yelling, "Duck and cover!"

The group just laughed and joked that the jam session was apparently over. Everyone packed up their belongings, said good night to one another, then headed to the coolness of their beds.

Colton was left alone with Saffron. The Milky Way glistened above as they walked towards her empty house.

"Look, I know this's been a crazy time in my life," she said, "but honestly, I don't want it to end. Would you like to spend the night with me?"

"I'd like to spend my life with you," he confessed, the words coming out of his mouth before realizing what he was saying. "Well, I, ah," he stammered, blushing inconspicuously in the dark, "I-I hadn't planned on letting that slip out so early."

Saffron launched herself into his arms, her happiness and passion delivered through her kiss.

It took an amazing act of strength for Colton to disengage from the embrace instead of following his instincts to carry her inside.

As they released, the air rushed out of both of their lungs.

"I'm sorry, Roni," he said as he kissed her forehead. "I'd love to stay here with you, believe me, but," he said regretfully, "it's probably best I go home."

No sense postponing the inevitable, he thought.

There was so much he wanted to say to his family, and probably a good deal more they wanted to say to him.

"Please, please, pretty please," Saffron pleaded, batting her eyelashes coyly. "With sugar on top," she purred.

Colton gazed down at her Betty Boop pout and wanted nothing more than to make love to her again. The pain of goodbye was crushing his sternum; his attraction to her momentarily rooting his feet to the ground.

"That's quite the invitation," he said, his voice a baritone of desire. "But I've got work tomorrow, and some family discussions to have." His pulse quickened with anxiety over the upcoming talk. "The faster I can unravel myself from my current situation," he said, "the quicker I can spend more time with you. Your dad offered me a job here, working on mechanical things and honing my woodworking skills. I said yes, but only if it was okay with you."

"It's real," she whispered.

"What?" he asked with confusion. "Climate change?"

She burst out laughing.

"Well, duh!" she said, teasingly pushing his shoulder. "No, silly, I meant *this,* us…it's real for me." Her blue eyes mirrored back starshine. "I just thought you should know."

There it was, beautiful confirmation; the truth spoken out loud.

"It's real for me, too," he said, kissing her goodnight.

"Come back to me soon," she said, walking up the path to her house, her hand trailing delicately along the soft folds of the tall iris flowers. "We've got a lot to look forward to."

Colton got in his car for the long ride home.

Tiny lights shone from several of the little houses that dotted the immense property. The bluffs towered massively behind them, an impenetrable force. Inside the still pasture, the animals sheltered and slumbered. Above, the night sky was a canopy of glimmering stars.

It already felt like home.

Driving out the gate through the thick adobe walls, Colton couldn't help thinking, *I am seriously going to marry this girl.*

"Give us strength to use our past
to help us persevere in the times to come."
- Bryn Divine, Invocation speech
at Aztec High School 2017

Chapter 26: I Don't Like Mondays

Saffron's day started with an uncomfortable weight in her abdomen, a heaviness in her center, followed by the unmistakable cramp of her period starting.

Well, she thought, reaching for a reusable cloth pad, *at least it had the courtesy to wait until after my sex-filled weekend. Thank God for small favors!*

Thanking God made her remember how much gratitude she had for her mother's recovery; for meeting Colton; and for her own life.

Thank You for the big ones, too.

Zia and Jack were expected home later in the day. The whole Sweetwater group was planning an epic feast. Saffron had overheard someone talking about paella. Picturing the party to come, she thought about her recent recreational and sugary indulgences and realized it'd been a few months since she'd done a cleanse.

It'd be smart to detox, she thought pragmatically, feeling mildly bloated, *but…not until after the party. Now's a time to celebrate.*

As a compromise, she mixed a wheatgrass and barley drink for the drive to work.

Mondays were her day to spend in town. She had two yoga classes scheduled, one in the morning and one in the late afternoon, which left time between for errands, lunch and the library.

The drive from Navajo Dam to Aztec took twenty-seven minutes, ambling along a lonesome strip of road surrounded by unfettered, high desert beauty; rocky outcroppings, lonely junipers, and mountains to the north. She always enjoyed the view, but today she felt even more profoundly affected; her spirit was in the clouds, ready to embrace the day.

The tiny downtown was lined with historic buildings, erected in the late 1800's and early 1900's during the Great Migration west. The shops had a way of coming and going, but overall, there was a stable variety of rural, small town businesses, including a feed store for local livestock, barbershops and beauty parlors, art galleries and knick-knack stores, as well as a florist, brewery, guitar shop and a handful of eateries. The yoga studio was at the end of the strip.

Saffron neared the parking lot and saw two police vehicles with a small group of people clustered nearby. The owner, Susan, was dressed in baggy sweatpants and a long t-shirt like she'd just gotten out of bed; her face was a white mask of disbelief.

Very un-zen-like, Saffron thought, walking with trepidation from her car.

"What's going on?" she asked, looking from one person to another.

"Someone-van-vandalized-our-building," Susan choked as if the words hurt to say. "This is Saffron LeMay," she said, turning towards the policemen. "She teaches here on Mondays."

"Ma'am," said one officer with a crew cut and a baby face, "we're asking everyone. Where were you last night?"

"At home," Saffron responded quickly. "I live at the Sweetwater intentional community in Navajo Dam. We stayed up playing music until midnight, then I went to bed."

A second officer, this one more seasoned, with greying hair and an expanding waistline, escorted her to the studio. The front window pane had been shattered. Inside was havoc; shredded yoga mats, broken mirrors, and obscene graffiti on the walls.

Fuck Liberals. Dumb Bitch. Die Hippie Cunt.

Saffron's stomach turned sour, the green smoothie threatening to return.

"Can you think of anyone who would do this?" the officer asked, notepad in hand.

"Ahhh," she stammered uncertainly, drawing a blank on who she knew who was immature and idiotic enough to destroy someone else's property; or anyone that violent and angry. "I-I don't think so."

"We have to cancel classes today," Susan said, her hands shaking as she typed into her phone, sharing the sad news on social media. "Maybe for the week."

Saffron felt horrible, and violated. She imagined Susan felt the same, times ten.

"I swear," Susan said, her tears threatening to spill, "I don't recognize this town anymore. It's one thing after another. First your mom, now... this." Her voice broke and her face squinched in anguish. Losing the battle to hold back her tears, she grabbed Saffron tightly and buried her cries on her shoulder.

Saffron soothed as best she could, feeling raw and exposed herself.

Things are speeding up, said a panicky voice in her mind.

Ignoring it, she whispered into Susan's ear, "It's going to be okay."

Having no desire to return home, she drove to Riverside Park to peer into the Animas river which meandered lazily through town. During the summers, it was becoming commonplace for the water to be incredibly low, reduced to a trickle and pockmarked by exposed river stones; snowpack in the mountains of Colorado was not as reliable as it used to be; some winters did just fine, while others left the stately peaks freakishly bare. In Saffron's opinion, there were few things as sad as a barren mountaintop in winter. It was a depressing glimpse into the future of the world.

She recalled the summer when the river had been running strong with a violent color of orange, the result of an environmental catastrophe from the Gold King Mine spill. The Animas, or 'river of souls', had looked sickly and poisoned. Her family and friends had spent hours sending Reiki to the waters, praying for Gaia to heal yet another injurious folly of man.

Today, the water was low but clear.; above her floated a puffy white cloud, riding the thin blue line of atmosphere encircling the planet. She sat on a rock in the shade of an immense cottonwood, shoes off, her blue toes enjoying the coolness of the river. Listening to its quiet persistence, she thought about the hate-filled words spray-painted in red, and the anger of the person behind the action.

Polarization and division were rife in America.

Her worries turned towards Colton; the challenges facing him were no laughing matter; politics, religion, and climate change were tearing families apart.

Why don't people realize how interconnected everything is, Saffron wondered for the umpteenth time. *We all share the same boat, for God's sake! The same soil, the same water, the same air! We should be joining forces,* she wanted to scream, *because there's literally no place to go if we screw up!*

She felt her anger swelling and blew it out of her cheeks in a puff, picturing the darkness spilling out of her like the prisoner in Steven King's 'The Green Mile'.

It was an everlasting battle in her mind, the fight to enjoy the gifts and blessings that existed in the world, against the stark reality that there was also struggle, ignorance and strife. Inhaling deeply, she took a moment to enjoy the sun on her skin and the wind in her hair.

Today is a good day, she thought, the familiar affirmation feeling a bit like bullshit but still helping her realign towards more positive thinking.

She sent a prayer for peace into the river with an impassioned plea that Colton's attempt to address his family would go well.

"Love and War are the same thing, and stratagems and policy are as allowable in the one as in the other."
- Miguel de Cervantes
from Don Quixote de la Mancha

Chapter 27: Prodigal Son

Saffron returned home with the daytime heat blazing around her. Her parents had not yet arrived, however the air inside the Earthship was heavy with the skunky smell of weed. Laughter and melodic punk music played loudly from her part of the house. She heard one of her favorites, 'Science of Myth' by Screeching Weasel.

Singing in her head, she walked down the sunlit atrium.

'Science and religion are not mutually exclusive / In fact for better understanding / We take the facts of science and apply them / And if factors keep evolving / then we continue getting information / But closing off possibilities / makes it hard to see the bigger picture.'

Inside her dim living room, she found Lorelei cross-legged on the floor next to the couch, with Ayden upon it.

Shirtless and splayed across the sofa, he strummed her unplugged electric guitar to the song. Even with his back turned, there was no mistaking him. Ayden's signature, platinum blond hair was a spiky, attention-seeking mess. Tattoos covered his arms, but his back was clean and lean.

Lorelei, her hair plaited into two long braids, wore a Ramones t-shirt with the Guy Fawkes mask perched on top of her head. Staring intently into the Magic 8 ball, she held the green bong with her other hand.

Neither one looked up when Saffron entered.

"Ah-ah-em!" she said, loudly clearing her throat. "How ya doing there, Cheech?"

"Oh, hey Roni," Lorelei replied with a sleepy grin, her eyes mildly unfocused as she showed Saffron the ball. "It says here the 'Outlook is Good'. How cool is that? Whoo-hoo!!"

"Well, someone's doing pretty good by the looks of it," she responded with a smirk before turning her attention to Ayden. Saffron desperately wanted to play it cool, but her heart was racing like a runaway train.

"Holy shit, Chong!" she exclaimed, pantomiming shock in order to mask her true surprise. "Is that you?"

"Nah," he said coolly. "Just some other douchebag."

He winked at her with his arctic blue eyes, capable of hypnotizing admirers and haters alike; his trademark brilliant smile, a bit more cat-with-canary than usual. The combination evoked a daring, come-hither quality, as if he were imagining her naked.

Saffron gulped, then recovered by saying, "I-I can't believe you're here. I thought you were going underground."

"I am," he replied. "In fact, I'm...not...even...here," he said in a deep, mesmerizing voice.

"Oh!" Lorelei exclaimed, bubbling with excitement. "Ask him how he got here."

Ayden looked irritated, but quickly shook it off.

"I have my own plane now," he answered smugly, "a bitchin' twin engine Piper."

"Oh my God," Saffron said with disbelief, "that was you last night?! That was crazy, you big goof! What the hell are you doing with a plane?"

In a thundering, movie announcer voice, Lorelei responded, "It's time to teach the big dogs a lesson!" She then lit the bong and took a hit, the water gurgling loudly over the music as the smoke clouded the room.

"Huh?" Saffron asked, having no clue what she was talking about.

Ayden's smile disappeared. His hands tightened around the neck of the guitar.

"Don't tell her, for cry-eye-sake!" he said sharply. "She's dating some conservative oil and gas guy now." Mimicking Lorelei, he said in a baritone voice, "She's the enemy and cannot be trusted."

Lorelei snorted and burst out laughing.

Saffron's patience was thin. She was in no mood to play games.

"Um, 'A', who says he's conservative," she said acerbically, her hands on both hips, "and 'B', what would it matter anyway? Half the population is. And 'C', he's probably not going to be working in oil and gas for much longer, even if he wanted to. Laws are going to change eventually." Her irritation spilled over. Squinting her eyes, she added sternly, "And most importantly, oh Cryptic Ones, what the hell are you two talking about? Or, more truthfully, *not* talking about, I should say."

Ayden's smile had returned.

She knew he'd always delighted in ruffling her feathers, seeming to thrill in the spark of her spirit, the rise of her intensity when she got passionate about something. In the past, it had always turned him on.

"Well, I don't know, Hoot," he said to Lorelei. "Should we trust her? She's gotten pretty soft these days. I don't know if she can handle it."

"You-can't-handle-the-truth!" Lorelei responded loudly, convulsing again into laughter.

"Ugh, soft," Saffron repeated under her breath, bristling at the casual insult. In the philosophy of survive and thrive, being soft was tantamount to being a victim, one that wouldn't make it when the shit hit the fan. "I'll have you know that my 'conservative' boyfriend and I," she said, using air quotes and a slightly bragging tone, "are planning a trip to DC together to protest global warming."

"Did I hear you say 'boyfriend'," Lorelei said gleefully. "I want to hear everything! And I mean, the full, x-rated version." She reached up towards Saffron, urging her to sit down next to her.

Saffron remained standing.

Ayden's complexion paled; his sultry good looks reduced into lines of worry.

"Y-you," he said, sputtering uncharacteristically, "you can't go to Washington now. It's not…it's not safe."

"Wha-a-at do you mean," she said slowly, "it's…not…safe?" In her head, she sounded like Captain Kirk from Star Trek. Her stomach twisted uncomfortably. "Are you planning a riot, like in Miami?" She wasn't sure she wanted to hear the answer. "Because innocent people have died because of that."

"No, no, no," he said dismissively, "no rioting directly." Then, shrugging his shoulders, he added, "Well, it *could* happen as a result, but at least with this plan, the *right* people will die."

"It's called Operation Silver Spoon," Lorelei shared.

"Why?!?" Ayden scolded, smacking her with a pillow. "Why do I tell you anything? You are a horrible, horrible secret agent!"

The two of them engaged in mock cat fighting, slapping each other like children and laughing maniacally. Lorelei put the mask over her face for protection and wrestled the pillow away from him to use as a shield, bumping into the coffee table and jostling the items on top of it in the process, including the bong which almost tipped over.

Saffron whistled as loudly as she could.

-233-

The mask had fallen to the floor; its mustachioed face smiled blankly at the ceiling. Lorelei and Ayden stopped in mid-headlock. Both sets of eyes turned towards her.

"Ex-cuse me," she said stiffly, irritated by the sound of maturity in her voice. "I have had a hell of a time this past week. Will one of you please tell me what's going on," she demanded.

"Okay, in a nutshell, we're done," Ayden said, his eyes and voice gone cold. "We're done waiting for them to get their heads out of their asses. And we're done with the obscene, selfish greed of the über wealthy."

"Fuck the rich!" Lorelei shouted, her fist in the air.

"They've had their chance to fix things," he said, "and they've failed miserably."

Saffron's spider sense tingled like the barometric pressure had radically shifted.

"So," he continued with a sneer, "we're gonna level the playing field." He held her guitar in a sexy, rock and roll pose, aggressively strumming the strings. In an obnoxious, metal-band voice, he sang, *"Gonna hit them right between the ey-ey-eyessssss! Yea!"*

"Oh-kay," Saffron said worriedly, "what, *exactly,* does that mean, and who are we talking about?"

"Timebomb has a plan," Ayden said excitedly, oblivious to the anxiety coursing through Saffron's being. "It's going to destroy hundreds, if not thousands, of 1%ers overnight. A nearly 99% kill rate." Smiling proudly, he added, "We're going to hit the zip codes where the average income is six digits and up, the richest counties across America."

Saffron felt ill, stunned mute. She sat down heavily on the floor next to Lorelei.

"We got the info online," he said laughingly. "The Internet loves sharing shitty lists like that. 'Top 100 Billionaires and Their Obnoxious Pleasure Palaces!' My god, it's almost like they want us to hurt them. I guess they think we're supposed to be jealous or something."

"Or," Lorelei said bitterly, "they just want us to be good little consumers, selling our souls and exploiting other people in the hopes we can make enough money to be just like them someday." She tilted her head to the side, placed both hands demurely under her chin and batted her golden brown eyes, smiling blankly and *blink blink blinking* at Saffron like a Hollywood starlet from the 1950's or a peppy Mouseketeer.

There were many websites that had a penchant for lists like that. Saffron had been using them for years, collecting the names and details for hundreds of millionaires and billionaires. *Know thy enemy* had been her rationale. However, she'd never once considered using the information to attack them.

Her body felt rigid with tension and her mouth was completely dry.

"We've got five planes in total," Ayden said in a conspiratorial tone. "They're set to fly over the Hamptons, Silicon Valley, one of the counties just outside Houston where all the biggiewig oil and gas guys live, and a couple counties near DC where those asshole lobbyists and fuckwad politicians are." Casually, he added, "It's my job to hit Los Alamos."

Saffron's stomach fell to the floor, like a proverbial stone. If she had not already been sitting, her legs may have collapsed. Unfortunately, Ayden wasn't done filling her in on the plan.

"I love the irony of giving the bombs-and-weapons-people a dose of their own fucking medicine," he said with a macabre excitement.

"They're using aerosolized anthrax," Lorelei said evenly, her voice low.

"Oh my god," Saffron said, horrified. "You know about this?!"

Lorelei's face had the decency to sober up at the tone in Saffron's voice before it hardened again in defiance.

"How much longer can we continue with their boots on our necks?" she said, her golden eyes bright with righteous anger. "Should we just sit back, let them extinguish us all, one by one? Massacring us like they did to my ancestors?!" Accusingly, she ended with, "At least Ayden's trying to do something about it."

Her bitterness hit Saffron like a punch. *Am I really not doing enough?*

"Yes, yes, I get it," she heard herself answer in frustration, and in a part of her, she really did. The same anger and resentment had lived inside her for years as she watched the government being dictated by people of means rather than We, the People. An image from an old, black and white cartoon suddenly popped into her head of a devil on one shoulder and an angel on the other.

The devil absolutely saw the appeal of striking out so brashly with vengeance.

"I'm angry too," she admitted.

It might not be bad to hit Houston, the devil whispered temptingly.

Immediately, she felt guilt and aversion to the darker elements within her, revolting at the blackness that wanted to rise up. Rage and fear were a dangerous combination, capable of turning normal, everyday people into monsters. She thought again of the destruction of the yoga studio, and the farmers market.

The angel on her other shoulder, her conscience, tugged at her. She remembered her advice to Colton to act 'respectfully, civilly, and to operate from love'.

"But an action like that," she said, "a *terrorist* action, isn't going to make those issues go away, Ayden. It's like the heads of the Hydra. You cut one off, another will simply grow in its place. All you'll accomplish is chaos and the death of innocent bystanders, but the money will not come showering back down upon us like a fucking piñata and the climate is still going to go to shit."

"You know the upper class is going to suffer and die anyway," he said, his eyes burning into hers with a zealot's fire, "with all that's gonna to happen on this planet, and honestly, they deserve to be punished!" He smoldered with rage, was poisoned by it. "All these other countries around the world," he argued, "making moves towards progress, and here we are, going steadily backwards under the sadistic wishes of a handful of greedy tycoons!"

"But Ayden," Saffron said, her sense of rationality returning, "first of all, not every rich person is an unscrupulous dirtbag, and secondly, not all the Richie Rich fossil fuel guys live in America, do they? I mean, is Timebomb going to take out the billionaires in China and Russia, too? Are you gonna spray death from the sky onto Dubai? No. I'm sorry and I can't believe I have to say this, but murdering a bunch of lobbyists and politicians in DC, along with their housekeepers and nannies, I might add, is not going to end global warming. It's not the right solution."

Scowling, Ayden opened his mouth in retort, then shut it with no reply. She could see him considering her words, calculating. His fiercely blue eyes flashed. Angrily, he swallowed his beer while giving her a silent, side-eye stare.

The music had changed, becoming more abrasive; hardcore; its intensity nearing the grating-on-nerves stage.

Lorelei hugged her knees and stared at the floor, her face drawn, lost in thought.

"But, I absolutely agree with you on one thing," Saffron said. "Money *isn't* going to protect them forever, but shouldn't we try to convince them of that fact?!? As suffering and deaths multiply, it's gonna be difficult to conduct business as usual, especially if governments and economies collapse. Shouldn't we explain to them, civilly and rationally, they've got the most to lose?

"Warn them, work with them, plead for our lives," she said fervently, her voice rising. "Anything, except killing them. Everyone should know this is a no-win game, no matter how much money they have."

"If things don't change soon," Ayden responded hotly, "it's all over, and you know it. We won't be able to stop the other tipping points. Lucky us, we might get our chance to see, up close and personal, what truly desperate people do during desperate times. One day, we too could be fugitives, escaping extreme weather, persecution and violence in search of a safe place. And think of it, we might not be spring chickens anymore when it goes down. No more survive and thrive for us, chickadee. Only heat, then meat."

He made a very convincing death thrall reenactment of the Wicked Witch of the West melting under a splash of water.

Well, that's a repulsive thought, her inner voice gagged.

Ayden had always exhausted her. It was like trying to wrap one's arms around a tornado; he spun and spun and spun so fast. At times, the ride had been supremely exhilarating; at the moment, not so much.

"We still have time to convince people," she interjected.

"That's bullshit," he sneered. "Those rich fucks are either oblivious, or so fundamentally twisted they don't care. Eventually, people'll rise up and take their share of what's left, getting their jollies off on punishing anyone who played a big part in letting this horrific catastrophe occur. Or hell, come to think of it, their own bodyguards may be the ones to finally take 'em out. It's gonna make the French Revolution look like a day at the park!"

"Yes!" Saffron said emphatically, shaking her head in agreement. "I know, and you know, but do *they* know that?! Isn't it possible many of them are in the dark? Clueless, like almost everyone else?! Come on! No one wants to look at this issue...not really. But our continued avoidance is going to kill us."

Her words hit her like a lightning bolt.

My god, how true is that!?

"It's imperative things change," she said passionately. "You're absolutely right about that, but we should be the ones trying to convince them! To reach out to them. Help them change. We do *not* need to kill them." She looked imploringly from Ayden to Lorelei as she spoke, wishing to burrow the message deeply within them. "Murder is not the answer."

Ayden was silent, looking both dumbfounded and disgusted. The music continued to blare.

"You're crazy," he said. "There's no way in hell you can make a big enough difference to save us. It's insane! You'll *never* get the elite class to change."

It was the straw that broke the camel's back.

Saffron blazed with a fiery rage in every cell of her body. Her hands closed into fists, her nails digging into her palms.

"NEVER?!?!" she yelled defiantly, like a child on the verge of a tantrum. "Have you just met me?!? When have I *ever* let *anyone* tell me what *is*, or is *not*, possible?" Every other word punctuated out of her like a bullet from a gun, her voice rising in pitch, her eyes on Ayden like daggers.

"Hmmph," she grumbled, exasperation pouring from her like a broken levee, "never, my ass. Never's just something that hasn't been done before."

Her words caused a lightbulb to turn on inside her head; a seed of a thought; a glimmer of something wanting to be born.

"Maybe this is the role I've been meant to fill," she said, a trickle of excitement beginning to build. "You know? Working to influence the world as an agent of positive change?"

"And what makes you think you can influence those people?" he asked with disdain.

The question caught her off-guard. It was so similar to what Colton had asked of her.

How can we motivate others to join us, she wondered. *To make changes peacefully, without carnage and mayhem?*

"We live on highly sacred ground," she began, the words coming from the ether. "It's like an epicenter of energy around here, actual holy land. Haven't you ever felt it? Maybe we can access its force to make a difference?"

Ayden looked at her with a mixture of anger and pity.

"You know I don't believe in that mumbo-jumbo, New-Age-y bullshit," he said, shaking his head dismissively. "You're a dreamer, totally delusional."

"Dreams are POWERFUL!!!" Saffron shouted. "Dreamers are the ones who've transformed this world before, and it'll be the dreamers who will save this planet for the future!"

She turned away from him, dismayed by his lack of faith and frustrated by her inability to convince him. She scooted closer to Lorelei, their knees touching, eyes locked together.

"I believe," she said imploringly, "we have the power to manifest the world we want to live in, don't you? If we truly want to ascend, to fully walk on a spiritual path, then we *cannot kill our enemies*. And definitely not the innocent. It's completely and utterly unacceptable."

Saffron thought of others who had radically fought back against oppression; Mahatma Gandhi, Nelson Mandela, Martin Luther King, even Jesus Christ himself. They each had toppled evil empires and corrupted institutions with grace and non-violence. It was true, violence had been committed against them, but they had never stooped that low.

Most importantly, they each had been triumphant.

It's what we need now, she realized with another epiphany. *Love is always the answer.*

She had a vision of people gathering, linked arm in arm, and leading the charge for change.

Lorelei began to choke up. She nervously looked at Ayden who was glowering. When she turned back, Saffron grabbed her hands and held them tightly in hers.

"Not only am I going to go to DC," she said resolutely, "but we're going to create a massive, viral campaign called 'Bring Us Back From The Brink'. We'll aim it at the world's wealthiest people to let them know we need their help, and to activate others to join us in our mission. We must convince them we simply cannot solve these problems without them."

From deep within Saffron, a still, small voice whispered, *We need critical mass.*

She looked at Ayden, at the man who customarily made her feel crazy. He was stubborn, with a mile-wide, overinflated sense of justice; not an inherently bad man, just one of many in the country brimming with anger. Convincing him to stop Operation Silver Spoon was going to be tricky.

And what about the others involved? How can I get them to abort the mission?

Saffron couldn't deal with a new headache at the moment. She shuffled the problem to the back of her mind like Scarlett O'Hara, putting it aside for tomorrow.

"Ayden," she said softly, grabbing his hand and squeezing it, "we need them. I feel it in my bones. It simply won't get solved without them. Don't do this. Please!"

Zia's bright sing-song voice suddenly called out, "We're hooooooome!!!"

"Mom!" Saffron yelled back nervously, like a kid about to be busted with a cigarette. "Dad! I'll be right there."

She continued glaring at Ayden and Lorelei.

"We aren't done talking about this," she said forcefully, leaving little room for dissent. "You two are both going to help me. If you want my silence and cooperation, then this is what it's going to cost you.

"Because just like you," she said, "I've got zero fucks left to give."

She hesitated, torn with the knowledge of their plan, sick in her heart with its implications, debating in her head how to best respond, and lacking much time in which to decide.

"You buy me the time I need to work my mojo," she snarled at Ayden, "to influence the masses in my own way, or else." She didn't have time to finish giving an ultimatum. They could hear footsteps coming down the long hallway.

"Please," she pleaded in desperation, "just give me some time. Why not give this a chance before it's too late and we do something we regret?"

Jack and Zia came in a second later, excited and surprised to see Ayden had returned. Everyone began sharing hugs and kisses as if nothing in the world was wrong.

For Saffron, the homecoming with her mother was bittersweet.

"Now is the accepted time, not tomorrow,
not some more convenient season.
It is today that our best work can be done
and not some future day or future year.
It is today that we fit ourselves
for the greater usefulness of tomorrow."
- W.E.B. Dubois

Chapter 28: Day of Reckoning

Colton arose before dawn to work in the barn with his horses. Inside was the sweet smell he loved; alfalfa hay and dust, combined with the surprisingly pleasant undertone of manure. HoneyLemon and Dusty whinnied their welcomes and nudged the pockets of his jacket.

"Things are going to change soon, ladies," he said, stroking their manes and looking into their soulful eyes. Faithfully, he gave them each apples and a good brushing.

With his chores completed, he arrived early enough at work to see the moon still hugging the horizon, reluctant to vanish. As he dealt with lingering issues, checking and deleting old emails and sifting through piles of paperwork, Colton felt mildly frantic, driven by an urge to clear everything away and make space for his life to take a new path.

Today he planned on talking to his family about the multiplying hazards in the world; the loss of diversity, the erratic nature of the weather, and the increasing impacts on economics and security. He intended to ask for their help in finding answers to protect the family and restore the natural world back to glory.

He had read his Bible the night before, hoping to find clues on speaking to them, in a way they'd, hopefully, be more receptive to listening to. Nothing seemed right until he found Matthew 10:19: *When they deliver you over, do not be anxious how you are to speak or what you are to say, for what you are to say will be given to you in that hour.*

He prayed he'd be blessed with the right words and tone, as he torpedoed the Millers' entire worldview.

Asa came in promptly at 7:00am, Gage directly behind.

His dad looked weary; his best friend, murderous.

"Dad," Colton said apprehensively, "can we talk for a minute? I've got something important on my mind. I hope you'll listen."

Colton felt strange returning home only hours after leaving. As the garage door rolled shut, blocking the late morning sun, he removed the key from its ignition and closed his eyes, taking a moment to appreciate the silent dark.

The one-on-one, heart-to-heart discussion he'd hoped for had been more like a two-against-one, no-holds-barred fight. Like a scene stuck on repeat, the conversation with his father and Gage had grown increasingly frustrating with every replay in his mind.

He'd begun by telling them he'd been reading lots of detailed articles on global warming, and not just the denial ones. Then, he'd mentioned some of the predictions, like water shortages and drier land, which was "gonna be hell for the ranchers". He shared a few suggestions to help folks avert disaster, like eating locally grown food, restoring native plants on homesites, and consciously using less electricity and gas, suggesting they factor in the impacts of shipping and manufacturing, too.

"How and where people shop," he'd said, "the stuff we all buy… that's more important than most people know."

Unfortunately, their eyes had glazed over, their lips tightening into thin lines of disapproval. As he'd feared, they'd reacted by repeating the old company line of criticism, telling him climate change wasn't proven, that oil and gas would never go away, stubbornly stating it couldn't go away, and that the economy would completely collapse if it did.

Their opinions on the subject had been hardline; hardwired; lamentably unshakable.

In distress, Colton had asked them to simply read more, to read everything they could, saying, "It's way too important a problem to stay ignorant of." He'd then warned them they weren't going to like what they learned, that the truth was ugly, but they owed it to themselves and everyone they cared about to get properly informed.

Asa had tried to end the conversation multiple times by reminding Colton how much work had to be done.

"The only urgency I can see," he'd said sternly, "is checking the inventory in the warehouse."

Gage, however, had burned with malice, making the issue personal rather than attempting to understand Colton's underlying concern. He'd been rude and insulting, especially towards Saffron.

"That granola-eating, mushroom-growing, treehugger has fucked with your mind, man," he'd raged.

It had taken every ounce of Colton's strength and inner resolve to keep his temper in check. Although he'd aimed to stay respectful, to be a strong man, he'd crumbled under their attack, getting more defensive than he'd liked.

"You can't be this damn hard-headed!" he'd yelled.

Use that brain the good Lord gave you, he'd wanted to shout, using a phrase of Asa's when his dad was really, really angry. Instead, he audibly muttered, "Stubborn jackasses."

He barely remembered leaving. He thought his final words had been, "I can't do this anymore."

When Colton opened his eyes, his hands were gripping the steering wheel.

It'd hurt to have his dad and best friend refuse to listen to him, but he hadn't been too surprised. The prospect of how his mother was going to react was a wild card; it was one thing to butt heads with his father, who could be as ornery as a mule, but if his mother didn't listen or understand…that would be a more painful blow.

Well CJ, he thought bleakly, *one parent down, one more to go.*

Entering the cool, air-conditioned house, he found his mother sitting on the floor of the living room surrounded by piles of folded and unfolded clothes. The radio was playing a popular contemporary Christian song. He heard the advice to surrender and have faith.

"My goodness," Cricket said, startled. "What're you doin' back so early?"

"I guess," Colton said surreally, "because I quit."

"Love is patient and kind;
love does not envy or boast;
it is not arrogant or rude.
It does not insist on its own way,
it is not irritable or resentful,
it does not rejoice at wrongdoing
but rejoices with truth.
Love bears all things, believes all things,
hopes all things, endures all things."
- 1 Corinthians 13:4-7

Chapter 29 : And It Was Good

"Ohhh, baby," Cricket said, letting her bedazzled t-shirt fall into her lap as her heart dropped into her stomach. For days, she'd been worrying about her son. Sadly, it appeared her fears were correct; Colton looked pale and drawn as he delivered the terrible news.

The last time she'd seen him this wrought was after the hurricane in Texas.

Asa had surprised her with a ten day cruise for their twenty-fifth wedding anniversary which had been lovely, a second honeymoon; a time to reconnect with her long-time sweetheart.

All of her children and grandchildren had gone to stay with her eldest son, Dylan, in the suburbs of Houston. It was supposed to have been a fun time for the whole clan, until Harvey landed on top of them, dumping four feet of rain in an hour, and then some.

When she'd learned her loved ones were in jeopardy, her and Asa had gotten off at the next port, rented a car in Mexico, and raced like bats out of hell. Communication had been horrible; weather and travel, exponentially worse. Hampered by the aftermath, all they'd been able to do was creep along the detours, chugging black coffee and praying for their family's safety.

It had taken time and every ounce of will to reach them; the destruction she witnessed along the way slicing through her and leaving scars. The 'storm with no boundaries' which had threatened rich and poor alike, had taught her the lesson that she could be robbed of everything she loved and held dear in a heartbeat.

When she'd finally seen Colton, he was changed; older; less the teenage boy he had been. The pain in his eyes that day was similar to what she saw in them now.

"I don't get it, mom," Colton said wearily, collapsing on the sofa like the Scarecrow from Wizard of Oz, as if his bones had turned to jelly. "You guys raised us to believe it's a parent's duty to protect and provide for their families, right? Well, I've been seriously reading about global warming, and I've got to tell you, it looks like everyone's in trouble unless we make some big changes. I-I tried to talk to dad about it. I bet you can guess how that went."

From the suffering on Colton's face, she imagined the discussion had gone badly.

She knew it was hard to stand in Asa's dominating shadow; sometimes, it wasn't easy for her either. On this issue, she imagined her husband hadn't done his best to listen.

Never in a million years had she thought a child of theirs would bring up global warming as a reason for leaving the family business.

Actually, she thought, the truth coming to the surface, *I'm not totally surprised.*

In fact, it felt sort of inevitable; she'd been noticing headlines mentioning problems in the environment, too.

Colton's face darkened, anger rising to the surface of his skin.

"I simply can't understand why people aren't learning more about it," he said in frustration. "And once they do," he continued, staring at the ceiling, "why don't they start working like crazy to make sure we reverse the damages?!? It makes no sense at all except, maybe, I don't know, I guess it's not really *real* to most folks. The changes seem to be happening slowly, so it doesn't *feel* like the crisis it really is. It doesn't seem…immediate, like an earthquake. Plus, I guess, it's just plain difficult to face, there's too much to think about, and most people hate change like the plague."

Colton rubbed his eyes and mussed his hair as if he was trying to scrub the knowledge out of his body.

"Well, okay," he added with a ghost of a smile, "maybe there're lots of reasons why we aren't dealing with it, but it's still no excuse to go on acting like nothing's wrong."

Exhausted, with seemingly nothing more to say, he laid facedown on the couch and covered his head with a throw pillow.

Cricket looked on her son's prostrate body.

From early on, her youngest son had had a big heart. As a teen, he'd stood up to bullies, been a good role model, and comforted people in pain. She knew it was in his nature to want to help people.

His words had brought a heavy weight upon her chest.

She'd always been protective of her children, wanting what was best for them. The notion that something horrible was coming, and she hadn't prepared them for it, made her uneasy. The possibility her family could be in danger, again, and she was ignoring the warning signs, gnawed inside her.

"I'll tell you what I'll do," she said, letting out a deep breath. "I promise to look deeper into it. I will. I-I'm at a loss about what I can do about it, but I'll see what's being said, okay? And I'll pray for you."

"We're all going to need prayers," Colton said, taking off the pillow and sitting to face his mother. "But mostly, we need prayers to turn into actions. Things don't have to be this way."

"Is this all because of that new girl you're dating?" she asked, getting up from the floor to sit next to him, her knees popping. "I've barely seen you lately, and when I have, you've been agitated and distracted. I'm worried about you."

"Don't be, mom," he said apologetically. "I'm actually very happy. If I didn't know the sky was falling, I'd be over the moon." He cracked a weak smile. "All she's done is open a door to what was already around me, and I chose to fall down the rabbit hole on my own. It was always there, under the surface, this feeling that things weren't quite right, but now I can't hide from it anymore." Taking her hand in his, he added, "But please, don't worry about Saffron. With her, I feel like I can face anything."

Cricket had planned on nagging him about Kaelynne, among other things, like sex before marriage, but she saw her son's face change before her eyes. It softened, a look of peace coming over him, his eyes growing in depth as they looked into hers.

Sensing the shift, a maturation, she choose to bite her tongue.

Briefly, she thought she had glimpsed the decent and fearless man he would become.

"You love her," she stated, sighing deeply.

Colton nodded and held his breath, looking expectantly as if he feared she'd argue with him as Asa had.

She had no intention to turn her back on her child.

"Well, baby," she said quietly, "I hope for your sake it works out."

The smile which erupted across his face gave her confirmation she'd said the right thing.

"Thank you," he gushed with relief, his eyes bright with gratitude.

"Um, m-mom," he added sheepishly, chewing his lip. "There's something else. I know I'm hitting you with a lot of stuff, like our planet's ecosystems are destabilizing and all that, so I'm really sorry, but Saffron's dad, Jack LeMay, offered me an apprenticeship in carpentry, and I said yes. I'll also be learning organic farming, and hopefully some homebuilding skills. This is about more than just Saffron, mom. It simply feels right." He paused and squared his shoulders. "I'm moving to Sweetwater…today. They've got an empty tiny house I can stay in. I know it's early in my relationship with Saffron," he said, "but I already know I'm going to ask her to marry me. She's the one."

Cricket went still, like an opossum feigning death to escape danger. She closed her eyes as thoughts buzzed in her head; it was so much to take in, so many ways things could go wrong. In stunned silence, she became conscious of her heartbeat and the sound of music playing in the kitchen. The song reminded her to trust in God's love and the path before her, giving the advice she needed in the moment like an omen.

Yes Lord, I hear you, she prayed, taking a deep breath. *I don't know what's going to come in this world, but please, I ask for You to bring peace and happiness for my son and family.* Thinking about Colton's distress about the climate, she added the intention, *Please bestow these blessings to the rest of the world.*

Her heart swelled as her words went out from her to Spirit, feeling as if her prayers had already been answered.

Thank you in advance for saving us, she thought. *In Jesus's name. Amen.*

"Well," Cricket said, exhaling loudly the breath she'd been holding, "you're too big to put across my knee, so I guess I'll just have to have faith that it'll work out."

Colton wrapped his arms around her, as if he didn't want to let go.

"I love you to the moon and back, CJ," she said into his shoulder, "and don't you ever forget it. You always have a home here. I'll talk with your father, and I'll keep my promise to learn more, okay? Just promise me you'll be smart and take care of yourself."

"Yes, ma'am," he said. "I love you too."

Four hours later, he had finished packing and loading his horses in a trailer behind his truck. He kissed her on the cheek before he left, dressed in a t-shirt and athletic shorts.

"If I'm gonna live in a new world with a new life," he said, driving off to see Saffron at the yoga studio for her late afternoon class. "I better get used to new experiences."

Cricket wondered how easy it would be for old dogs like Asa to learn new tricks.

"These are times in which a genius would wish to live.
It is not in the still calm of life
that great characters are formed.
Great necessities call out great virtues."
- Abigail Adams

Chapter 30: Operation Eyes Wide Open

Zia's homecoming party was set in the large yurt in the center of Sweetwater. The spacious tent bustled with all of the Colonists and their guests.

Saffron had been uncharacteristically silent, her ability to perform small talk having been severely limited by shock. The last thing she wanted was to be around Ayden and Lorelei, the Assassin Twins. Seeking refuge away from them, she lingered by the bookcases.

A substantial library filled the left side of the structure while the right included a kitchen and small platform, typically used for group meetings and performances. Above the stage was a large white board, known as the Big Board, scribbled with notes, timelines and project plans. On a stool beneath it, Jack was taking requests and playing his acoustic guitar.

Four long tables radiated from the center like spokes on a wheel towards the bookcase side. This arrangement gave readers a place to sit when they found a book they liked and made room for people to congregate near the kitchen and stage. On either side of the entrance were love seats for private conversations or reflection. In the very center was a wood-burning stove surrounded by a stone wall to protect people from getting burned and to better retain heat during the colder months.

The yurt was hot, but not unbearable. Two fans on either side of the room kept the air circulating. The mood was high and lively, but Saffron was oblivious to it. She felt lost in a daze; her body buzzed, uncomfortably numb, as she blindly looked over the titles on the shelves.

Struggling to make sense of Ayden's murderous intentions, she felt like she lacked a sufficient language to process her feelings which bordered on panic and shell-shock. The words, 'Dastardly Plan', rambled repeatedly inside her brain like an album stuck in a groove.

Mindlessly, her fingers scrolled up and down the spines of the books.

She took down a weathered, yellowed favorite, 'Living On The Earth' by Alicia Bay Laurel; in her opinion, the ultimate hippie bible. She flipped through its original drawings and handwritten pages, staring blankly at its sage advice for existing as a human being with a simpler life. The beauty and hopefulness in it was in stark contrast to the turmoil raging within her. She returned the book to the shelf unread.

Suddenly, she was startled by a hand on her shoulder.

"Roni, are you okay?"

She turned to see Colton's worried face.

Saffron was momentarily confused by his question and level of concern. Her first thought was, *How does he know about the Dastardly Plan?*

"I was just at the studio," he said. "I wanted to take your class and saw what had been done to it." Protectively, he wrapped his arms around her, pressing against her. "Are you okay?"

Shaking off her confusion, she fully awakened to her position in the noisy but happy-sounding room, coming out of her thoughts and back into her body.

"Oh, yeah," she said, a note of exhaustion in her voice. "What a clusterfuck. Susan hopes to have it cleaned up and ready by Thursday. Hopefully, I can return to work the next day." She leaned in to touch more of Colton's body. "I'm glad you're here."

"I quit my job today," he said over the sound of a woman's laughter. "It didn't go so well with my dad. I just let my horses out into the pasture with yours. Jack told me there was a tiny house I could move into."

"Well," she answered, "you may be moving in with me instead. The former occupant returned home today. Remember my old bandmate, Ayden, the one I told you about?"

She gave the room a quick once over and found his shockingly blond head angled closely towards Lorelei's glossy dark-haired one. They were sitting together on a loveseat, utterly engrossed in conversation.

"By the way," she nervously admitted, "he's kind of, um, my old boyfriend."

"Well...okay then," Colton said slowly. "I guess I'll take my bags to your place? I-I can sleep on the couch, if it'll make you feel more comfortable."

The sweetness of his statement made Saffron smile and want to squeeze him even tighter.

If only my biggest issues were proper etiquette and decorum, she thought wistfully.

"I believe it'll work out, gentle sir," she said softly into his chest, inhaling his scent. Touching him, she already felt more steady, less numb.

Zia's voice rose faintly over the group's revelry, but was overwhelmed by the noise of the yurt.

"May I have everyone's attention," she repeated, clinking her glass briskly until the room was quiet.

Standing on the platform, she was a striking vision, wearing a form-fitting, off-the-shoulder dress with vibrant embroidered flowers. Her long hair was piled on the top of her head with a white rose behind her left ear. Above the neckline of her dress was a daring square of gauze, boldly displayed, as if to tell the Universe, and anyone who saw her, that she'd never give in to tragedy.

Fearlessly, she would choose to flaunt her scars, and do so with style and aplomb.

She reminded Saffron of Frida Kahlo, the provocative and political painter.

Only, her brain reminded her, *she's more like her red-headed, distantly-related cousin.* Briefly, she wondered how many generations of separation a DNA test would show between the two.

"I'd like to say a few words," Zia said. "First, I want to thank you, each and every one of you for being there for me. Most of you know I like to think of myself as a pretty badass motherbleeper, which technically I am," she said with a flourish of her hands, "but, I'm so grateful to you all for lending me your strength these past few days."

She smiled warmly as her eyes met with Saffron's.

"What we have here together is truly exceptional," she continued. "Not everyone's so lucky. We're a committed, loving group of people, like a tribe, whom I trust to stick together, weathering whatever changes and obstacles we'll encounter. Life isn't always easy, or pleasant, or pretty, but I believe we'll never give up on one another. We won't run from trouble, because I think we can agree that it's worth it, that the hard times always get better, and sometimes, life is so good, it takes your breath away."

She stopped speaking to inhale deeply, filling her lungs as fully as she could. Exhaling, she smiled at the faces around her.

Saffron squeezed Colton around his waist, buoyed by his presence and her mother's words.

"I truly believe we're entering a powerful time, a crossroads," Zia said. "A time when we need to consider precisely how we want the world to transform…and, what we're prepared to do about it."

Standing near Zia was Lorelei's grandmother. She came forward, a quiet diminutive woman with well-earned wrinkles and a mile-wide smile, dressed in a denim shirt and a colorfully rainbowed skirt that billowed as she walked. Silver and turquoise jewelry bedecked her neck, fingers and wrists; an impressive piece fashioned into her twisted bun of greying hair.

Softly, she whispered into Zia's ear.

"Oh, yes, please," Zia responded happily. "I'd like that very much. Thank you." She stepped aside and let Shimásání walk towards the stage.

Everyone stayed silently attentive.

"Yá'át'ééh," she began with the Diné greeting for 'hello' and 'all is good.'

"This land knows and remembers many songs," she said. "People have been on this soil for thousands of years, emerging from the earth and born into the light. Our ancestors knew how to live in harmony with the beings around us. Today," she said, looking up through the center of the yurt at a slice of blue sky, "that way of thinking is needed again."

She began to sing a mesmerizing chant, an old blessing song used in healing ceremonies. The ancient dialect danced from her, landing on the hungry ears of the audience.

Saffron had heard it many times in her life. Once, when she'd been little and fighting a fever, Shimásání had sung it just for her. She'd later asked what the song meant.

Shimásání had answered that Bilagáanas, or white people, had given it many translations, but the best way to understand it was to know its intention; the song was meant to restore balance and peace.

It reminded Saffron of Kundalini mantras, born on the other side of the world. Listening to Shimásání's hauntingly compelling voice, Saffron felt transported. The hypnotic singing rose and fell as she gazed around at the loving, friendly people who enriched her life. She watched her mother, her eyes closed, drinking in the song's prayerful intention as she held hands with her husband; her lover; her rock.

She saw Lorelei and Ayden sitting on the opposite side of the circle. Lorelei was rocking slightly to the music, a wistful smile upon her face, mouthing the Navajo words; Carla had insisted her and her daughter learn some of the old ways of their culture to honor and retain it.

Ayden was busily playing with his cuticles. Intermittently, he would look up at Shimásání's performance, then back down, his attention diverted back to his hands. To Saffron, he seemed detached from the moment, a mismatched frequency, out of tune with the space around him. As if he could feel her eyes on him, he looked towards her, and Saffron immediately turned away.

Looking for a distraction, she glanced at the Big Board's calendar.

Less than a month until the August harvest moon, she noted. *Where was time going?*

Still feeling and fearing Ayden's gaze, she glanced past Colton's shoulder at the ring of bookcases behind them.

Sweetwater's collection was highly impressive. Their library was the envy of every survivalist they'd ever met. As expected, they had books on the global warming conversation, some dating back over six decades which were kept mostly for nostalgia's sake and out of respect for the earliest responders like Rachel Carson and Bill McKibbons. Nowadays, they typically used the internet to keep up to date on emerging statistics and facts.

There were also books on engineering and design, everything from windmills to grain mills. Among the shelves were ones about health and first aid, including some intense medical books. There was even a detailed research dissertation on how to feed every person on the planet if there was ever an asteroid strike, an atomic bomb detonation, or an eruption from a super volcano. Saffron had only read it once, unnerved by the thought of eating nothing but crickets and fungi grown on dead trees during a decades-long, sunless winter.

The vast majority of their collection, however, centered around different societies and civilizations with their secrets of adaptability over the centuries. Their shelves contained the histories of the collective journey through time; tales of the enigmatic and repetitive circle of life; details of people at their shiniest bests and most traumatic lows; the story of humanity itself.

In Saffron's opinion, these books proved people were excellent at problem solving, capable of creative inventions and advancements for the betterment of Mankind.

Where there was a will, there was a way, she thought.

The group had gathered this knowledge, building an archive, a lexicon to be passed down from one generation to the next, safeguarded in case the Grid ever went down. She'd been absorbing these texts since she was a child, hunting for answers and for a way of life that would feed her heart and soul.

She thought of her argument with Ayden, her defensiveness about the conservatives-versus-liberals polarity, and the strife between the Haves and the Have-nots.

Why're we so prone to picking sides, she wondered. *Is it part of our DNA?*

Suddenly, an electric thought came into her: While every single person was related in some way to each other, each person who'd ever lived was also unique, an individual with their own personality, experiences, and perceptions, plus a multitude of opinions, peccadillos and lifestyles specific to that person.

No two people on the planet were ever exactly alike.

Diversity was the essence of life itself.

In that moment, she realized the only thing every person had in common, the only quality which was uniformly shared, came down to one solitary thing: we were human, members of the Homo sapiens species. It was the only thing that united us. After that one defining similarity, everything else became mere adjectives, descriptors of individual selves.

Rich/poor; black/white; male/female; gay/straight; fat/skinny; etcetera/ad nauseam.

Unfortunately, she realized, too many people defined themselves by their descriptions instead of embracing the unifying truth they were all human beings with common needs. This tendency to divide into subgroups had created a cultural feeling of 'Us versus Them' which had repeated over time.

Only, Saffron thought, *our separateness is a lie. We're more like cells in a body, interdependent, and if the host gets sick and dies, everyone will suffer.*

She listened to Shimásání sing and an idea took hold of her, entering her head from the crown chakra, impregnating her.

Effortlessly, her energy field, her aura, expanded.

If we must change to survive, she thought with amazement, *then I must change too!* Her heart started racing. *I need to let go of my hatred and biases, my ego, and embrace a more loving approach.*

The truth came into her at a subatomic level, like she was receiving an upgrade to her energy system.

What would happen if we stopped judging people, placing value on some adjectives over others, like rich over poor? White over black? What if we truly followed in Christ's footsteps and loved everyone, including our enemies, as He had mandated?

Jesus's message had been an astoundingly powerful truth in his day, and it was no less earth-shattering today. Other prophets and religious visionaries had preached the same lesson. It was universal. A Universal Law. Do unto others as you would have them do unto you.

From Buddha and Krishna to John Lennon and Lenny Kravitz, the message was the same: let love rule.

Saffron realized for her to be effective in changing the world, she would have to turn away from the devil on her shoulder, learning to love the greedy and the self-absorbed as her brothers and sisters; to reach out to them and kindly show them how they could fix the Hot Mess together.

Shimásásaní's undulating notes swept across the room. Saffron took the healing song into herself and her heart chakra opened. She had a vision of a seed sprouting, the moment when the stored, hidden potential explodes into a living entity, into a viable, thriving being as the green shoot reaches for the light.

There's so much to do, she thought incredulously, *but it all could unfold effortlessly, like a growing plant.*

Her inner voice exclaimed, *It may even be fun!*

Closing her eyes, she began praying her deepest desires.

Lord, I pray that the challenges we face today propel us to a future beyond our wildest expectations, if we believe in it, and work towards it. Please help us unite. Do not allow the possibility of a dystopian universe to exist. Fully and completely, I embrace this vision and version of Your Kingdom on earth.

Feeling recharged and hopeful, she opened her eyes and peered again at Ayden. He looked both bored and defiant, his leg twitching restlessly.

Man, this isn't going to be easy, she thought.

It was going to take work, but as her mother had said, it was worth it. Somewhere, she imagined, there were wealthy individuals taking stock, forecasting the future, and searching for solutions like she was.

They had to exist!

Saffron committed, then and there, to finding the right people to help her transform the world. Her mother was right; it was a powerful time. What was needed now was action and a great dissemination of knowledge. People needed to be activated by role models and visionaries; unifiers and creators; music and art; and above all, acceptance and love.

The world was aching for another Renaissance, to open their hearts and minds.

Maybe Colton's song idea isn't that farfetched, she considered.

Shimásásaní's chanting ended and in the brief silence before the applause, Saffron felt energy from the earth and from above coursing through her. She turned to Colton who'd been raptly watching the performance, oblivious to her metamorphosis.

"I got it," she whispered excitedly into his ear. "I know what we're going to do."

She bounced on the soles of her feet with glee.

"Is it so crazy that it just might work?" he said half-jokingly.

"Oh," she answered, "you have no idea."

"An idea that is developed and put into action is more important than an idea that exists only as an idea."
- Gautama Buddha

Chapter 31: Trauma Transmuted

Colton spent the rest of the afternoon and into the night with Saffron talking about The Master Plan, hatching ideas and bouncing them off one another, a major brainstorming session which coalesced more and more deeply as they talked.

Like a rug on a loom, each thread added to the rest until a pattern emerged.

Saffron was unstoppable, riffing one idea after another like a tommy machine gun; words pouring loquaciously from her mouth in a cascade.

She wanted to reach out to moguls and politicians, to movie stars and scientists, as well as grassroots activists and union leaders. She foresaw a revolution in media and education; the creation of more responsible websites and tv shows, and a return of civics, ethics and philosophy classes, as well as shop and home economics courses.

"For both sexes," she adamantly insisted. "A penis is not required to fix an engine and a vagina is not necessary to make a casserole."

And of course, she talked about a huge departure from fossil fuels.

Colton pointed out the need to transition people like himself and his family who worked at the lower levels in the industry. Regular people, he argued, had already taken enough hits economically. He stressed that the working men and women in America, including San Juan County, would have to be taken into account.

Saffron told him she couldn't have agreed more, that the changes the country needed to undertake would create tons of new jobs. Oil and gas employees could be paid very well doing the necessary environmental clean-up that should occur, as well as receiving training and getting jobs in the construction of renewable power grid structures.

"Plus," she gushed, "it'll be good for their karma."

He also pointed out that petroleum was used in a multitude of products such as plastics, make-up, tires and lubricants.

"Algae is the future!" she proclaimed excitedly.

Begrudgingly, he was able to get her to admit there were probably several uses that people wouldn't be able to get rid of right away, if ever.

"Fine," Saffron acquiesced, "just know that bioengineers will be working to replace them entirely." Then, as an afterthought, she said, "But I don't think I'm wrong about algae."

Colton enjoyed her exuberance. He simply allowed her the space to spin and dream. The good news was that the majority of her ideas were balanced and sound. He too added some ideas into the mix, ones which were less exotic than hers, but mostly, he let her do her thing.

She was the one with the vision.

She's been learning and thinking about this stuff for a lot longer than me, he thought pragmatically. *It's probably smart to see how her ideas and the solutions suggested by scientists work out before shutting them down.*

His grandfather had taught him that you don't always get things right the first few times you do them, but it doesn't stop one from trying. Anything society attempted to do now would be a work in progress. It could be refined over time...if they had the time.

It was minutes before midnight when they finally quit talking about it.

"I'm going to take a quick shower," she said, "then you're welcome to take a turn."

Colton had a different idea in mind.

"Why don't we conserve water," he suggested silkily, "and take one at the same time?"

In the long list of good ideas they'd come up with, he thought this one ranked easily in the top ten.

The image of Colton's nude, soapy body rubbing up against hers burst into Saffron's brain. It was an incredibly appealing thought, followed by dismay.

"Well, for one thing," she said with a pout, "I don't trust showering together would actually save any resources whatsoever. And sadly, I started my period."

"Awww, we can do it," he drawled. "We can make it fast, just a quick tease in the shower to make us hungry for more." He put his arms around her and kissed the space between her neck and shoulder, her secret spot.

Saffron's knees almost went out from under her.

"And," Colton added, his breath on her ear, "I'll never stop wanting to make love to you, no matter what. If you don't want to do it that way, then I'm sure we can think of other things we can do."

He smiled at her, performing his own Groucho Marx impersonation, his eyebrows dancing across his forehead.

If you spend years denying yourself actual sex, she remembered him saying, *you get pretty good at doing all the other things.*

Saffron felt herself getting aroused.

He really is sexy, her naughty voice chimed in. *It'd be a shame to waste him.*

"I'll compromise with you," she said. "Give me two minutes by myself and I'll meet you in my bedroom when you're done."

Saffron was eager to get clean; she'd been stewing in negative emotions for much of the day and was ready to wash off. In the shower, she rinsed at lightning speed, hastily inserting a reusable menstrual cup before wrapping herself in a towel and bounding down the greenery-lined hallway into her cozy den.

Norah Jones was again playing on the stereo. The room smelled of piñon incense. Colton stood naked in the middle of her living room, fully erect. Saffron's wet feet slipped out from under her. Her towel came loose and she caught her balance by reaching for the bookcase.

"Well," he said, grinning a sideways smile, "I think that's the least graceful thing I've ever seen you do."

Saffron was speechless, feeling a combination of surprise and fury. Just before she opened her mouth to tell him off, he laughed and extended a hand towards her.

"Come here, you," he said, beckoning her to come closer. "I've missed you, my little rebel."

There are moments in life that are pumped full of more juice than others, times which leave a deep impression. Saffron felt the planet tilt, her center shifting.

This was true love. It was silly, it was kind. It was intimate, and sometimes, passionate. What Saffron suddenly understood was when it was unconditional, love had an inherently magical quality.

She took him to her dome at the top of the spiral staircase where they spent time getting to know each other better, the sounds of their mutual pleasure resounding off the curved walls like a choir in a cathedral.

Before morning, Saffron's sleep turned uneasy.

She dreamt she was lost in the darkness of The Bunker, discovering a strange door she'd never seen before leading deeper into the earth. Inside was a long tunnel, lined on both sides of the aisle with burbling aquariums, each one a perfect microcosm of a different environment.

There was a dim Amazonian river simulation, a brightly colored coral reef brimming with diversity, even a replica of her first fish tank with its angelfish and tetras swimming merrily through their ceramic pagoda.

As she walked deeper in, the tanks began to cloud, the specimens, darting in and out of algae-streaked rocks, slowly morphing into monstrous deformities and devolutions. At the end, the tanks brimmed with an oozing black slickness; a primordial goo.

Red eyes peered out at her unwaveringly through the murk.

Saffron's unease grew.

"They won't let you say all the things you plan on saying," a deep voice muttered threateningly.

It was not her own.

"Not without retribution," It continued. "Do you really want to put your family in jeopardy?"

"My family's already in jeopardy," her dream voice responded.

"You are going to piss off some powerful people," It hissed.

"I'm pissed off too," she retorted sharply, "and powerful in my own way."

Her hands found another mysterious opening at the dismally dark end of the tunnel. A door opened, and Saffron found herself standing in the center of Sweetwater in the bright light of day.

Looking up, she saw black op soldiers rappelling down the cliff face towards her home. Her friends were lined up at the openings in the adobe wall, firing guns to ward off an attack coming from the other side. The first soldiers from the cliff touched ground and a landmine exploded beneath them, reducing them to rubble.

"What do you think happens to people who try to change the world," the voice spoke again.

This time Saffron gave it a name; Darkness.

Drones flew the fence and began systematically shooting at the people around her. The scene of her family and loved ones getting brutally murdered was interspersed with a view of a native village, an ancient people being massacred before her eyes like a hologram, like an echo.

It was chaos; an evil which felt as old as the universe.

The use of force against innocent people was forever an abomination.

In response, Saffron felt her dreamself expanding and radiating light, pushing goodness into the field beyond her. Suddenly, she saw the world from outer space, the planet encased in a black cloud and thousands of white lights shooting up like beacons. She focused her energy and sent her own white light up and out into the world to join the others, driving the black clouds away.

Her heart chakra flowered within as a tsunami of love erupted from her core. She was immersed in it, a vessel of water among billions of others, floating in the spiritual essence of the ocean, wave upon wave pulsing around her. She could sense every other conscious soul that had ever existed, the magic E of Einstein's famous $E = mc^2$.

Everything was truly united at the singular point of creation; and, at the center of it all, it was good.

Yá'át'ééh.

"I will never back down from this fight," she told the Darkness.

It was both a statement and a commitment deeply forged.

"You can't win," It rasped.

"Watch me," Saffron said fearlessly, and awoke with her arms and legs wrapped around Colton.

"I believe if one always looked up at the skies,
one would end up with wings."
- Gustave Flaubert

Chapter 32: Dream Weaver

Colton's first major project was nearing completion. Soon, he was going to surprise Saffron with a canoe built for two. Jack had been very enthusiastic about the idea ever since Colton had first mentioned it to him at the hospital. In fact, the older man was almost as excited about the special gift as he was, although Colton had not yet told him that when it was completed, he was going to ask for his daughter's hand in marriage.

For the first time in his life, he was sure what he wanted; to spend his days with a smart, loving woman who made his wildest dreams come true, and who inspired him to do the same for her.

Over the past month, he'd been following some of Saffron's New-Age-y wisdom.

As he had carved the secret boat, coaxing its hidden form out of a large piece of timber, he'd been furiously daydreaming about the future he wanted to see. Of course, she'd used the word 'manifest', as in, '*Focus on what you want to see manifest*', but he knew what she'd meant. In his upbringing, he'd been taught 'ask, believe, receive…amen.'

They were different words, but in his mind, the same intention.

Either way, it felt like the sensible thing to do.

In his musings, he pictured the two of them surrounded by happy children, feeling blessed to watch them grow older in a stable, healthy environment, on a planet that had averted catastrophe. It had become a daily practice for him to pray for these things and more, the visions growing clearer every time.

Dusting wood shavings off of his clothes and out of his hair, he left the work shed to walk towards the LeMay's double-domed Earthship.

Most of his fellow Sweetwater members were outside, putting the harvest moon to good use as they gathered the produce from the fields. The vintage truck was nearly full for the haul to the market the next day. They were expecting a large crowd as the stalwart Aztecians had shown their strong spines once again; ever since the blackout and riot, record numbers of people had been actively supporting local growers and farmers; it seemed their community spirit remained alive and well.

Colton wished he could say the same about his family.

Communication with his parents and siblings continued to be strained. His mother had told him to give them time, they were still grappling with his change of heart and address. On the upside, she'd kept her word and had begun reading more. She'd even enrolled for a master gardener's class and had bragged about her newfound frugality.

"I cut our electric bill in half last month," she'd told him excitedly. "It's crazy how much energy is wasted in homes. Your dad likes saving money, but not the nagging about turning off the lights. Don't worry, honey, we'll get them turned around."

At the moment, however, the Millers were as divided as the nation.

Above him, the full moon was an amber celestial eye. He could almost sense its gravitational force on his being, exerting a tidal effect on his blood and tissues, much like the pulling of waters across the globe. In the distance, he heard the plaintive cries of coyotes who may have felt the same sensation as he. Their lonesome howling made him think of the Diné myths about cunning Coyote.

For some reason, thoughts of the trickster god made his mind turn to Ayden.

Colton wasn't sure what to make of him. The tension between Saffron and her ex was like watching two people navigating a tightrope; rigid motions, no nonsense attitude, with an undercurrent that things could go badly, quickly.

For the most part, they seemed to ignore each other, rarely looking each other's way unless Saffron had a task for him. Then, she would get bossy, more forceful than normal. She was never overtly mean, but she wasn't exactly friendly either. They could have been office co-workers; one, a demanding boss, and the other, an employee dreaming of being anywhere but where he was.

Saffron had not yet given many details into their relationship, but then again, neither had he. The last thing he wanted was to go into specifics about Kaelynne who was still leaving erratic and threatening messages on his phone. He'd begun deleting them without listening. The last one he'd heard had been full of expletives, including the words, 'hippie cunt'.

It had unnerved him to think she may have been behind the yoga studio's destruction, but Colton was reluctant to call the police with his suspicions. Unfortunately, he didn't know what else to do except bless Kaelynne and let her go.

As for Ayden, he truly didn't want to know much about him either, so it was okay with him if Saffron wanted to keep her stories to herself.

Overall, he was enjoying life in the intentional community. Working with his hands, planting, repairing, carving the canoe, it all felt productive and helpful rather than repetitive and mere busy work. At the end of each day, he had a sense of accomplishment and an increase in his self-confidence which made him feel less like a cog in a mindless machine and more like part of something greater. It was a feeling he wished others could experience for themselves.

He had plans to voice his opinions when they went to Washington, DC in two weeks.

Inside the Earthship, Colton found Saffron toiling in the darkened room of The Bunker where she'd spent most of her evenings over the past month. The computer screen flashed hypnotically, casting her silhouette in a play of light and shadow.

The day after Zia's homecoming celebration, Saffron had called for an emergency meeting, asking everyone to help her on the #Brinker Project, or The Kumbaya Solution, as they were now calling it.

Tomorrow was the planned unveiling of their efforts, the start of a new day.

"Looks good," he said, peering over her shoulder at her work and kissing the top of her lavender scented hair. He handed her a mug of chai and began rubbing her shoulders.

On the monitor was the video they'd created, intercut with performers from other intentional communities and friends from around the world. In addition to Saffron's singing, Lorelei's fiddle, Jack's guitar, Kristen's stand-up bass, and John Perry's banjo, the video showed other musicians playing more exotic instruments like Aboriginal didgeridoos, Tibetan lutes, Indian sitars, as well as footage of a Navajo drumming circle.

Watching her perform in person had thrilled Colton. Passionately, she had belted out the lyrics, dancing in her ecstatic style around the pavilion's bandstand like she was conjuring a better world through sheer will.

She had worn the flowing red skirt from the last full moon, with black combat boots and her favorite t-shirt; on it was a drawing of Joan of Arc with her quote, 'I am not afraid…I was born to do this'. Her hair had been wild with curls and a few small braids interlaced with ribbons. More ribbons had wrapped her wrists. As she'd danced, her crystal necklaces had twirled with her movements. Exuding joy and strength, she'd appeared like a Gaelic princess or a powerful gypsy, beseeching her tribe to rise and vanquish the enemy, only with love, not war.

As Colton watched the computer, the song ended and Saffron's face came on the screen. She was dressed in white, the red highlights in her hair aflame with sunlight, as she sat cross-legged on a blue mandala tapestry at the edge of Navajo Lake. This was the part of the video where she delivered the 'Message to the Masses' she'd felt compelled to share. As she spoke, the names and contact information for a litany of politicians, celebrities, CEO's, and hundreds of billionaires and multi-millionaires scrolled constantly at the bottom of the screen; a who's who of the most powerful and influential people in the world.

Colton's arms suddenly erupted in goosebumps as a passage from the Bible came to his mind: *So shall my word be that goes out from my mouth; it shall not return to me empty, but it will accomplish that which I purpose, and shall succeed in the thing for which I sent it. Isaiah 55:11.*

For all of their sakes, he prayed for it to be true.

"Are you in earnest? Seize this very minute;
What you can do, or dream you can do, begin it;
Boldness has genius, power and magic in it."
- Johann Wolfgang von Goethe

Chapter 33: The Big Rant

Manically driven, almost possessed, Saffron had rushed to complete her project as quickly as she could. Blessedly, the other Sweetwater members had not only been open to her ideas, they'd improved them, making some even better than she'd imagined. Everyone had chipped in, spending hours in Aztec's library, studiously typing at their banks of computers, looking up names, finding addresses, in order to expand their reach.

The entire plan centered on ways to maximize the message's impact.

Ayden had been reluctant to help at the start. On the day of the emergency meeting, his only contribution to the conversation had been to suggest one way to ensure the campaign would go viral was if they hijacked a television station.

"Hey, we'd definitely get everyone's attention that way! 'We now interrupt your regular broadcasting of the Family Feud to bring you a message of your pending demise and our plan to avoid it!'," he'd said in a schlocky, radio announcer voice. "Brought to you by Cliff's Organic Lentils!"

Everyone had laughed, except Saffron, who'd responded only by handing him a piece of paper with her list of demands. One of them she thought was so brilliant, there was no way he could refuse.

'Get on your damn soap box, dude,' she'd written, *'and get the punks together, country punks, city punks, old ones, new ones, I don't care. Just get out there and use your voice and powers for good.'* She'd signed it, *'Or Else'* with the postscript, *'Once everyone realizes we don't need fucking permission to do the right thing, it'll be transformative. Think how hella cool it'll be if punks help solve the urban food desert problem or lead the way in sustainable living. It could be epic!!!'*

Whether her late night, feverish insights had made common sense to him or the threat of exposure held more influence, he'd grudgingly provided the technical support she'd needed, agreeing to everything on the list except appearing in the video. She suspected it was because he still wanted to keep his identity and location a secret…just in case.

His co-conspirators had purportedly agreed to postpone D-day to November 5th, the anniversary of Guy Fawkes's attack on Parliament.

Anarchists could be so predictable, she briefly thought with a smirk.

It was far from perfect, but it did buy her some time.

Lorelei had been much more amenable to the new plan, throwing herself completely into the new project and working long hours to help meet the deadline. Saffron believed it was because she felt guilty for initially going along with Ayden's evil one.

Saffron thought she understood the underlying frustration and rage which lay behind someone supporting such a macabre act; nobody liked to feel trapped and oppressed, between a rock and a hard place. Sometimes when the autonomic nervous system kicked in, the body's response was to fight, instead of run away. She wouldn't be surprised if more violence began occurring in the years to come if things didn't turn around, and quickly.

Regardless, it was still her opinion that people needed to do right, even if it was the harder thing to do, which it usually was. Lorelei's change of heart, plus her contributions to the more peaceful approach, had made it easy to forgive her best friend's transgressions.

However, the angel on Saffron's shoulder was more critical with her own abject failure to report the Dastardly Plan to the authorities. It gnawed at her. When she allowed herself time for self-reflection, she realized that even with her newfound desire to emanate love to all, deep down there was a small part of her which felt if there was no Plan B for the majority of earth's inhabitants, then it wasn't fair for there be a Plan B for the billionaires.

The devil on her shoulder was less vocal than it used to be, but it was still there, and it thought it was perfectly okay to keep their options open.

She wasn't proud of herself for these thoughts and typically pushed them away, replacing them with the overpowering and determined belief that Timebomb would be thwarted by her plan's definitive and resounding success.

Still, the weight of the secret felt like a cancerous lump in her belly. She hoped she would have enough time. She prayed no harm would ever have to come because, if her plan failed, she'd be forced to turn Ayden in. It would be hard, but she knew she couldn't allow his plot to follow through, regardless of what her darker nature thought.

She was committed to never letting the devil win.

She brought her attention back to the computer screen. On it was her performance of one of her favorite songs, 'Haven', from an Irish band called WeBanjo3. She hoped people would embrace the concept of being a haven for others, to be supportive, helping each other to flourish.

It was key in her vision for a world that was more nurturing, less 'Lord of the Flies'.

When she'd added the other musicians' diverse interpretations and tribal influences to the Celtic-inspired song, it had been enriched beyond anything she'd thought possible. It had transformed into Earth Music; one song and a multitude of voices, sounds and cultures to create it. She hoped it would be the song heard round the world, a catalyst to inspire millions.

Colton came up behind her, carrying the faint scent of sawdust and the fragrant spices of hot tea.

"Looks good," he said, his fingers working gently into her tired muscles.

As he kissed the top of her head, her nagging thoughts dissipated instantly. This had become one of her favorite moments of her day, the time when he'd interrupt her all-consuming obsession to remind her of why she was doing it in the first place.

Tonight, they were planning to ride Dusty and Bernie, her aging silver stallion, out into the desert to watch the moon sail across the sky. She'd already packed the Pendleton blanket and some potent cannabis in case the urge to fuck him senseless should arise, which she predicted it would.

Her feelings for Colton continued to astound her; her giddiness, horniness and sense of balance growing stronger by the day. Like a key in a lock, they felt right together…with the exception of one small, yet potentially earth-shattering, hiccup; she couldn't remember if she'd told him why she couldn't get pregnant. She vaguely recalled telling him she wouldn't get knocked up their first time, but that wasn't exactly the same as saying, "Hey, I had my tubes tied. This factory is closed to manufacturing."

It'd seemed a minor thing not to talk about to a guy she'd only been dating a month, but with each day, the 'secret' felt more pressing. Then, last night, she'd overheard Colton talking in his sleep.

"Daddy's got you," he had said, along with "Say hi to Mommy."

The seven small words and contented, blissful look on his face had stunned her.

Even more shocking was a certainty that somehow, sometime, she would have kids with him, just...not her own. On the trip to DC, she guessed there'd be plenty of time to talk.

Cringing, she realized if there was one thing she hated more than talking about climate change, it was discussing overpopulation.

Man, she thought, *is this how a mother feels, having to be the bad guy sometimes?*

The video shifted from the music portion of the clip to the heart of her message. The song was, in her opinion, merely a means of attracting eyes in an overly-saturated social media realm. The 'sermon' afterwards was her real intent.

One of her grand ideas had been to apply a principle of physics; the law stating that when a force is exerted, there must be a reaction. Her intention was to make as big of a noise as she was capable of producing, like a little Who trying to be heard by Dr. Seuss's Horton, with the faith that the Universe and God would decide how big the outcome would be. She hoped the right people would hear the call and be moved to take the appropriate actions.

Initially, the intensity of this part of her mission had overwhelmed her. There was so much she wanted to say. Deciding on what to focus on had been very difficult. Her overactive brain and worries had begun to exhaust her. Sometimes, when she was very tired, the dark voice of doubt would creep into her sub-conscious and whisper, *What if no one cares?*

In order to clear her mind and best prepare herself, she'd gone alone to the lake, spending an hour in meditation before filming, chanting 'Sat Nam' and repeating 'Glory be' quietly to herself, purifying her thoughts, grounding her body, and releasing her ego and expectations.

When she'd finally felt ready to speak from the heart, the words had flowed easily. She'd gazed into the camera as if peering directly into the eyes of the intended viewer, someone she'd imagined sitting in front of her on the rocky beach.

"Thank you for your attention," her video self began speaking. "You probably don't know me since I'm one of eight billion, but I'm someone who believes we each serve a purpose, we each have value...You matter." Saffron watched herself take a deep breath as the water rippled behind her. "My fellow humans, we are in a defining time in our collective history. What happens here and now has ramifications throughout all of the future days to come.

"Climatologists are warning us we have less than five years to commit to massive changes, a 'Radical Conversion to Sustainable Solutions'," she'd said, making air quotes. "And, if we don't, the likelihood of rampant extinction across the planet is greatly increased in the next few decades."

Scrolling beneath her image was a steady stream of names and addresses; the extensive list included CEO's and their corporate headquarters; politicians and their locations in the nation's Capitol; high-profile celebrities and the addresses of their managers in Hollywood; as well as deep-pocketed aristocrats, tycoons, and the names of their younger heirs, all due to inherit inconceivable fortunes.

"I suspect," Saffron continued, "most of you don't want to learn the ugly details about climate change and global warming, and it's probably true that the vast majority of you don't want to change either, not even minimally, let alone, radically.

"Well, too bad," she had said strongly, but not unkindly. "Man up, warrior princess up, cowboy up, do whatever it takes to take a serious look at these issues, and then, I ask you to be a part of the greatest emergency mobilization in all of human history. We...are...in...crisis. It's pivotal we act now, logically, ethically, and humanely in order to bring ourselves back from the brink of destruction."

The image shifted to footage of the Aztec ruins, the ancient Anasazi village which had existed in the area over a thousand years ago; its crumbling rock walls still holding doorways and windows into the shadows; its round, ceremonial kiva still reverberating with the sacred vibrations of past prayers.

"If you study history," her voice continued to speak over the images, "you'll learn that societies have collapsed many times over the millennia. What's different now is we know it's coming, and we possess a million ways to combat it. The solutions exist, all that's missing is will. Unfortunately for us, the window of opportunity is closing rapidly. That's what we're being told by the world's majority of scientists.

"They've been trying to warn us that with each passing day, we're missing chances for success."

The film switched to a close-up of Saffron's face.

"It's time to act in a manner worthy of our souls. I don't know about you, but being a victim doesn't sit well with me. Wringing my hands and waiting for Doomsday to come…this is not what I came here to do!

"It's time to multi-task and be the hardcore, full-on, problem-solving MotherFixers we're capable of being."

Zia and Carla had added that last sentence to the speech. They'd each taken charge of creating bumperstickers and t-shirts which read, 'MotherFixers' on one side and 'Stop Climate Destabilization' on the other. They planned to use the proceeds to fund various efforts in the community.

"Start by asking questions," Saffron had continued. "Are you doing everything you could be doing? Of course not. Nobody is. Do you know everything you should know? Impossible, but we can try to learn more every day. Collectively, if we each make improvements, you, me, everyone, then the challenges we face today are actually opportunities in disguise. Maybe we can heal more than a dying planet by focusing on what we share in common, by understanding everyone is a soul in a different body, some born in California and others in Calcutta.

"Maybe we can come through this horrific time better than we've ever been before."

The camera shot pulled back and Saffron was again sitting serenely near the water, blue sky and white clouds behind her, wet sand near her shiny, aquamarine-painted toes.

"Basically," she'd continued, "there're many ways our future can go, various timelines if you will, or statistical probabilities, all of which are dependent on the actions and choices each of us are making today. The good news is we're only in trouble based on decisions we've made yesterday. Anything we want to see happen in the future starts with what we're choosing to do with each present moment.

"So please, take the time and learn what it'll take to fix these problems. Afterwards, take what you've learned and apply it. I'm sure there'll be many ideas about what *other* people should be doing, but I beg of you to be open to what you personally could be doing better. Then, make a commitment to do it.

"Technically, this isn't the end of the world," she'd said, "however, it could be for a significant number of us. And it's not going to happen like a switch on the wall, when it suddenly goes from 'okay and tolerable' to 'Holy Shite End Days'."

Saffron was secretly pleased with herself for not cussing.

"Instead, it's going to happen slowly, until the new normal will be hardship and suffering, loss of diversity, and death.

"But it doesn't need to happen like that. We're capable of tremendous vision and spirit. All we have to do is decide to do it, take responsibility for our situation and then," she broke into a sardonic smile, "well, then, all we have to do is transform our systems, institutions, our thinking, deep-rooted ways of living, and...oh yeah, diet."

Easy peasy, she thought mockingly. *Piece of cake.*

"I know it's not going to be easy," she'd said with a Mona Lisa smile, "but I want to offer some secrets of survival: surrender yourself to a vision of hope, not despair. Be gentle with yourself, and with others. What you're going to learn about our current environmental status will probably frighten you. Fight back the fears by dreaming of a healthier world, by picturing a more harmonious, just and equitable one. Don't just prepare for the worst, *expect the best!* With the many different pathways our future can take, isn't it smart to picture the best case scenario and work towards it?

"Personally, I believe it's possible, necessary even, *if* we are brave enough to dream it into existence. So please, join us in pushing the boulder up the mountain. Look to organizations and individuals who are already working diligently on solving this crisis. They exist! Search them out, listen to them, and to each other. Who knows where the next great idea is going to spring from? It could be you.

"Now," she had said on the screen, taking in another deep breath, "let's talk about the names listed below. These folks are some of the wealthiest, most influential people the world has ever seen. What the scientists have been trying to tell us is we've gotten to the point in the environment where bottoms-up changes alone are not going to cut it.

"Sadly, you and I will not turn things around based solely on our individual sacrifices. The only approach which will currently save us are top-down solutions. We simply must have the key world players step up. I know it sounds crazy, but nobody else can get us out of this Hot Mess like the multi-millionaires and billionaires can, and should.

"I have a message I'd like to say just to them: I know many of you have worked hard to amass your riches, to build your empires, and make contributions to society. I admire many of you for it, but sacrifices need to be made across the board. You and your families are not immune. We cannot do this on our own. Your help, your resources, your compassion and your courage are needed now like never before.

"I have to say that if you were saving up for a rainy day, then that day has truly come."

Next came a montage of black and white footage from old movies; clips of people furiously writing letters, of postmen strolling down sidewalks next to white picket fences, and old-fashioned newsrooms and mailrooms piled high with stuffed mailbags.

"Everybody knows someone with more influence than them," she'd said. "Start writing, letters and emails. Make videos. Be seen at non-violent protests. Believe it or not, snail mail may be the most productive. They won't be able to delete and ignore copious bags littering their offices.

"Please, tell them your stories, about you and your families, about your hopes, dreams and accomplishments. Open yourself to them so we can open their hearts. Let them know why you're worth saving. What do we have to lose by trying? The answer is, everything.

"Now is not the time for insults, or threats, or blame. This may be the hardest thing I'm asking of you. Please act respectfully, but firmly. Be civil, and eloquent. Appeal to their sense of responsibility and honor.

"It's true that reversing global warming trumps all other endeavors at this point in time, but the beauty is that in solving it, we'll make monumental strides in fixing most of our other problems too. Because of this, the 1%ers alone have the ability to make the biggest contribution ever made in the history of mankind. They could potentially be our heroes."

Again, Saffron had stopped to breathe deeply and enjoy the idyllic landscape surrounding her.

When she spoke again, she'd said earnestly, "It's important you don't let everyone else do the work for you. Don't sit out and put the burden onto someone else's shoulders. Every single one of us is not only capable, but needed, to bring our special mark on the changes we need to see. Yes, sacrifices are to be made, but when we do them together, it'll bring about the transformation we're yearning for. Many hands make short work."

The last scene came on the screen, with Saffron standing in tree pose in the center of Sweetland's labyrinth, the beauty of the desert in the background.

"I believe in you. I believe in humanity! I believe we can again regain common sense, as Benjamin Franklin thought possible, and we can actively choose to put aside our differences for a common goal, for the common good, and for the Commonwealth of this country.

"This is the version of the future we should be demanding to come into existence!

"Or," she'd said in a serious tone, "shall we choose to do nothing and perish like the arrogant, haughty people the Bible mentions in Revelations? Shall we simply allow the planet and its inhabitants to languish in a sabotaged landscape? Or, are we going to elevate, to rise to this occasion like the loving, creative beings we were meant to be? I believe we can, and must.

"I ask you to pray for the best outcome," she'd added, "for the obstacles to be quickly removed, to pray like you mean it to the Love surrounding us, even if you've never prayed before. Give thanks and use your light and positive energy to show whichever god you believe in you are committed to being a part of the solutions.

"I love you. I've never met you, but I love you. We're in a time where we can experience a phenomenal level of healing…or we can destruct.

"Personally," she had concluded, looking heavenwards, "I pray for a world that is beautiful, pure, and lasting."

In the video, the next shot shifted to the blue sky with its wisps of clouds. Finally, the words 'Ready, Steady, Go!' appeared on the screen before fading away.

With those last parting words burned on her retinas, Saffron sat in the dimness of The Bunker with her eyes closed, channeling Reiki and her intentions to the world, then decided to hit Send, releasing the message instantly to thousands of individuals, corporations, colleges, churches, and politicians across America.

Tomorrow, other intentional communities worldwide would be

releasing their own video performances and messages. She couldn't wait to see the ripple effect of their efforts. It warmed her heart.

Exhaling a loud sigh, she thought with optimism and hope, *Today is a good day.*

"Let's go ride and see the moon," Colton said softly into her ear. "It's stunning."

With a blue glow lighting the land, they soon headed into the empty desert.

Saffron tried to imagine the reaction to come. She purposefully pictured a massive gathering of people; Millennials and Boomers; young and old punks, hippies, and cowboys; accountants, preachers, and teachers with school kids and pimply teenagers at their sides; mothers and daughters, fathers and sons; all linking, arm in arm, on the streets across America and in Washington, DC.

She visualized wealthy people, from first generation money to old-world legacies, receiving the pleas and cries of the multitude and having their hearts crack open. She foresaw a vibrancy renew across the land, an elevation of millions who'd been formerly oppressed, and blessedly, the madness of the world dissipating and a gentleness returning to all people.

Stroking her horse's neck, she mentally sent the prayer, *Please let them see the light.*

Acknowledgements

First, my sincere and utmost gratitude to those living in San Juan County, Southwest Colorado and the Navajo Nation. You've been the most incredible neighbors, enriching my life tremendously over the past fifteen years, whether you knew it or not, helping me grow as a holistic physician, as a mother, and as a human being. Thank you from the bottom of my heart for opening your hearts to me.

I especially want to thank my husband for his unshakeable faith in me, his unconditional love and support, and for being the best travel buddy a girl could ask for on this wildly spinning ball in space.

To my kids, there is not enough gratitude in the world to give you for accepting your crazy mama with all of my quirks, and loving me anyway. I love you to the moon and back. All of this is for you, babies.

To my friends, family, neighbors, patients, congregation members, bar mates and flat-out strangers who let me babble for the past three years about things which made them uncomfortable, I am eternally sorry and forever grateful. I learned something important from our discussions and interactions every single time. It absolutely takes a village. You all matter.

To the many girlfriends who supported me the most, aka my Original Brinkers, my tribe, I cannot stress how much you've helped me over the years. I hope you remain in my life forever. Your Lights are blinding and the world is a much better place with you in it.

My deepest thanks for my early readers who encouraged me and made my writing better: Sue Kuzmuk, Stephanie Burnell, Nicci Unsicker, Rebecca Larivee, Jacques Ritchie, and Suzanne Arms. And to my editor, Katia Ariel, thanks for helping me unravel the knots, twists, and convolutions so the pattern could appear on the loom. You brought much needed sanity in a very insane time.

There's a litany of authors who tickled my brain and inspired my imagination, as well as provided clues on how to proceed with my first novel. As I'm a freakish bookworm, I'm afraid to start listing names for fear I'll never stop, but three in particular stand out. First, thank you, Lawrence Wollersheim, for shaking me out of my complacency. And, my heartfelt thanks go to Anne Lamott and Elizabeth Gilbert, whose advice about creative writing were a beacon to guide me throughout this process. You ladies were my wingmen, even if you never knew it. To all the other writers and scientists whose studies and books I read, I'm forever grateful for your observations and insights. Keep sharing all you know.

To every one of my teachers, both academic and spiritual, I give you my utmost thanks for molding and shaping me. Neale Donald Walsch and Deepak Chopra, you two gentlemen have extraordinary brains that helped pull me through the dark on more than one occasion. Keep sharing your Light. To the United Church of Christ Protestant Church in Beecher, IL, Unity Church in Mt. Prospect, IL, Fellowship of the Spirit in Farmington, NM, and the Unitarian Universalist congregations in Oak Park, IL, Evanston, IL, Farmington, NM, Pagosa Springs, CO and Durango, CO, thank you for helping me develop a compassionate and strong faith. A special thanks to Reverend Katie Kandarian-Morris, for just being you. To the many ministers, preachers, shamans, Reiki practitioners, Lightworkers, ecstatic dancers, and energy healers I've had the privilege to encounter, you've opened my mind to realms outside the box. Thanks for helping me keep my feet on the ground while I explored the ether. (Kim, I miss you but I had to stretch my wings and fly on my own. Thanks for making it possible.)

Shout out to my alma maters: John Hersey High School- thank you for your excellence in ethics and for hiring Chuck Venegoni, who taught me deductive reasoning, critical thinking, and how to write like a badass, and Ed Moon, who gave me the theatre as my playground and creative outlet. (And to my fellow classmate, Nora Herold, the metaphysical queen, who graciously shares her channeled insights to the social media masses like a boss. The instructions to 'emit joy' and to 'operate from love' came through her.)

Thank you William Rainey Harper College for my National Merit scholarship, to Columbia College in Chicago for opening the doors into the film industry and literature, and to Chicago National College of Naprapathy (now named National College of Naprapathic Medicine) and Southwest University of Naprapathic Medicine for teaching me how to heal myself and others. I am still trying to fulfill my obligation to 'correct suffering' in the world.

A h-u-u-u-u-g-e thanks to the many musicians who graciously shared their songs and who lift me up when life gets me down, or when I just need to shake what the good Lord gave me. There's too many musicians, bands and singer/songwriters to count, I just know that I love and appreciate you all.

And a very special 'Thank You' to Ben Foster for Everything, including an unforgettable and invaluable twelve years. Sorry I was such a crazy mess, but I needed to go and eat the moon.

I would not be the person I am today without ALL of you.

Lastly, thank *you* for coming on this journey with me, dear Readers. I hope you enjoyed it. Now the 'hard' part. The conversation has just begun, so feel free to write me online or via mail.

Together…we can move mountains.

Made in the USA
Las Vegas, NV
28 April 2021